On the Hook

A cozy boat club mystery

Rea Keech

Real
Nice Books
Baltimore, Maryland

ISBN 979-8-9932747-4-4 Hardback
ISBN 979-8-9932747-5-1 Paperback
ISBN 979-8-9932747-6-8 Ebook

Library of Congress Control Number
2026938351

Published by
Real
Nice Books
11 Dutton Court, Suite 606
Baltimore, Maryland 21228
www.realnicebooks.com

Publisher's note: This is a work of fiction. Names, characters, places, institutions, and incidents are entirely the product of the author's imagination or are used fictitiously, and any resemblance to actual persons, living or dead, or to events, incidents, institutions, or places is entirely coincidental.

Cover picture of Laser (trimmed) from © Etnoy / Wikimedia Commons / CC-BY-SA-3.0 / GFDL
Set in Minion Pro.

On the Hook

—a cozy boat club mystery

by the prize-winning author of *A Hundred Veils*

OTHER NOVELS BY REA KEECH:

Saint Sergey's Head

Nebulous Enemies

Uncertain Luck

First World Problems
    (Shady Park Chronicles, Book 1)

Shady Park Panic
    (Shady Park Chronicles, Book 2)

Shady Park Secrets
    (Shady Park Chronicles, Book 3)

A Hundred Veils

AUDIOBOOKS NARRATED BY THE AUTHOR:

A Hundred Veils

Uncertain Luck

Chapters

1 The Maritime Republic of Westport 7
2 Laser butt 13
3 On the hook 19
4 Further questions 24
5 No business on Sundays 30
6 Thanks for 36
7 Drawn together 42
8 Got their man 47
9 Sailing ladies 52
10 Hair control 59
11 About Saturday night 63
12 Mean or heartless? 67
13 A transported cuddle 72
14 Hating to lose 76
15 The abandoned boat 81
16 An artificial eulogy 86
17 Eviction 90
18 Stakeout 96
19 Revenge 101
20 A fingerprint 105
21 Hurricane party 110
22 Purple shorts 115
23 A desirable disqualification 121
24 No sail 126
25 Observing an observer 132
26 Swimming ladies 137
27 Partners 142
28 Initiations 148
29 Not what it looks like 154
30 A hard deal to close 160
31 No call or message 166

32	No playing with dolls	172
33	Pretend wife (1)	178
34	Pretend wife (2)	184
35	Bad battery	190
36	A fake button	197
37	Suspicious congratulations	206
38	Sails and kimchi	212
39	A snoop	217
40	The smell of blackmail	223
41	A torn suit	228
42	A holding tank	234
43	A gambling problem	240
44	Sleeping arrangements	246
45	Good sportsmanship	253
46	Could have been yours	260
47	Oooh, Ahh	267
48	No problem	274

Sherlock Holmes: *"You know my method. It is founded upon the observation of trifles."*

—Arthur Conan Doyle, *The Boscombe Valley Mystery*

1

The Maritime Republic of Westport

The clanking of halyards against the masts of the docked sailboats woke Anne Bateman early. There was a good bit of wind, which she hoped would continue for the regatta the next day. She brushed her chin-length sandy blond hair, threw on her Friday blouse, stepped into the black jeans she'd worn for the past few days, hurried down the creaky steps of her rented bungalow on Windward Street, and headed for the Small Boat Tackle Shop down on Tiller Street, its bell tinkling as she entered.

"Hello there," the young clerk sang out. "Those sailing gloves you bought back in November must have worked." He pointed to a printout from the *Westport Voice* taped to the wall behind him alongside ads for turnbuckles, sail slides, double-braid line, and marine glue. "That's you, isn't it?" he said, pointing. In the picture Anne was at the front end of the team pulling for the Maritime Republic of Westport against Colonial City in the women's tug of war.

"That was four months ago. I can't believe you still have that up." Anne's face in the photo wore a grimace, a wavy strand of hair plastered by sweat to her cheek and her blue eyes flashing in the sun. Another printout showed Westport men in the annual sock-burning ceremony. She said, "I just need some thin double-braid line."

"You sailing in the Laser regatta tomorrow?" His eyebrows lifted. "Those shallow boats are a challenge to keep upright when it's windy. I'll be rooting for you. I'm just getting started in a two-person Snipe myself. I'm Bill, by the way. I live on the next street over."

Anne gave him her name. She recalled him shyly flirting with her when she'd bought the gloves. He probably did that with every female customer, but just in case, since he looked to be about twenty and she was forty-three, she said, "Thanks. It's a Women's Over-Forty regatta."

Bill lowered his gaze and asked how many feet of line she needed.

Westport, or the Maritime Republic of Westport, as many residents only half-jokingly insisted on calling the village, was a narrow peninsula jutting into the Chesapeake Bay, separated from the state capital by Town Creek on the north and Bay Creek on the south. Anne had moved back to the village eighteen years ago to take a job at an elementary school. Well-off Westport parents sent their children to private schools, but Westport Elementary, with its mix of Black, Hispanic, and White children, was the kind of school Anne loved teaching in.

There were only two more days of school until summer break. Anne checked her phone. Still time to stop at the corner for a coffee at Clyde's Café before the first bell. An old photo of the original Clyde standing in front of his store next to a horse-drawn cart hung on the wall by the entrance. The cart itself was still on display in an alcove behind the café, but no living Westporter had known the original Clyde. The café had passed down to his grandson, also named Clyde.

Anne looked for a place to sit with her coffee and found only one empty chair, at a table where John Neucomb was sitting. He was studying what looked like legal documents, his gray eyes framed by his reading glasses and his light brown hair teased up at the top of his head in a style that had been current among some actors and TV personalities a few years ago.

"Mind if I sit here?" Anne observed his deck shoes and sockless feet as she pulled out a chair. He was dressed like many of the sailing set who had moved into Westport, despite the small size of its old Sears kit houses and post-war bungalows, because of the availability of docking for their boats. John was about the same age as Anne, but you couldn't tell it from his appearance. To Anne, he and the Westport newcomers seemed to dress themselves as their mothers had dressed them when they went to school in the late seventies or early eighties—polo shirt, often yellow or pink with an alligator logo, tucked in to Bermuda shorts, khaki, with a multi-colored stretchable belt. And of course deck shoes without socks—perhaps to imply, Anne conjectured, a readiness to slosh through water to get to their boats. In John's case, it would be to get to the boat he hoped to buy and learn how to sail someday.

John waved his hand towards the chair. He was a lawyer for a Colonial City manufacturing lobby and married to Ruth, a gray-streaked redhead neighbor of Anne who also taught at Westport Elementary.

"I don't want to interrupt your work," she apologized.

He whisked the papers into a leather shoulder bag. "I guess you know—I guess the whole village knows since I told Ms. Beatrice—Ruth and I are getting divorced. And it's not going smoothly."

"I'm sorry. You have no children, so that wouldn't be—"

"It's the house. She wants to buy out my half. I don't want her to have it."

Anne wondered why, but didn't ask. Her own husband had died suddenly at twenty-eight after a run fifteen years ago. She couldn't imagine them ever having fought over a house. It was probably because they'd had such a loving relationship that she hadn't re-married. She said, "I guess there's no way you two could reconcile?"

"Ruth hates her job at Westport Elementary. Since she got her Ed.D., she thinks the job is beneath her. I told her I make enough money. She could quit and take up some hobby, I don't know, like learn how to sail or something."

"Heh-heh."

"Yeah, I know." John started to change the subject when there was a shuffle and tap of a cane next to the table. Ms. Beatrice, the neighborhood sentinel, stood there stiffly in her pastel blue granny dress, eyeing them.

"Oh! My!" she said.

That afternoon the kids in Anne's fifth-grade English lesson were getting restless because it was Friday. They rushed out at the bell, but Tonya stopped in the hall to talk to her. "Ms. Anne, I hear you're racing tomorrow. I've never been in a sailboat. Maybe someday. I made you a bracelet for a good luck charm but Ms. Ruth—"

Tramping down the hall with a scowl on her freckled face, Ruth interrupted, "Tonya, school's over. You need to go home now. Leave Ms. Anne alone."

"Yes, Ms. Ruth."

Ruth grabbed Anne's arm with her cold, thin fingers. "Come into my office, will you? We need to talk."

Anne shrugged, called "Thank you" to Tonya, and followed Ruth into the teachers' room, which Ruth referred to as her office. She sat in the chair beside Ruth's desk and noticed a bracelet of little beads strung on a string lying on top of a thick red psychology textbook. Ruth brushed the bracelet off and quickly slipped the book into her bag.

"What a cute little bracelet," Anne said.

"That? I took it from Tonya, who was making it during my class. She apparently wasn't interested in learning about the capitals of Ecuador and Chile."

Anne picked it up and slipped it on her wrist. "I like it."

Ruth's phone in its leopard skin case sounded *Rahr-Rahr* on her desk. Anne thought she recognized the caller's picture as a well-known local realtor. Ruth glanced at it and quickly shut it off. "Anyway, Anne, I understand tomorrow's yet another regatta. Which means cars will be parked in front of our houses again." Ruth lived only a block down from Anne on Windward Street.

Anne grinned. "Not in front of mine. My van's going to stay parked there."

"You can walk to the Westport Sailing Club tomorrow. But what about me? If I drive across the drawbridge to Colonial City to get my hair done, when I get back somebody will be parked in front of my house."

"I know. I'm sorry. But there's nothing I can—"

"I've done something about it already," Ruth sniffed, lifting a pointy chin. "I've contacted the commodore—apparently that's what they call him—of your Westport Sailing Club. He told me the club's board of directors had narrowly voted not to ask the Westport Civic Association to put up *Parking for Residents Only* signs along Windward and Tiller Streets. They fear the Maritime Republic of Westport committee will object. The Republic nincompoops say customers of the sail lofts, rigging shops, cafés, and marinas need to have a place to park. Parking restrictions would be bad for business."

Anne nodded. "That's what I've heard."

"Maritime Republic, indeed," Ruth scoffed. "I understand the idea was made up by a bunch of men drinking in a bar."

Anne said she'd heard that, too. "Yet their organization still has a lot of pull in the neighborhood."

"We'll see about that. Your sailing club commodore said if I joined the club as a board member, I might sway the club to change their mind and ask the Westport Civic Association to put up those parking signs."

"But you don't sail, Ruth."

"Commodore Dan said some Board members don't sail anymore, either. They just oversee the books and serve on what he called the race committees."

"You'll serve on race committees?"

"That's what I wanted to ask you about. What would that involve?"

"They judge the races. They go out on the course in a boat and make sure the sailors follow the rules."

"Oh. I was thinking meetings and paperwork," Ruth pouted. "I'm a little afraid of boats. I guess they wear life jackets?"

"Of course."

"I don't know if I could do that."

"Maybe you could try it tomorrow. See how you like it. There's a race committee meeting in the clubhouse tomorrow morning where they go over the rules for the regatta. Commodore Dan would probably let you join them for the day."

Ruth frowned for a moment as if Anne had been suggesting hara-kiri. But then her face relaxed. "You know, I just might surprise you and do that. I could cancel my hair appointment. I'm sure if I meet this commodore or whatever and join the board, I can convince them to find a way to put an end to this parking outrage."

"Maybe. You should get to the club by eight."

On the way home from the school, Anne met Tim Griffin, the Westport Sailing Club dockmaster and race facilitator. They'd been friends since a regatta two years ago. Tim had helped her repair her boat when a fitting tore loose from the deck. He didn't have to. It wasn't his job, and he had to delay the regatta until he fixed her boat. He felt sorry for her, she assumed. But after that he made a point to talk to her and encourage her whenever she showed up at the club for practice.

It was hot, and Tim's light brown hair was tousled and his tanned face was glowing in a light sweat. He showed her a sample T-shirt he'd ordered for the club to sell to regatta participants at the awards ceremony on Sunday. It had the Westport Sailing Club logo and a picture of a Laser, the one-person open sailboat they would be sailing in. "Like it?"

"I love it."

"Walk you home?"

On the way, Anne was toying with the bracelet Tonya had made for her and tripped on a crack in the sidewalk. Tim grabbed her hand to steady her, then to her surprise kept hold of it part of the way to her house.

2

Laser butt

Early Saturday morning Anne checked the NOAA local report for the bay on her little VHF scanner. Southerly winds ten to fifteen miles per hour. That meant Tim would set up the windward mark of the race out in the bay beyond Greenthumb Point. Flood tide in the bay would be at 9:30, about when the race would start. So the best strategy on the windward leg of the race would be to stay in the shallower water at the sides of the course where the adverse current was weaker, then to sail down the middle with the current towards the leeward mark. She chuckled to herself, aware that making these calculations never did her much good.

The twenty-nine women in the regatta had carried or wheeled their light Laser sailboats on dollies up to the club's carpeted platform that sloped down into Town Creek, ready to raise masts and sails, slide the boats down into the water, and sail out into the bay. But first they all had to go sit on the wide stairway up to the second-floor clubhouse meeting room to hear the race committee announce the rules. It would be a two-race regatta, Olympic course. Any infractions of the rules could be remedied by sailing two 360-degree circles before proceeding. Low point scoring, with no throw-outs. The sum of each boat's finishing places in the two races would be that boat's score. Lowest overall score wins.

The women started to get up to go to their boats, but Commodore Dan, a short ex-Marine with a white moustache and matching eyebrows, held up his hand. "Before we start, I want to introduce one of our club's benefactors who's here with us today, Mr. Lawrence A. Bullock." The women, some of them muttering, sat back down.

"Doctor Bullock," Bullock corrected the commodore. "I have a Ph.D."

A husky, reddish faced man in a tight-fitting suit, Bullock looked to be in his sixties. He had large hands that he tossed back and forth as he talked. "Ladies," he boomed. "So happy to meet you all. I want to announce that, at my urging, the Fellowship Club has agreed to provide steamed crabs for your awards ceremony tomorrow. As you know, crabs are scarce this time of year. I'm sure you'll appreciate my Fellowship Club's generosity."

Anne started to get up, but Bullock wasn't finished. "I understand the daughter of the chair of the Board of Trustees for Severn Heights College is sailing in this race. Lily, are you here? Stand up, please."

Lily, a neighbor and friend of Anne's, tried to wave off the request but reluctantly stood when Bullock insisted, her pale face turning rosy.

"I'm pulling for you, Lily. I've never sailed in a regatta—football was my sport. Check out State U's record in the eighties. I was starting center for four years. But, as B.F. Skinner says, behavior can be modified for the better with the proper system of rewards and punishments. And I say sport of any kind can provide that system. Tell your father I'm rooting for you, Lily. And tell him I hope to be accepting the position of president of the college soon."

"Oh brother," Anne muttered into her lap.

Lily sat back down and whispered, "You have a Ph.D. too, Anne. How come you don't have people address you as Doctor?"

Anne whispered back, "I don't want people constantly asking me about their ailments."

Bullock went on. "I've docked *Knot on Call*, my Beneteau 38, here for this regatta to show my support for this little racing club. Actually, I'll probably keep the boat here a couple of weeks, at least. It's for sale. You can't see it from here, but it's docked beyond those big sailboats on trailers on the Bay Creek side of the club. I invite anybody who wants to come aboard and look at it after the race. Up until about eight o'clock, that is." He gave a nasal snicker. "My wife doesn't allow me to sleep on the boat."

Several women gave Lily a sympathetic pat on the back as they headed for their boats. Anne saw that Ruth, her red curls dangling out of a beige headscarf and sporting an inflatable life jacket, had indeed joined the race committee and with them was heading towards the committee boat, *Baited Breath*, a wide decked fishing boat that a local marina owner brought up to the club dock for the club to use at regattas. Tim had gone ahead in the club's Boston Whaler to set the course.

At the launching platform, Anne found herself next to Petra Fields, a tall, trim blond whom Anne had heard of but never met. Petra was a member of the South Bay Racing Club and was said to be the top woman Laser racer on the east coast. She was arguing in a low voice with Rob Green, an enterprising young sailmaker in Westport. Anne heard Rob mutter, "You can't use this sail. It's a prototype I made you just for practice races."

"I've used it in every regatta this season," Petra hissed. She pointed to a little red *International Laser Class Association Authorized Sailmaker* button."

"You put that on the sail yourself? You can't do that."

"Keep your voice down."

"What about that letter you got?"

"Don't worry about it," Petra snapped back.

Muttering a curse, Rob turned and hurried away.

Anne marveled at the toned muscles of Petra's arms as she lifted her boat's mast without help and set it onto her boat. Petra never made eye contact with Anne and didn't talk to any of the other women.

Anne noticed Petra's sail seemed to have a slightly fuller cut than the regulation Laser sail, but she couldn't be sure. Anne fastened her hiking strap with the new line and strapped on a hiking pad to avoid getting what the sailors called "Laser butt" when leaning out or "hiking" to keep the boat level in heavy air. She gathered her hair into a short ponytail that she pulled through the gap behind her ball cap. Like the other women, Anne wore shorts and a

T-shirt over a bathing suit, with a life jacket. Most had switched to the thin, comfortable jackets that inflated automatically when they hit the water.

The Laser fleet sailed out of Town Creek towards the bay. Anne could see that Tim, in the Whaler, had already set the marks of the course and had boarded the committee boat at the starting line.

The start was the most difficult part of any race. These twenty-nine identical boats had to maneuver behind an imaginary line between the committee boat and a buoy about fifty yards away and sail across that line just as the race committee signaled the start of the race. If you were late to cross, the sails of all the boats ahead of you would slow you down. If you crossed the line early, you were disqualified—or in this race you had to return behind the line and sail two complete circles before moving on.

The fleet of Lasers reached the starting area just before the warning horn sounded on the committee boat indicating ten minutes until the start. Anne saw Commodore Dan, his head covered by a safari hat, talking to Ruth, pointing towards the buoy at the other end of the line, and handing Ruth a megaphone.

Avoiding the boats on starboard tack, Anne sailed up and down the line as close to it as possible without crossing it. At the one-minute signal, she looked for a place among the jumble of boats that were fighting for position, ready to trim their sails and cross at the starting gun, preferably at full speed.

At the gun Anne had to avoid another boat, which forced her to cross the line more slowly than she wanted, but her position close to the committee boat side of the line was good. Then she heard the megaphone. "Two-Two-Six-Nine-Four-Two—Over." Anne looked back at the committee boat. It was Ruth who had called the boat over early. It was a high sail number, indicating a very new boat. Anne took another look back. It was Petra—she recognized her long blond hair streaming from under her cap. Anne heard Petra shout a curse at Ruth. But Petra had no choice but to sail back behind the line and do two complete circles before following behind the rest of the fleet.

Anne had no thoughts of winning the regatta. She would be happy to finish anywhere in the middle of the fleet. When the wind picked up halfway to the windward mark, she had to hike far out to keep from capsizing. There'd be groaning about Laser butt when the regatta was over. She was starting to wonder if she was getting too old for this. But as she trimmed the sheet slightly to keep the boom out of the water, she noticed the bead bracelet on her wrist. The boat surged onto a plane, skimming across the water. An instant rush of energy told her that the thrill of Laser racing was still her thing.

When Anne rounded the windward mark, there were about ten boats ahead of her. She held her position on the reaches, then lost another boat or two by the windward finish. Not bad.

As each boat crossed the finish line, it made a wide circle back to the leeward mark for the second race. Anne was surprised to see that Petra had gained on a number of boats and would not finish last.

The wind held for the second race. No one was called over early. The only incident happened on the first leg of the race. Anne was on starboard tack with the right-of-way when Petra, on port tack, bumped Anne's boat and made her deviate slightly from her course. Anne could have cried "Protest" and made Petra do two circles right there but didn't. Nobody else saw the infraction, and Anne didn't like the thought of having Petra as her enemy. In no time, Petra was far ahead of her.

After that second race, the Lasers sailed back to the floating dock. Petra was the first one back by far. She stood glaring at Ruth as the race committee got off the boat and went up into the clubhouse meeting room. Anne, Lily, and the other club members slid their boats onto the Laser rack for storage while non-members helped each other carry their boats to car racks or lightweight trailers hitched to their cars or vans.

'Doctor' Bullock stepped out of the clubhouse meeting room

onto the platform at the top of the stairs and repeated his invitation for "any of you beautiful ladies" to join him on his large cruising sailboat for a drink and a tour. In the boatyard, however, the talk was of going to Blake's Pub, a tradition after the regatta. A few women headed for the spartan showers on the ground floor of the clubhouse, but most went directly to Blake's dressed as they were.

Anne put away her boat and went to help Tim cast off the borrowed committee boat after everyone had left. The scores for the regatta wouldn't be announced until the next day at the awards ceremony, but Anne asked Tim if he knew the results.

"They're not supposed to be announced until the ceremony," he said, "but I have a copy. Let's see. Petra placed 19th out of 29 in the first race and took first in the second race."

"So she obviously didn't win the regatta. How about me? I'm really out of practice, but I know there were some boats behind me."

Tim grinned. "Already checked it. You came in 10th and 11th." He gave her a high five.

"And I'm just curious. What about Lily? She was embarrassed when 'Doctor' Bullock drew so much attention to her."

Tim scanned his copy of the results. Beat you by five boats in the first race. You beat her by four in the second. So she beat you by a point."

"Good for her. Are you coming to Blake's tonight?"

"I can't. I have to meet with the race committee, then help set up tables for the awards ceremony and cookout tomorrow."

"Right. Well, I'm going to take a shower in my own house, then go to Blake's at least for a little while."

"You should. The post mortems are fun."

"But I wonder. Could I maybe stop by to ask you something about the race on my way back home?"

"Sure. I'll be in my mansion." It was what he called the little cabin on the grounds that the club gave him to live in.

3

On the hook

Blake's Pub, a hangout for sailors and boaters, was the traditional gathering place after Westport Sailing Club regattas. The pub was packed when Anne got there. The regulars—crabbers, fishermen, boat builders, sailors—were rowdy from beer and the rare appearance of lots of women in shorts and T-shirts or tank tops standing around drinking beer. Anne saw Petra, still in her purple South Bay Racing Club shorts and the only sailor who hadn't thrown a shirt over her bathing suit top, near the bar surrounded by a group of grinning men. "Come on!" they drawled. "Over early? No way! That woman must've had it in for you." Petra had obviously been complaining about Ruth's call in the first race. Anne suspected the men actually had no idea what she was talking about but just wanted to egg her on and buy her more drinks and maybe get lucky.

Anne, who had changed to a blouse and jeans, squeezed through a throng of women to the bar to order fish tacos and a draft beer. She looked around and didn't see Ruth. Blake's wasn't Ruth's kind of place.

"Weren't you racing today?" Reggie, the bartender wiped some spilled beer from the counter in front of her. "Oh, you were? How'd you do?"

"Middle of the fleet."

"Um-hm." He poured her a pint of beer and called out, "William, one order of fish tacos."

Petra seemed to hear this and, bored with the men crowding around her, made her way to the bar and took the only empty stool, next to Anne, probably planning to order some tacos herself. Anne said hello, but Petra was tipsy and didn't seem to recognize her. She ordered a shot of Tequila and tossed it down in one gulp. William the cook, a young mahogany skinned man in a white apron, came from the kitchen and squeezed between Anne and Petra to put Anne's order on the bar. Assuming it was hers, Petra slid the tacos over in front of herself.

Anne heard William whisper to Petra, "I need to talk to you. You still owe me."

"Huh? Oh. For the bennies. And I need more of them. I just spent all the money I brought with me. There's more in my van. When do you get off work?"

"Eleven. Keep your voice down."

"Meet me at the club when you get off. Not by the clubhouse. Back by the boat launching dock. I'll pay you then. And, like I said, I need more."

William backed away from the bar, sliding the tacos back in front of Anne. He winked at Petra. "You want your own tacos? Guess you can ask Reggie to put them on a tab."

Anne picked up a taco, and Petra gave her a sidelong glance. Anne tried to sidetrack her. "I understand you took first place in the second race today. Nice."

"Huh? You were racing, too?"

This was the second time tonight somebody wasn't sure Anne was one of the racers. She was about the same age as the rest of the women. She kept herself in shape. Was it because she'd showered and changed into clothes that made her look like … what? More like a teacher? Petra should have recognized Anne as the sailor who rigged her boat next to hers—if not as the woman who let her get by with a port-tack infraction.

Finally Petra said, "Oh you're the one who … well, it was just a little bump anyway." She cursed. "Like that over-early call. I couldn't have been over by more than a foot or two. That call probably ruined my chances of qualifying for the Olympic tryouts. I could strangle that woman."

Anne knew that with twenty-nine boats it would be impossible for a race committee to detect only a foot or two. Most boats were probably over the line by a foot or two. Petra wouldn't have been called over unless it had been by a good bit more than that.

Petra pulled out her wallet and seemed surprised to find it empty. She'd obviously had too much to drink. Anne said, "You live in South County, right, Petra? Are you driving home tonight?"

Petra said she'd be sleeping in her van.

A well-built, tan-skinned man in a sleeveless black shirt with an eagle tattoo on his arm squeezed in on the other side of Petra. "Bad luck today, *mi amor*? Let me buy you a drink to cheer you up." Petra nodded.

Anne decided the fish taco was the best she'd ever tasted, probably because she was so hungry. She looked through the window over the bar. The sun was getting lower in the sky. She finished the fries, too, just as William brought Petra her order.

"What's this?" Petra growled. "I didn't order this."

Anne got up and nodded to the tattoo man that he could have her seat next to Petra.

"No," he pleaded. "Don't get up, Miss. I'll buy you both a drink."

Anne declined with a smile. In the crowd of women standing with their drinks in the narrow pub, she found her friend Lily and a few women she knew from the days when they all sailed in the junior program at the Westport club. They had scattered long since then, gone to college, got jobs, married, had babies, but still came back to sail in regattas when they could. Anne, Lily, and a few others who had grown up in the village had moved back to Westport. There was a good bit of showing pictures of children and even some grandchildren on their phones. One of the women remembered Anne's husband, Neil. "Is he still a keen jogger?" She seemed shocked to hear that Neil had died rather young of a heart problem he didn't know he had. "It was after a long jog," Anne explained. She suddenly found herself feeling lonely. At seven thirty she said goodbye and walked back to the sailing club to see Tim.

Tim was sitting on a chair outside of his cabin, his black lab

Molly beside him, with a book on his lap. He seemed to be waiting for Anne. It was late June, but the air was chilly, and, for the first time, he invited her to come inside.

The dark-stained wooden cabin was basically one room with a separate kitchen area and an enclosed toilet. Tim's bed stood next to his desk. Besides one chair, a large bookshelf, and two wooden filing cabinets, there was no other furniture. Anne sat in the chair at the desk, and Tim sat on the bed.

"I was talking to Petra tonight," Anne said. "She says the over-early call was unfair."

"It wasn't. She was over early. I was the one who made the call, as always. But Commodore Dan wanted to let Ruth have the fun of announcing it over the megaphone. I told her exactly what to say."

"So Petra got caught. She's probably used to getting away with it."

Tim rubbed his chin. "Something else, though. On the committee boat Ruth said she regularly sends posts to the *Westport Voice* website. She told everybody she plans to send a report on the regatta."

"Hmm. Maybe she actually enjoyed it. Do you think?"

"I know she was enjoying the scuttlebutt in the committee boat. There were some questions about whether the sail Rob Green had made for Petra was legal and whether it gave her an unfair advantage. When Ruth started taking notes, Rob asked her not to mention the sail in her *Westport Voice* report. But Ruth insisted she was going to include that discussion when she sent in her report first thing tomorrow morning. She told Rob, 'I'm not in the habit of omitting any details that might be significant.'"

"That's so like her."

"Well I don't know if the sail was legal or not, but I know the accusation that it was a cheat could damage Rob's career."

Anne sighed. "Ruth doesn't listen to me. If I asked her not to report it, it would only encourage her to do it."

"Oh, no, Anne. I didn't mean for you to get involved in this."

Tim had dropped his book on the desk. Anne sneaked a peak. It seemed to be about tall square-rigged ships. This man with light blue eyes had been a mystery to her since she met him. He was a few years older than her—she'd asked him—unmarried, intelligent judging by the nautical and historical books on his shelf, and conscientious about his job. *Sympatico*, some of her students might call him. She had lots of questions she'd like to ask him, but she decided to hold off for now. Go gently, she told herself. You don't want to be called over early.

She left Tim's cabin after he fixed her a cup of frothy Malaysian *teh tarik* tea, which he said he'd learned to make in Kuala Lumpur. Tim walked her home and watched until she went in the door. Exhausted from the regatta, she dropped into her bed and fell into a deep sleep.

Police sirens and the wailing of an ambulance woke her up. It was daylight, seven in the morning. Anne rushed to the door. The blue lights of police cars and red lights of an ambulance flashed down Windward Street and turned onto Tiller Street just past her house. They were heading for the Westport Sailing Club. She threw on a clean T-shirt from the last regatta, pulled on the jeans from last night, and rushed to the club without combing her hair.

She ran towards the launching dock at the Bay Creek corner of the boatyard behind the row of twenty-six-foot sailboats lined up on trailers where police were directing a crew from the ambulance with a stretcher—and stopped, gasping. Hanging at the launching dock by an inflatable life jacket from the hook of the boat launching crane was a limp human body, dripping wet, its head taped up in a plastic bag.

4

Further questions

Her hand over her mouth, Anne took a tentative step towards the area where uniformed cops were photographing the body. Tim was talking to a portly cop with gray hair who seemed to be in charge. Anne stepped forward to ask Tim what had happened, but a young cop with a thin, pale face and sharp nose stopped her. "Crime scene, Ma'am. You'll have to move back." He stretched a roll of yellow barrier tape to block off a large area around the launching dock.

Anne stood outside the tape, gaping as a van with a forensics team pulled into the boatyard and a man and woman got out and put on white coveralls. They seemed to approach the hanging body as if it were a curiosity more than a human being. It looked like they were searching the ground and fingerprinting the hook, the plastic bag, and the push button switch which hung from a thick electric wire that operated the launching crane—all without any obvious signs of pity for the dead person.

Neighbors and club members started trickling onto the club grounds. Held back behind the tape, everyone craned trying to see who the victim might be. Finally a white gowned forensics woman nodded approval for the ambulance crew to take the body down and lay it on the stretcher. Anne climbed to the top of the clubhouse stairs to get a better look. She saw the forensics woman delicately cut the plastic bag away from the head.

Anne gasped and screamed out. "Ruth!"

She held her breath as the forensics team covered the body with a white cloth. Ruth was wearing the same clothes she'd had on the previous day except for her scarf, but now the barely noticeable white life jacket the club had lent her was fully inflated. Anne thought she saw red marks around her neck.

The young cop ducked under the barrier tape and called Anne down from the steps. "Do you know the victim, Ma'am?" He took out his notebook. Anne was able to give him Ruth's name, address, and place of employment. She didn't know the names of any of Ruth's relatives other than her husband.

"Do you know if she had any enemies? Anybody who might want to harm her?"

"There might have been people who were annoyed with her, but I don't know anybody who would want to kill her." While he was questioning Anne, more people started trickling into the boatyard, recording everything they saw with their cell phones. The young cop asked for anybody else who might know the victim. Anne saw Ms. Beatrice shuffle up, tapping her cane, and take hold of the young cop's jacket.

When the ambulance left, probably to deliver the body to the medical examiner in Baltimore, the gray haired cop—Captain Blunt the tag below his badge read—put Tim into a police car and drove away. Anne had no chance to ask Tim if he'd been the one to find the body and call the police. She'd had no chance to get the whole story from him. She ran her fingers through her uncombed hair—she probably looked like a madwoman—and was heading back to her house when the young cop, whose sharp nose seemed suited to sniff out evil, stopped her.

"Ms. Anne Bateman? I have some more questions for you if you don't mind." He opened his notebook. "Is it true you've written comments on …." He checked his notebook. "… the *Westport Voice* website, opposing Ruth Neucomb's posts complaining about what she called excessive historical preservation restrictions for the neighborhood?"

"Um, yes. Ruth and I teach at the same school. A couple of times I've told her in person and on the website when I thought she'd been mistaken about some of her claims."

"I suppose the website is available to the public, yes?" He made a note. "Let me ask you something else." He cleared his throat.

"Are you having an affair with Ruth Neucomb's husband?"

"Of course not."

"I understand she and her husband were planning to divorce. Is that correct?"

"Yes."

"Did you and Mr. Neucomb plan to get married after the divorce?"

"Certainly not."

The cop checked his notebook. "Is it true that you had coffee with him at Clyde's Café yesterday morning?"

"Yes. It was crowded, and there was an empty chair at his table."

"Mr. Neucomb had his legal shoulder bag with him, is that true? Yes? Did you discuss his divorce with him?"

"He told me there was a dispute about the house. That's all."

"Can you be more specific? Did Mr. Neucomb want the house after the divorce?"

"He said he did. I don't see why—"

"Let me ask you this." He looked at his notes. "Do you currently own the house you live in?"

"No. I rent it."

"I see." He wrote down her answer. "And where were you between about nine and midnight last night?"

"Home."

"Alone?"

"Yes."

He wrote more in his notebook. "We may have some more questions for you later. I'll have to ask you to notify us if you intend to leave town." He gave her his card. Sergeant Carrs. Anne had to tell herself he was just doing his job. She was scared, though.

Commodore Dan arrived while the forensics team was driving away. Panicked club members and neighbors rushed to tell him what they knew. He immediately said the awards ceremony would have to be canceled. "So Larry," he said to one of the board members, "we have the phone numbers of all the participants. Would you notify them that we'll mail out the awards? I'll call Doctor Bullock and ask him to postpone the order for crabs until our Fourth of July feast."

Anne went home and called her mother in Florida. "Just in case you hear this on the news, Mom, there's been a death at the club. It's a woman I worked with at Westport Elementary. I wanted to assure you I'm all right."

"That's great, Dear."

Anne could never be sure her mother heard her correctly. "I don't want this incident to discourage you from the idea of moving up here to Westport, Mom."

"Move to Westport? First you've mentioned anything about that. Your dad and I just moved down here."

"That was two years ago, Mom. It's was Dad's idea. Since he died, you're there all alone."

"Who died?"

"I'm talking about Dad. Put your hearing aids in, Mom."

"Well, thanks for calling, Dear." The phone buzzed off.

Anne had been planning to go to Florida as soon as school was over to convince her mother to sell her house there and move back to Westport. She never imagined herself being told by the police not to leave town without notifying them. As for Tim, they'd taken him to the police station, leaving a police woman to guard the taped off area. Was it because Tim had discovered the body? Or was he actually a suspect?

Westport, despite declaring its tongue-in-cheek independence from Colonial City as the Maritime Republic of Westport in 1998, had actually been annexed to Colonial City in 1951. It was served by the Colonial City police department. Tim would have been taken to the police station there, two miles across the drawbridge near the narrow end of Academy Creek. How long would they keep him there?

She sat by her front window waiting for the police to pass by bringing Tim back to the sailing club. Or for Tim to call her. But when the phone rang, it was John Neucomb.

"Ruth has been killed, Anne. What did you tell the police? They're suggesting I might have done it. That you and I are having an affair." His voice trembled in anger.

"I told them we're not having an affair."

"They searched our house on Windward Street, took some things from it, and taped off the door. They took me into the station for questioning. Did you tell them Ruth and I were divorcing? That I'd already moved out?"

"I think Ms. Beatrice told them that. They already knew it."

"They asked me where I was last night at about the time Ruth was killed. I told them I brought some papers to our house for her to sign around six o'clock. Ruth wasn't there. I waited there and fell asleep until almost after midnight and she still hadn't come back. Then I went back to my apartment."

"Did anybody see you there?"

"That's what the police asked. They used the word alibi. I want to warn you, Anne. If you're the one giving them the idea I did it, I'll file a defamation lawsuit against you." He ended the call.

Could John Neucomb actually have killed Ruth? He sounded angry, not the least bit sad that Ruth was gone. Anne had just had a glimpse of his personality that she'd not seen before. She supposed the police would keep an eye on what he did now that his wife was out of the way and he had full possession of the house.

A police car passed her house and turned onto Tiller Street towards the sailing club. Returning Tim, she hoped. Anne didn't want to confront the police again and waited until the car was heading back to Colonial City. Then she took out her phone. But it rang before she dialed. Tim.

"Anne, are you OK? They asked me a lot of questions about you?"

"It seems Ms. Beatrice told them I had a reason to want Ruth dead."

"Because of an affair with her husband. They mentioned that to me. I told them it was ridiculous."

"It is ridiculous, Tim. I swear." She was fighting back tears.

"I know, Anne."

"Was it you who found Ruth hanging there?"

"Yeah. I don't think they suspect me, but who knows? When they brought me back just now, before they took down the yellow barrier tape, they put a plastic bag around the launching crane's control switch, then asked me to show them how we use it to lift big boats off their trailers and drop them into the deep water at the dock."

"I'm scared, Tim."

"Let's talk. Can you come over here?"

5

No business on Sundays

Tim's job required him to live at the Westport Sailing Club. Besides being the dockmaster and race facilitator, he took it upon himself to act as an unofficial security guard. He seldom left the boatyard for an extended time without notifying Commodore Dan. Anne brushed her tangled hair, put on a silky blouse, and went to his cabin. It was past noon when he opened the door, letting out his dog Molly and an aroma of crab cakes and Old Bay seasoning. Molly gave Anne's leg a touch with her nose, and Tim greeted her with a smile. "I'm hungry. I thought you might be, too."

"I am." She'd eaten nothing yet that day and figured Tim hadn't either. He poured out two coffee cups of Riesling, and they ate from his desk. Anne put everything out of her mind until she'd eaten a large crab cake and finished her wine.

"So here's the story," Tim said. "I walked you home about eight thirty last night. As soon as I got back, I crashed onto the bed and fell asleep right away. That must have been no later than nine. Then a little after eleven, I woke up to use the toilet. I thought I heard something in the boatyard and opened the door to listen. Molly ran out barking, and I followed her to the Bay Creek corner of the club grounds. I had a glimpse of a Black man running towards the narrow passage that leads out to Tiller Street. Molly stopped when the man disappeared down the path. I've trained her not to leave the club grounds."

"Did you recognize the man?"

"No. There was heavy cloud cover, too dark. He wasn't carrying anything, so I figured he wasn't a thief. I gave a quick look around to see if anything had been moved and went back to bed. I should have checked more thoroughly."

"Do you think that was the man who killed Ruth?"

"Maybe. I went back out just at daylight. This time I checked closer to where I'd seen the man. I walked behind the line of big Solings on trailers to the launching dock where the crane is and saw her hanging there."

Anne asked if he was sure it was a Black man?

"Yes. I could tell that much."

"Then I might know who it was." She told Tim what she'd heard Petra and William talking about at Blake's that night.

"William, the cook at Blake's Pub? He hangs around here sometimes on Laser regatta mornings to see if anybody needs help carrying their boats from their car to the ramp. Some of them give him a tip. Anne, if you know William was here last night, we should tell the police."

"Yes. Of course." She frowned. "But I wonder. Why would William kill Ruth? I don't think he even knew her. You always read about police wanting to solve cases too quickly and—"

"Not the Colonial City police. They have a great reputation."

"I know. You're right." She tapped a finger nervously on the desk. "I'd just like to see what William says about it before I give the police his name." She pushed back her chair. "And I feel like it's best to act fast."

"What? You're going to Blake's right now to find him?"

"Believe me, I'd like to stay, but—"

"I can't go with you now. I told the police I'd be here all day."

"That's all right. I can go by myself. Thanks for a great lunch, Tim." She stood up. "I'll call you and let you know how it went."

Blake's was much quieter Sunday afternoon. Anne went up to the bar and asked Reggie if she could speak to William.

"William's off today. Kitchen's open, though. Get you something to eat?"

"No, thanks. I just wanted to talk to him. Do you know where he lives?"

"On the Bay Creek end of Independence Street, west side."

Reggie gave Anne a glare of disapproval. "He doesn't do business on Sundays, though."

"Oh, no. Not anything like that. I just want to ask him something."

"Yeah? His mother's a church lady. Just so you know."

"Don't worry. This is a social visit. That's all."

The bartender narrowed his eyes skeptically as she left.

The light gray clapboard house that William lived in with his mother, like many in Westport, had a covered front porch, hers, like many, featuring a rocking chair. Anne walked up and knocked on the door. A gray haired woman in a beige flowered dress welcomed her in. "I think I know you," she said. "You're a teacher at the elementary school, aren't you? I've seen you on the playground at recess time."

"Yes. I live on Windward Street, next to that house with an anchor by its mailbox." It was how she usually described to people in Westport where she lived.

"My son William went to school there until he was ten," William's mother said. "That was twenty years ago."

"I've taught there for eighteen years, so I just missed him."

"I already made a donation to the PTA fund this year, but if they need more, I'll be glad—"

"Oh, no. That's not why I'm here. They told me at Blake's where William lives. A friend of mine wanted me to give him a message." It sounded a little lame, but it was the best Anne could come up with.

"William's out back in the shed working on that dinghy he's been building for almost a year. I'll go get him."

"Don't bother, please. I'll find him myself."

William's mother led her through the kitchen and opened the door to the back stairs. "The shed door's open. Just go in."

Anne knocked on the door jamb. William was gluing a stern rail to the boat and looked up. "Huh? Just a minute." He wiped off the excess glue.

Anne stepped into the shed. "What a beautiful boat. It looks like it's just about ready to launch."

The pained look on William's face softened immediately. "Will be soon. I plan to take it to the Eastern Shore of the bay and catch some crabs."

Anne stroked the gunnel with her hand. "Beautiful finish."

"Yeah. But I got to say, I don't do business on Sunday."

"I'm just here to ask you something."

"You a cop?"

"No. Last night at Blake's I heard you talking to Petra. She said she'd meet you at the Westport Sailing Club after you got off work at eleven."

William only stared at her.

"You might have heard a woman was killed there last night."

"Yeah? You say you're not a cop?"

"Word of honor. But a witness told me he saw somebody last night near where the dead woman was found. The cops are probably going to question me tomorrow. If it was you, I wanted to get your side of the story first."

William paced around the dinghy, staring down at the dirt floor. "If the cops ask you, I know you'll tell them what you heard. Maybe somebody else saw me, too. So yeah, I did go to the club a little after eleven and waited. But Petra never showed up. As soon as I heard a dog bark, I ran down the narrow path onto Tiller Street."

"You didn't see the woman hanging from the boat launch crane?"

"No."

"You didn't hear anybody else in the boatyard?"

"No."

"Did Petra contact you after that?"

"No. She was pretty drunk. I figure she probably doesn't even remember telling me to meet her there."

"All right, William. If you're telling the truth, the police will figure that out. I'm not going to say anything to them unless they ask me." And in the meantime, she thought, I need to find Petra and try to find out if you *are* telling the truth.

Tim called Anne as she was walking back to her house. "Everything OK, Anne?"

"Yeah, you didn't need to worry. William said he did come to the club to meet Petra, but she never showed up."

"Hmm."

"Tim, the club has a list of emergency contacts for the women in the regatta. Can we look at them if I stop by?"

Wagging her tail, Molly ran to greet Anne as she came in the boatyard. Tim was already upstairs in the club office, the regatta entry forms spread out on a table. "Here's Petra's form," Tim told her. "South County address."

Anne called Petra's number. A woman answered. "She hasn't come back yet. I'm her partner, Jessie. I haven't heard from her. She usually calls to tell me how she did in the regatta."

"I'm sure there's no need to worry. But if you hear from her, would you call me?"

So Petra didn't go home. "Or at least she didn't *get* home," Anne said to Tim. "She was tipsy Saturday night at Blake's. Might have been the combination of Benzedrine and alcohol. I hope she didn't have an accident."

"I wonder if that combination could have pushed her over the top in another way," Tim said. "She was furious at Ruth."

"You mean ...?"

"Yeah. I've been thinking about that."

"I guess I have, too." Anne gave out a long sigh. "Anyway, tomorrow's the last day of school. I have to figure out something to tell the kids about Ruth, then I need to get some rest."

"Without dinner?" Tim teased. "Come look at this." He led her to a refrigerator in the club's kitchen. "Shrimp salad that the club had prepared to serve with the crabs at the ceremony today. We wouldn't want all of it to go bad, would we?"

6

Thanks for

The news of Ruth's death had spread through the small Westport community, and Anne's class sat motionless, staring at her as she walked into the room. "It looks like you've all heard the sad news already," Anne began. "I'm so sorry. Ms. Ruth is no longer with us, but she will be remembered. We'll say some departing words for her this afternoon at the last day of school convocation. I thought it would be a nice gesture if my students would all write a short goodbye note to her that I can read then. So everybody please take out paper and pencil. If you don't have paper, raise your hand. Or if you need a pencil." Anne knew this would be a challenge for the Spanish-speaking kids who'd been dropped into her class a couple months ago without knowing a word of English. She said, "I'll come around to see if you need help." When Anne passed Tonya's desk, Tonya pointed to the bracelet on Anne's wrist and grinned. Anne smiled and nodded.

The students were asking each other what to write, borrowing paper and pencils, and groaning when the principal, Lucia, a bubbly ebony faced woman with glasses that magnified her eyes, came to the door and called Anne out into the hall. "Anne, a Sergeant Carrs from the police is here to see you." Lucia took over Anne's class, and Sergeant Carrs escorted Anne to his car.

She sat clenching her hands in the back seat, wondering if Ruth's husband John Neucomb had told the police anything to make them more suspicious of her. And then wondering if John, who'd showed her in his phone call how angry he could get, might actually have killed Ruth in order to get possession of the house. Anne took out her phone and checked the *Westport Voice*, which she'd given up reading months ago. There were lots of complaints by Ruth about any- and everything, but her latest posts on the theme of community regulations had become more specific. It was absolutely unacceptable, Ruth wrote, to restrict any new development in Westport to marine related businesses. "If I want to turn my house into a four-story condo, why shouldn't I be able to?"

The idea would also have been repellent to her husband, who had bought into the Maritime Republic ethos with the fanaticism of a religious convert. Sock burning—check. Tug of war against Colonial City—check. Maintain the quaint style of the houses—check. Anne herself shuddered to think what a monstrous modern four-story condo would do to the early-American small town charm of Windward Street.

The police station had a stale, air-conditioned odor. Sergeant Carrs pointed Anne to a seat beside his cluttered metal desk. "We need some more information from you," he began. "Can you confirm the deceased's husband John Neucomb's whereabouts the evening his wife was killed?"

"No."

"Phone records show he called you yesterday. What did you talk about?"

"He told me he told the police he was at their house between six and midnight."

"But you can't confirm that?"

"No."

"He and Ruth were separated, he told me. Can you confirm that?"

"I knew they were getting a divorce. Ruth never told me he'd actually moved out. But he mentioned it in that phone call to me."

"Would you say that John Neucomb has a hot temper?"

"I really don't know him that well."

"Have you known him to threaten anybody?"

"Um, he did warn me not to spread around the false idea that he might have killed Ruth."

Carrs leaned towards her with his sharp nose. "What did you think when he gave you that warning?"

Anne had seen a few students who cheated react with aggressive denials like John's. She saw what the sergeant was getting at but didn't think it proved anything and said nothing.

"Let me ask you again. Were you having an affair with John Neucomb?"

"Believe me, Sergeant Carrs, we weren't having an affair. I hardly know the man."

"All right. Let's change tack for a moment. Isn't that what you sailboat guys say? I wanted to ask you something else. Do you know a Colonial City real estate developer named Ronald Whitby? Real Estate Ron is the name he goes by in his ads."

"Yes, I've seen the ads."

"Have you seen him in Westport talking to the deceased, Ruth Neucomb?"

"No."

"Are you aware that he has applied for a zoning exception to build a four-story condo at 306 Windward Street?"

"306. That's—"

"The Neucombs' house. Right."

"No. I didn't know that."

"Yet you seem concerned. We've read your comments on the *Westport Voice* defending the community's prohibition of any new development except for small maritime-related businesses."

"It's true. I'm in favor of keeping Westport as close as possible to the maritime village it's always been."

"And I understand John Neucomb feels the same. That seems to mean both you and Mr. Neucomb will have your way now that Ruth Neucomb is dead."

Anne felt a sudden lump in her throat preventing her from speaking.

"You say you were alone in your house between nine and midnight when the murder must have taken place according to the medical examiner's report, but nobody can corroborate that, am I right?"

Before Anne could answer, Captain Blunt burst into the office holding what looked like a flash drive his hand. He nodded to Anne. "Would you excuse us a minute? I need to talk to Sergeant Carrs in my office."

Anne waited, drumming her fingers softly on the desk. The dark skinned woman with hair braids whose desk sat next to Sergeant Carrs offered to bring her some coffee. The woman's desk plate said Darlene Trimble, and she wore civilian clothes. Anne thanked her and drank the coffee slowly, wishing she had strongly discouraged Ruth from serving on the race committee.

Sergeant Carrs whisked out of Captain Blunt's office. He didn't sit down. "That's all I have for you, Ms. Bait-Man."

"Bateman. You can just call me Anne."

"Yes. Sorry to make you wait. I'll drive you back to school now."

In the car Anne asked if they had found some new evidence.

"We might have," Sergeant Carrs answered laconically. He said no more until he dropped Anne off at the school. Anne watched him drive away, surprised that he didn't head back towards the drawbridge leading to Colonial City but turned down onto Tiller Street.

Anne was in time for the end-of-year convocation in the gym. The principal had already given out the final report cards and achievement certificates. "Oh, just in time," she trilled. "Ms. Anne is here to help us pay our respects to Ms. Ruth." She pulled a handful of papers from her bag.

Anne looked at the children's expectant faces, most of which, she thought, showed signs of hoping this would not go on very long before they were let out of school for the summer. She cleared her throat, glancing through the papers. Most of them were blank. The first said simply *goodbye*. The second said *bye miss*. Anne supplemented those with a few words of thanks for Ruth's excellent teaching. *Hope you are with god* another said. Anne changed *Hope* to *I'm sure*. The third said simply *Thanks for* followed by empty space. Anne finished it with *all your help*. She looked around. John

Neucomb had been invited, but he hadn't come.

As the students rushed out laughing and shouting, the principal commented sarcastically to Anne, "They seem to be managing to cope with the tragedy well."

Walking home, Anne came across Ms. Beatrice shuffling towards her brown shingled Victorian house on the corner. The woman's rouged cheeks were pinker than usual. She tapped her cane to stop Anne. "This is terrible. We have a quiet neighborhood, and now the police are everywhere. Do you have any idea what they were doing at the Small Boat Tackle Shop? That old policeman was there all morning. Now the young policeman just left."

"Maybe they're getting interested in sailboat racing."

Ms. Beatrice huffed into her house. Anne waited until she saw her face peering out from her watch post in the third-floor turret. She was actually grateful for the information Ms. Beatrice had given her, and decided to go back to the shop to see what she could learn.

Before going in, she took a look at the narrow passage at the side of the shop. Tall weeds and broken boat rigging jammed the way. Anyone who didn't know that the path led to the Westport Sailing Club wouldn't have guessed it did. Anne took a few steps and saw that a line of weeds had been trampled down. She looked at the wall of the shop. Up at the roofline there was a security camera she'd never noticed before.

The bell jingled when she went in, and the young clerk said hello in a perfunctory tone almost as if serving a customer at the moment was a nuisance. He said, "Can I help you? Oh, you're the girl, uh woman, who was getting ready to race in the regatta Saturday. I guess the whole thing was a disaster, right? I never imagined anybody would be murdered in Westport."

"Me either. Um, Bill, somebody saw a policeman talking to you today."

"Yeah. The shop has a motion-detecting security camera. It sends a notice to my phone when it records something. This morning I saw that it had picked up something Saturday night. The *Westport Voice* reported the murder happened at the sailing club behind this shop, so I called and told the police."

"And they came today to get the footage?"

"Yeah, an old cop was here this morning. He copied the footage from last night and took it. Then a young cop came back and showed me part of it on a tablet. The camera caught a man coming through the path beside the shop at 11:15 and leaving at 11:25. The cop asked me if I recognized him."

"Did you?"

"Yes, but I don't know his name. He was in the shop about a week ago buying marine glue. Said he was building a wooden dinghy."

7

Drawn together

Anne's head was aching. All she wanted to do was go home and get some sleep. She picked up a novel that let her escape into a happier world, fell asleep dreaming of sailing to a Caribbean island, and didn't wake up until late the next morning. It took a few minutes for reality to hit her again. Whether William was guilty or not, the police had a video of him running from the boatyard the night of the murder. She made an instant coffee—no way she was going to Clyde's, where she might run into John Neucomb. She wanted to go and tell Tim what she'd found out. Before she left, not wanting Tim to feel obliged to feed her again, she warmed up the leftover half of a large casserole of beef ragu lasagna to bring along.

"Do you think the police can identify the guy caught on video?" Tim asked her.

"I guess they'll be showing his picture around the village, so …."

"What if they show it to you?"

"Assuming it's William, I'll have to tell them."

"You don't think William did it, do you, Anne?"

"I know, he sells Benzedrine on the side for people like Petra who might want to get an illegal boost now and then. But I just feel like he was telling me the truth."

"It'll be hard for him to explain to the police what he was doing there. He might have to admit he was selling bennies to Petra. It wouldn't be as bad as murder."

Anne nodded. They were sitting at the boat club picnic bench overlooking Town Creek. A long stratus cloud drifted across the sun throwing a deep shadow on the water. Anne had set her casserole on the table, and Tim had managed to supply two plates and two forks from his cabin. No serving spoon. No glasses. No napkins.

They were starting to eat when Petra's partner Jessie called Anne. She sounded desperate. "Have you found her?"

"No," Anne said. "Sorry. I was hoping she had returned home by now."

Jessie was crying. "Something must have happened to her."

"I think we should call the police." Anne didn't want to interact with the police again. She suggested that Jessie call them.

"No." Jessie was nervous. "I can't call them. And please don't you call them."

"Why?"

"It's my parents. They don't know I'm living with Petra. If they find out, they wouldn't approve."

"But if Petra's missing—"

"They think I'm living with a man."

It took a moment before Anne understood. She couldn't help wondering what Jessie saw in Petra. Maybe Petra had a human side, but Anne hadn't detected it. At Blake's Pub, Petra had been angry enough to say she could strangle Ruth for calling her over early. It was a common hyperbole, but coming from Petra, it had given Anne a chill. "I'll let you know if I hear anything," Anne told Jessie. "And please let me know if you hear from her."

When Anne ended the call, Tim asked, "Do you think Petra ran away?"

"You mean killed Ruth, then ran away?"

"Seems like we have to consider that."

Anne knew they did.

"Forget it for now." Tim tapped her knee. "Yesterday was your last day of school. I should have congratulated you."

"Thanks. Later this summer I'll be doing some volunteer tutoring at the school, but—"

"But for now you're free, right? We should celebrate. Wait here." He went back to his cabin and brought out two plastic cups and a bottle of Chianti. It was weird, but Anne felt like the murder at the club was drawing her and Tim closer together. She'd always been charmed by his good looks and slightly foreign-seeming good manners and curious about this man who, in her opinion seemed out of place as the dockmaster of a fairly small, unremarkable boat club in a village where he seemed to have no relatives.

Just as they finished lunch, a van with *Green Sails* on its side panel drove into one of the club's few parking spaces. Rob Green came up to the table, nodded to Anne, and asked Tim if he could help with taking some measurements on one of the fifteen-foot Snipe sailboats kept on trailers in the yard.

"On a Snipe, not a Laser?" Tim asked. "I thought you were working towards getting certified to make official Laser sails?"

Rob rolled his eyes. "I'm putting that project aside, at least for now. The market for Laser sails is huge because it's an Olympic class boat, but, as you know, the International Laser Class Association only licenses a few sail lofts to make the sails. On the other hand, boats like the Snipe that aren't sailed in the Olympics have different rules. The Snipe association allows any loft to make sails for Snipes as long as they stick to the approved specifications." Rob shrugged. "The market for Snipe sails is pretty good, too."

Anne watched as Tim and Rob ran a measuring tape up the mast of a Snipe and straight down the mast to the boom to check the length of the luff, then out to the end of the boom to check the leech. They measured the length of the boom itself to find the maximum length for the foot of a sail for that type of boat.

When Rob left, Anne asked Tim why Rob didn't just look up the Snipe association's sail specifications.

"Of course he did. But the specifications give only maximums. A sailmaker needs to make sure the boat's mast and boom can effectively handle the maximum lengths."

Anne told Tim what she'd heard Petra and Rob arguing about before the regatta. "Petra used an unofficial sail made by Rob with a fake ILCA button she put on the sail herself."

"So the rumors were right. No wonder Rob was so angry when

Ruth Neucomb said she was going to publish those rumors in the *Westport Voice*. Whatever's in the *Westport Voice* gets around. If people found out it was Rob who made the illegal sail, he would have shared the blame for Petra's cheating. He'd never get a license to make official Laser sails."

"Did Rob make any threats against Ruth on the committee boat?"

"Not really."

"What do you mean?"

"Let me think. I heard him mumble, 'Somebody needs to teach that woman to mind her own business.'"

While Tim was washing the plates, Anne looked over the books on his shelves more closely than before. One particularly attracted her attention. *Sailing Elcano's Route from the Philippines to Spain.* She pulled it out. The author was Timothy Griffin. "Tim, this isn't you, is it?"

"That book? Yeah. I wrote it after I got back to the States after some time in Southeast Asia."

She'd been waiting for an opening to ask about Tim's life before he came to Westport. "How long were you there?"

"About five years. I was married once. To a girl from Manila. She died, and I got the idea of taking a sailboat and re-tracing Juan Sebastian Elcano's route from the Philippines back to Spain when he completed Ferdinand Magellan's circumnavigation of the world."

"That's what the book is about?"

"Yeah. After Magellan was killed in the battle of Mactan, Elcano continued the expedition and arrived in Seville in the one remaining ship of Magellan's original five with only seventeen or eighteen of the expedition's original two hundred forty Europeans. I wanted to see what sailing challenges Elcano's guys went through, then write a detailed description."

Anne needed to let all that sink in before she asked any more questions. She asked for another glass of wine.

"You're quiet," Tim said. "Are you wondering whether Rob Green could have taken Ruth's life?"

Anne had been thinking about Tim, but she said, "Well, if Rob did it, it was about money. If Petra did it, it was about fame."

"Mm. And if John Neucomb did it, it was money, too, I guess."

"And not wanting Ruth to ruin the ambiance of the neighborhood because he wanted so badly to fit in as a true Maritime Republic of Westport resident." Anne sighed, checked the time. "That little TV over there, Tim? Does it work?"

Tim tuned in the local evening news. A weather forecast was interrupted by a "Special Report." A slightly fuzzy but recognizable picture of William's face appeared, with the newscaster's message. "Police are looking for this man in connection with the recent murder of Ruth Neucomb. Anyone having information about his identity is requested to contact the Colonial City police." The police phone number was posted on the screen.

Anne was clenching her hands after that report. The police hadn't said where they got the picture. It was taken from a video clip, she knew, but it looked like it could have been taken on someone's phone. That's what William might think—that she'd taken it surreptitiously when she'd gone to talk to him. And now William might actually be the murderer. What if, before he was identified and arrested, he came to find her, or just happened to see her on the street?

"You can stay here with me, if you want," Tim offered. "You can stay here until he's caught."

"Thank you, Tim. But would you walk me home instead? I just want to go into my own house and lock the door."

8

Got their man

Anne checked the late TV news before going to bed—no announcement that William had been arrested. She slept only restlessly, getting up once at 3:00 a.m. to eat a cup of pineapple yogurt before going back to bed. She slept late, and by the time she got up, the all-news radio station noon report said that the police had just brought in a person of interest for questioning in what they were calling the "sailing club murder." His name was not being released yet, but Anne knew it must be William. She wondered how long they would hold him. In William's favor was the fact that he had no motive for killing Ruth. Against him was the undisputable fact that he had been caught on camera in the area where she was murdered at about the time the murder had been committed.

She was still in her yellow terrycloth bathrobe when somebody knocked on the door. It was William's mother, tears running down her smooth chestnut cheeks. Anne led her to her embarrassingly shabby couch in her narrow living room, where the old woman sat holding her black quilted purse on her lap.

"Ms. Anne, I'm so disappointed," the elderly woman sniffled. "My poor William. He told me he thought you were a nice lady. So did I."

Anne handed her a tissue.

"He said you …." William's mother swallowed hard. "He said you liked his boat. Ms. Anne, building that boat meant so much to him."

Anne took her hand. Her own throat choked with emotion, she managed to say, "I only talked to William that one time, and I liked him, too. Believe me, I wasn't the one who—"

"He said you took a picture of him. Gave it to the police. Told them he was a mur …." She couldn't finish the word.

"I didn't. I never took a picture of him. I never mentioned him to the police. Trust me, Mrs. ….”

“Jamieson. And now he’s arrested.”

“Mrs. Jamieson, the police might be asking him some questions. That’s all. I’m sure William didn’t even know the woman who was killed. She was a teacher I worked with. She never mentioned his name.”

William’s mother blinked and wiped her eyes. “But why him?”

Anne knew the answer, but it was the police’s job to tell William’s mother about the security camera. “Did William call you from the police station, Mrs. Jamieson?”

She nodded, sniffling again. “He said he didn’t do it.”

“Well, they won’t hold him if he didn’t do it.”

William’s mother stood up, steadying herself on the arm of the couch. Anne offered to walk with her back to her house.

“No need. Thank you. I’ll be going to see Pastor Brown at the Mount Zion Church.”

Summer vacation from school always made Anne feel restless. She’d find herself spending time at the Westport library looking for the perfect book, often a classic she’d always told herself she should read one day. Maybe now she could find a book about Magellan’s circumnavigation, which she knew almost nothing about. With her nerves rattled from talking to William’s mother, going to the library now seemed like a way to settle herself down.

She never went there in the old jeans or shorts and T-shirt she wore to the sailing club. Too great a chance other teachers or students would see her there. She tied her thick, wavy hair into a short ponytail, put on black stretch pants and her only clean blouse, a collared beige one, and added just a touch of lip gloss. But she’d skipped breakfast and needed to eat first. The only food in her refrigerator was leftover stir fry from two days ago. She wanted the special chips and fries that were served at Clyde’s for lunch.

On the way there she met Ms. Beatrice tapping along with her cane. “Terrible, isn’t it,” the old woman rasped. “What have we come to? They've arrested a man in our village for murder. They didn't say who it was on the news. I'm thinking the young man at the Tackle Shop might know. I'm going there to ask him."

"I'm sure the police have a good reason not to give out his name," Anne said, but Ms. Beatrice had already shuffled off, her sensible shoes scraping the sidewalk.

Pleased to find an open table, Anne signaled Pedro, the waiter-busboy-dishwasher, and father of Anne's student Luis.

"Fish and chips, yes, Ms. Anne? Rockfish today. Fresh from the bay this morning." He poured a glass of water. "Very bad news that teacher killed."

"Yes."

"Man asking for you this morning. Don't know his name. He had coffee and left."

"Oh?"

"With *portafolio*." Pedro mimed putting a bag over his shoulder.

Anne shook her head as if she had no idea who that might be. But she feared it was John Neucomb.

The fish and chips with vinegar were so good she finished them in no time. Pedro cleared the table and brought her the check. She was searching her phone for an idea of what book to get from the library when she heard a voice behind her. "Hello, Anne." It was John Neucomb. He sat down. "I was hoping to find you."

Anne stood up. John Neucomb was the last person she wanted to see. She had assumed he only went to Clyde's in the morning before going in to Colonial City for work.

"Please, Anne. I know. My angry phone call to you after the police questioned me. I'm sorry about that. I want to apologize."

Both Anne and John Neucomb glanced around as if to make sure Ms. Beatrice was nowhere in sight. Anne cautiously sat back down. John Neucomb said, "I was afraid the police were going to blame me for Ruth's death when I called you. Things have changed now. May I sit with you a minute? Thanks."

"What's changed?" Anne asked.

"The police have caught the guy who killed Ruth. Maybe you haven't seen the news. I'm not a suspect anymore. The police have taken the yellow tape off my house door." He leaned back and breathed out a sigh. "You're looking very good today."

"John, the Westport Elementary principal notified you of their ceremony to honor Ruth. You didn't come."

"Yes, I hated to miss that, but I had an important meeting with another lawyer in the city. Actually, it was related to Ruth. To her death, I mean. House deed, probate details, matters like that." His eyes seemed to be examining her. "I plan on making sure the house continues to look like a traditional Maritime Republic house. And I think you would support that, Anne. Am I right?"

Anne gave a reserved nod.

He straightened in his chair, putting both hands on the table as if about to make a legal proposition. "I'd like to propose something to you, Anne. As you know, Ruth and I disagreed on the value of keeping Westport a nautical community." He sniggered. "She didn't even want me to buy a boat. But I think you and I are on the same page. You're a boat person. You know this community from when you first took sailing lessons at the Westport Sailing Club as a child. You returned later to live here. I want to be a true Maritime Republic of Westport citizen. Anne, I think if you and I were together, that would be possible."

"Together? What do you mean?"

"We're both single now. I don't know you well, but I find you attractive. We're about the same age. You don't own your house. You're only renting."

"I don't like where you seem to be going with this."

"Let me finish. I've recently been promoted to partner in my law firm, with a substantial salary increase plus valuable perks. I could support you in a style that, as a teacher, you're not accustomed to. And as for me, you could be my link to the sailing society I long to join. I want to buy a boat. You could help me find just the right one and teach me how to sail it."

"Hold on. This can't be a marriage proposal, can it?" Anne sat up straight and slid her chair back a few inches. The scraping sound echoed in the room, but Anne seemed to be the only one who noticed.

"I know it comes unexpectedly, Anne. But if we got married, it would enhance both of our lives. Ruth told me once that you dreamed of going on a Caribbean cruise in your own sailboat."

"How can you talk like this to me after Ruth has just been murdered?" Anne was starting to suspect that John Neucomb had in fact murdered his wife and had possibly been planning this all along.

John said, "Do you realize that Ruth and I had no longer been living together? I've been living in an apartment in the new condo out beyond the drawbridge to Colonial City."

"Ruth never told me that, but …." Anne didn't remind him that he'd implied as much in his angry call to her.

"Probably because Ruth didn't want to mention her affair with Real Estate Ron."

"What? No."

"It's true. Hard to believe, isn't it. That creep. Have you seen pictures of him? And I've looked into some shady dealings he's made. I'm not going to let that rest."

Anne tried to think of anything Ruth might have said or done that would suggest she was having an affair. She did mention Real Estate Ron a good bit. And Anne remembered Ruth getting a call from him in her office. But that's all Anne could come up with.

John Neucomb put his hand on hers. She quickly snatched it away. John was undeterred. "What do you think? You and me, taking state legislators on cruises up and down the bay. Sailing off together to Newport or Fort Lauderdale for vacations."

"I think you're out of your mind. And you'd better not let the police hear you talking like this. For both of our sakes."

"I told you. Don't worry. They've got their man."

9

Sailing ladies

Anne wasn't going to be able concentrate on looking for books in the library and was happy to come across her friend Lily before she got there.

"You look like you've seen a ghost, Anne."

"Oh, I guess I was thinking about Ruth. It's still shocking. But look at you in your Bay Warden uniform." The petite Lily was dressed in a dark green shirt and shorts with a walkie talkie hanging from a wide leather belt and a Natural Resources badge pinned to her breast. Her auburn hair drifted out from a slit in the back of a dark green cap featuring the Natural Resources star and logo. With their son and daughter both staying for summer classes at college, Lily and her husband were empty nesters, and Lily had taken a volunteer job checking for violations of oyster and crab conservation laws in the bay and its tributaries. She said, "I found a guy with a bushel of female crabs in his boat today."

Harvesting female crabs had been forbidden until the next year in order to increase the crab supply. "What did you do when you caught him, Lily?"

"I'm not allowed to arrest people or give tickets or anything. I told him if he didn't dump them back, I would report him, then wrote down his boat registration number."

"Good for you."

"And his outboard engine was leaking oil into the water. I told him if we don't take care of our bay and rivers, the water will become a polluted mess with nothing living in it."

When Anne only nodded, Lily said, "I can tell something's wrong, Anne. Why not stop by my house and I'll fix you some tea?"

Anne was always surprised to walk into Lily's small off-white stucco house that looked similar to the other houses on Chart Street on the outside. Inside, however, walls had been moved to enlarge rooms, the floors and stairway were now of polished Brazilian cherry, a candle style chandelier hung in the hall, and, most impressively the whole house had been expanded towards the back without changing the house's front façade.

Lily poured Anne a cup of tea from a porcelain pot into a matching cup painted with a delicate river scene. The sofa they sat on and all the furniture was in the Queen Anne style favored in Colonial City homes. Lily and her husband managed to live in Colonial City elegance without giving up the charm and access to the water of Westport.

"Tell me what's worrying you, Anne. I feel like it's not only what happened to Ruth."

"Yeah. Let me ask you. Did you know Ruth and her husband were getting a divorce?"

"No. I hardly knew Ruth."

"Don't tell this to anybody, Lily. Promise? Ms. Beatrice told the police she suspected I was having an affair with Ruth's husband."

Lily started to laugh, then stopped herself. "You're not saying they believed what that old gossip says?"

"I don't know. But it gets worse. Right before I ran into you today, Ruth's husband sat down at my table in Clyde's and ...."

"What?"

"Actually proposed marriage to me."

Lily brought her hand to her mouth to stifle a laugh. "Was he joking? You don't really know him, do you?"

"No."

"And this was just a few days after his wife was killed." Lily wrung her hands. "It almost makes you think he ... I don't want to say it. Anyway the police already caught the man who killed Ruth."

"They only announced they have a person of interest. And if they find out John Neucomb asked me to marry him right after Ruth was killed—"

"Oh, Anne. Don't tell anybody. Stay away from that man."

"I plan to."

Lily stuck up her little finger. "Promise? And I'll never tell anybody, either. I promise." Lily frowned. "But what about Ruth's husband? Is he going to tell people he wants to marry you?"

"He'd be stupid if he did."

"This whole thing is terrible, Anne. Do you think the police really have the right person? At first I suspected it was Petra."

"Me, too. At Blake's Pub I heard Petra say she could strangle Ruth for calling her over early."

"But after what you just told me, now I wonder if Ruth's husband did it."

"I know. He's cold, calculating. He told me Ruth wasn't satisfied with her life, that she wanted to be more than an elementary school teacher. Today I found out John Neucomb hasn't been satisfied with his life either. And it's been Ruth who was standing in his way."

Lily put her hands to her cheeks. "I can't think about this. Out on the water I can always clear worries from my mind."

"I know what you mean."

"Anne, there's still time before Vince gets home. Come take a ride with me in my Whaler. A friend called me and asked if I wanted to see an eagle's nest. Give me a minute to get out of this uniform."

"I'd like to change, too. I don't want to get these clothes wet."

"I can lend you something to put on." Lily laughed. "My own little shirts might not fit. I'll get you one of Betty's that she left here when she went away to college. You don't want to ruin those pants, either. I'll get you a pair of Betty's shorts, too."

Lily put on a *Save the Bay* T-shirt and gave Anne one picturing Taylor Swift.

Lily kept her little boat at Harvey's Marina on Town Creek at the end of Westport near the drawbridge. The dockworkers all knew her. A suntanned man with long yellow hair tied back in a ponytail said, "Hey, Lily. Where you going? Take me with you."

"Next time, Travis," Lily laughed. She handed Anne a spare life jacket and started the rumbling forty-horsepower engine—big for her thirteen-foot boat. Yellow Ponytail and a brown skinned co-worker came to cast her off.

Lily carefully kept to six knots in the creek so as not to disturb the docked boats and the fish and other sea life. But when she turned out into the bay, she threw the throttle forward, jolting the boat up onto a plane. Anne had to hold on tight to the seat and siderail. "It's over there by Greenthumb Point," Lily shouted above the engine and wind noise. "You can see the tower."

The boat slowed again and turned into a cove on the Greenthumb shore where three abandoned wooden fishing shacks stood next to a newly-built concrete slab supporting a tall steel cell phone tower. Lily shifted into neutral and they drifted up beside a boat bigger than hers that was tied to a huge tree stump. A powerfully built man with olive skin and short black hair standing straight up watched them get out and step over some rocks to come ashore. "Ms. Lily, good to see you. Not in uniform?"

"Not today, Jorge. I just came to show my friend Anne the eagle nest."

Jorge pointed up to the top of the tower. In a massive nest of sticks, a bald eagle was feeding her fledglings, whose beaks peeped above the ridge of the nest. Anne had heard bald eagles were re-appearing in the bay area, but this was the first nest she'd seen so close to Westport. She took a picture with her phone. It was then that she noticed an eagle tattoo on Jorge's arm and wondered if he could be the man who had bought Petra a drink at Blake's after the regatta.

"Let me introduce you, Jorge," Lily said. "This is my friend Anne."

Jorge looked closely at Anne. "My nephew goes to Westport Elementary. I pick him up sometimes after school. Are you a teacher there? I think I've seen you in the schoolyard."

"Yes. What is your nephew's name?"

"Roberto."

"Roberto's in my class. A clever boy. Very polite." Roberto was the student who'd written *Thank you for ….* as his farewell note to Ruth.

"Roberto told me he learned so much from you this year." Jorge touched his chest. "Thank you."

Anne was becoming more sure Jorge was the man she'd seen buying Petra a drink after the regatta. She playfully asked if he ever went to Blake's Pub.

"Sometimes." Jorge grinned. "I was there the night all those sailing ladies came into the pub. *Ay, Dios mío!*"

"I think I saw you there."

Jorge flushed, possibly remembering he'd also offered to buy Anne a drink. "You …. That was you? Roberto's teacher? If I knew I would never have—"

"No problem, Jorge. You were talking to somebody I know. Petra."

Jorge relaxed a bit. "Yes, I remember. Big blond?" He breathed out a sigh. "I thought sailing ladies would be *sympática*. This woman was not."

"What did she talk about? Do you remember?"

"She was angry at some woman. She didn't say why. Probably had too much Tequila. I left her and went to talk to someone else."

Lily chimed in, "To talk to another woman, right? Still looking for the perfect someone, Jorge? You had the right idea, though," Lily encouraged him. "A 'sailing lady' might be right for you."

"I had a woman for a long time," Jorge said, "but we never married. No children. Then she left me for my second cousin. And they married." Jorge shrugged. "Maybe for the best. I don't know."

A loud peep sounded from the eagle nest. With a flutter of wings, a baby eagle dropped from the nest and hit the ground in front of Jorge.

Jorge bent to look at it. "He hurt his wing when he fell. I'm afraid foxes are going to get him."

Lily took out her phone. "I'll call somebody from Natural Resources to come and take him to their rehabilitation center." She took a picture of the baby eagle. "The poor little thing."

Jorge said he'd stay and guard the baby eagle until the Natural Resources arrived.

As Lily and Anne motored back out into the bay, Lily remarked with a grin, "Jorge might be a good match for you, Anne. He likes 'sailing ladies.'"

Anne said she still wasn't thinking about getting married again. "But I'd prefer Jorge to John Neucomb, that's for sure."

"Jorge helped me set up an oyster growing cage in an inlet near here. The Bay Foundation gives you baby oysters. You keep them protected for a year until they grow a couple of inches long, then give them back to the foundation, which plants them on sanctuary reefs, where no one is allowed to harvest them. We need more oysters in the bay to filter the water."

"I know about oyster farming. I've never seen one of the cages, though."

"We still have time. I'll show you mine." Lily steered the boat towards a narrow inlet along the Greenthumb shoreline.

"Grab that line on the piling," Lilly said. They stepped onto the shore, and Lily pulled up a rope attached to the oyster cage. "Oh look. They're even bigger than the last time I checked. Almost ready to go."

They motored back into the bay and towards the Westport Sailing Club heading for Town Creek and Lily's dock. When they passed the club, Anne said, "I see Dr. Bullock's boat is still there. I guess he's leaving it there until after the Fourth of July feast." She laughed. "He'll probably give another pompous speech hoping to sell it."

"What a blowhard."

"Is your father really going to appoint him as president of Severn Heights College?"

"It doesn't work that way. The Board of Trustees can hire a president, but the normal procedure is that the college faculty and administration form a selection committee. They check credentials, past experience, recommendations. Then they vote. Their selection has to be approved by the Board of Trustees, but that's usually just a formality. And, by the way, the chair of the board has no special authority or input. In fact my dad's planning to vote against Bullock. His main qualification is that his golfing buddy is one of the trustees."

"Your dad doesn't think he's qualified to be president of the college?"

"No. The background check didn't turn up anything except that back in college Bullock was suspended for two games from the football team for repeated unnecessary roughness penalties. But my dad's main objection is that Bullock's only academic qualification is that he taught some continuing education courses at a community college—things like 'Creating Your Personal Impact' and 'Confidence Building for Career Advancement.' But he's never taught a credit course."

"Does it have to be a unanimous vote by the trustees for the president to be appointed?"

"No. Just a simple majority."

10

Hair control

On her way home, as Anne turned onto Windward Street, a dark-skinned bald man in a Roman collar waved to her. "Ms. Anne? I'm Pastor Brown. I'm bringing William Jamieson's mother to see you. She's very upset."

William's mother was trembling and didn't seem able to speak. She clutched her heavy breast, breathing hard. Pastor Brown took her arm in his. "We called the police station. Mrs. Jamieson's voice was weak, and I spoke for her."

"What did the police say?" Anne asked.

Before the pastor could answer, Mrs. Jamieson's legs seemed to give way, and he and Anne held her to keep her from falling. "I worry about her heart," Pastor Brown said. "She's had some problems before."

"Let's get her to my house," Anne said. "It's only a few doors down."

Anne sat William's mother on her couch and found a cloth to wipe beads of sweat from her forehead. "Are you feeling dizzy, Mrs. Jamieson? Is there any pain?" Anne remembered asking her husband Neil these questions before he passed away. Her own hands were shaking now as she took out her phone. "I'll call an ambulance."

"No, no," William's mother finally spoke. "This happens sometimes when I get to worrying." She sighed. "There. I'm much better now."

Anne wasn't so sure. "Or maybe I could drive you to the emergency room and let them check you out."

"I'm fine, Dear. I just need to sit a minute."

Anne brought her a glass of water. She wanted to know what the police had said about William, but she didn't want to upset his mother again.

Pastor Brown said he didn't think William's mother should be alone in her house for a while. "I'd bring her to my own house, but with four young children, my wife and I are—"

"Understood," Anne said. "Mrs. Jamieson, you can stay here with me."

William's mother protested, but her hands were shaking. Anne asked if she'd had any dinner. "Can you stay with her here for a minute," she asked Pastor Brown, "while I go warm something up?" She microwaved a bowl of Irish stew from her refrigerator. Anne always ate at the little white kitchen table, but she brought the stew to the bare dining room table at the other end of the single room that served as a living room and dining room. Anne was relieved to see Mrs. Jamieson eating it. When she finished, Anne said, "I have an extra room with a bed upstairs. Let me take you up. I have a nightgown you can use."

Pastor Brown was still there when Anne came back down. "Bless you," he said. "Mrs. Jamieson has had a hard life. William is the only joy she has left. And now …."

"What? What did the police say?"

Pastor Brown closed his deep brown eyes. "They did *not* say it was you who identified William. I stressed that to Mrs. Jamieson, and she believed me. But they said a security camera had footage at the time of the murder showing him going into a back entrance to the Westport Sailing Club and coming out of it."

"But William didn't even know that woman." Anne knew why William had gone there, but she saw no reason to bring that up. He was being held as a suspect in a murder, not a minor drug deal.

Pastor Brown frowned and shook his head. "William told the police he'd gone there to meet a friend. That late at night! I can't imagine. And why would they meet there? I don't think the police believed him." The pastor gazed steadily at Anne. "It wasn't you he was going to meet, was it? I know you're a member of that club. And Mrs. Jamieson says you came to her house to talk to William at her house after the murder was discovered."

Anne felt her throat tighten. "No," she said, shaking her head. "It wasn't me he was going to meet."

Pastor Brown gave her a pat on the hand. "I didn't think so. I told Mrs. Jamieson I didn't think so." He rubbed his bald head. "Although Mrs. Jamieson says the woman who was murdered taught at Westport Elementary like you, and you knew her."

Anne looked the pastor in the eye. "I did. And I found out about her murder the next day when everybody else did."

"Yes. Yes. Well, the police say their investigation is ongoing. They can't comment on it. They're conducting interviews and reviewing evidence. The good news, I guess, is that they have until noon tomorrow to charge William. If they don't have enough evidence to charge him, they have to let him go."

"Besides his picture on the security camera footage, what other evidence have they found? Did they say?"

"No, but they asked me if I'd ever seen William with a woman who wore a black satin scrunchie in her hair." The pastor shrugged. "I told them it's not something I would have noticed. I only see William at church, and not every Sunday at that."

Pastor Brown left saying he would pray for the murdered woman, as well as Mrs. Jamieson, William, and Anne.

William's mother was asleep when Anne looked into the room. The street light coming through the window gave her dark face a more peaceful look than Anne had expected. Anne touched her hand and leaned close to check her breathing before whispering "Good night."

Before she went to bed herself, Anne went down to the kitchen to find something she could serve for breakfast. Pancakes. She would make pancakes. Now to clean up a little. She washed and dried the dishes, chuckling as she put them away. She hadn't had this feeling since her own mother had been able to visit her. She tiptoed up to her bedroom to pick up clothes before William's mother could see them scattered all over the chair and carpet. Her pine dressing table was covered with jars and tubes of cosmetics and skin creams, comb, hairbrush, and assorted scrunchies, all of which she shoved into a drawer.

Maybe Pastor Brown didn't notice whether a woman wore a scrunchie or not, but Anne did. Almost all women sailing in a regatta who didn't have short hair would tie it in scrunchies and feed the ponytail through the opening in their ball caps. Anne closed her eyes recalling the sight of Petra raising her sail with her long blond hair tied back in a black satin scrunchie.

11

About Saturday night

That picture of Petra was still in her mind when she served breakfast to William's mother early the next morning. "I have some sausage to go with these pancakes, Mrs. Jamieson. And some orange juice. You probably need to build up your strength."

"Thank you, Dear. My house is so empty without William. Thank you for letting me stay here last night. I'll be out of your way as soon as—"

"No. There's no need to go. I like having you here. We'll go get some of your clothes and things and—"

"Oh, my. Here I am thinking only about myself. You live alone, too." Mrs. Jamieson put her hands to her face. "Tell me how you do it. But, no, Dear. I have to go back home. I need to be there in case William tries to contact me."

"All right. I'll walk you home. And can we exchange phone numbers in case either of us gets news about William?"

At the door to her house, William's mother said, "Why don't you come in for a spell? I'll get you some tea." She served it with some home-made cinnamon buns on a dining table covered with a floral pattern linen cloth. The room was larger than Anne's little dining area, its walls papered with a rather old fashioned red and black stripe design like that on Anne's mother's house when she was young. Anne sipped the tea slowly, to extend her visit. "That's a beautiful little lampstand," she said.

"Thank you. My William made it. He's clever working with wood." William's mother clasped her hand over her mouth. "Oh, my! Today's Thursday. William usually goes up the street to the church meeting room on Thursdays at noon to help some of the children with their projects. They'll be expecting him. What will Pastor Brown tell them?"

"I'm sure he'll just say William is busy with something else."

"Busy is right. My William always has two, maybe three jobs going at once. Cook at Blake's Pub, doing woodwork on sailboats at Miller's Marina, building his own boat, cutting people's lawns—Lord, he'll always find a way to make money for the crab and fish business he's got his mind set on opening up."

Anne wanted to say William could be out of police custody soon. The video footage of him at the crime scene in itself might not be enough to charge him. But it didn't seem wise to give his mother false hopes. She asked about William's work with children at the church.

"He leaves some tools and wood there. This week they were going to make napkin holders." Mrs. Jamieson began to fidget with her own cloth napkin. "I usually go with him. It's not just William. There are four or five groups working on different things. I usually work on needlepoint with some of them." She looked at a pendulum clock on the wall. "It starts in fifteen minutes, and I forgot all about it."

Pastor Brown smiled to see that Anne had accompanied Mrs. Jamieson to the church. "Another volunteer for the children's workshop?" he trilled. "Perfect. We have some children struggling with basic writing skills."

William's mother winked at Anne. "Told you you'd fit in."

In the open room at the back of the church, groups of elementary-school aged children sitting at tables stopped talking and looked up when the pastor introduced Anne as a new writing tutor. Mrs. Jamieson went to her needlepoint table, three other women went to their tables, and the pastor led Anne to a table with two girls and two boys who looked less enthusiastic about their project than painting plaster of Paris figures or making dioramas. Anne was surprised to see Lily's friend Jorge at a table pouring water from a jug into one of the glasses he had lined up. Jorge smiled at her, put his hand to his heart, and gave each child a set of tablets.

"Well," Anne said to Michael, Susan, Anita, and Juan, all of whom she already knew from school. "We don't want to make this like schoolwork, do we?"

A chorus of *NOs* rang out.

"OK. I see you have pencils and paper. But first"—she took out her phone—"we're going to tell a story, one part at a time, as I pass this phone around."

Anne was in her element. The kids, all of different ages, worked with each other well since they were all having problems with writing English. Michael and Juan set Susan and Anita into fits of giggling with each of their additions to the story. They all worked together trying to put it into writing. Before Anne knew it, the workshop was over.

Pastor Brown flashed the room lights. "That's all, everybody." In a louder voice, he called out, "See you on Sunday."

He stopped by Anne's table. "I can see working here has put Mrs. Jamieson in a better frame of mind. Thanks for your help. I reminded her if the police don't charge William today, they'll have to release him. She's more settled now, breathing easier, and I'm going to walk her home."

As Anne was leaving, Jorge walked up beside her. "Nice to see you here."

"Yes. What was that project you were doing with the kids?"

"Testing bay water. For absorbed oxygen level, pollution, sediment—things that affect aquatic life."

Anne took him aside. "Can I talk to you a minute?" They stood in the churchyard after everyone was gone. "Maybe you know William Jamieson?" Anne began.

"Yes. He works with me at Miller's Marina. And he works here with the kids on Thursday mornings." Jorge pursed his lips. "I don't think he did it. None of us do."

"So you saw his picture in the news."

Jorge nodded.

"Can I ask you something about last Saturday night at Blake's?"

He bowed his head. "Again, So sorry. I think I tried to buy you a drink. I had no idea you were a teacher. And my nephew Roberto's teacher at that."

"Please, don't apologize. That's not what I wanted to talk about. I want to ask you about Petra." Anne smiled. "The woman you actually did buy a drink for."

"Yes?" Jorge shifted his weight uneasily.

"Do you remember what she was wearing?"

Jorge rolled his eyes. "I do, but …."

"What about her hair?"

"Blonde."

"Was it tied back? Like in a ponytail?"

"I think yes."

"Was it tied in a scrunchie?"

"This word I don't know."

"It's like a thing to tie up a woman's hair. Like mine. See?"

"Very pretty."

"Well?"

"Ah, yes. I remember."

"Was it thicker than mine? Satin? Do you remember what color it was?"

Jorge tilted his head. "The light was dim in the pub. And I wasn't looking so much at … I mean it might have been dark blue. Is that important?"

"I don't know. Could it have been black? Black satin?"

"Sure. Maybe."

"Did you leave the pub before Petra did?"

"No. She left about nine thirty. She was staggering and stumbling. I remember Reggie at the bar asking her if she was driving. She told him she was going to sleep in her van that night."

Anne thanked him. "And great project you did with the kids."

"How about you? Will you be coming back next Thursday?"

"If I can."

12

Mean or heartless?

Anne wanted to stop by and catch Tim up on some things she'd learned. He was putting a *Boat for Sale* notice on the club's outdoor bulletin board. *38-foot Beneteau. Like new. Hardly used. Call for price.*

Anne laughed. "Is that *Knot on Call*, 'Doctor' Bullock's boat? I'm sure it's definitely like new. I doubt he's ever put up the sails."

"Yeah. He came by and asked me to help him sell it. He said he would give me the key in case any potential buyer came by to look at it. But he forgot to give me the key before he left. The boat's in good shape for somebody looking for a second-hand cruising boat."

"I might know somebody. Ruth's husband John Neucomb."

"Get serious."

"With Ruth out of the way, I guess he feels free to become a full-fledged Maritime Republic guy. He told me he plans to buy a sailboat." Anne hesitated. She didn't like to spread gossip about a dead woman, but she'd learned of another motive John Neucomb might have for killing Ruth. "He also told me Ruth was having an affair with Real Estate Ron. I don't know if it's true or not."

"So you've been talking to him?"

Anne felt the blood rush to her face. She didn't know if she wanted to tell Tim that John Neucomb had actually made her a marriage proposal. She settled on saying, "I saw him in Clyde's. That man's crazy. His wife's probably still lying in the morgue and he's talking about buying a boat."

Tim closed the glass door over the bulletin board. "I've met John Neucomb a couple of times when he comes poking around here. Something about him gives me the creeps. We know the police have him on their list of suspects."

Anne ventured to make another referral to her recent conversation in Clyde's. "John Neucomb told me he felt safe because the police had 'got their man.' Meaning the guy whose picture was on the news. William, the cook at Blake's Pub. Also," Anne added quickly to change the topic from John Neucomb, "I met Pastor Brown. The pastor said the police asked him if he'd seen William with a woman who wore a black satin scrunchie in her hair."

Tim raised an eyebrow. "What do you make of that?"

"We know William said he was going to meet Petra here at the club that night. And I know Petra was wearing a black scrunchie."

"But William said he looked around and Petra didn't show up."

"Right. I heard Petra tell him to meet her here at the club when he got off work at eleven. But I just found out Petra left the pub about nine thirty."

"So Petra could have been here and gone by the time William got here. She would have had time to ...." Tim stroked his chin. "Petra had motive and opportunity. Isn't that what they say on police dramas?"

"And why did the police ask Pastor Brown about the scrunchie? I bet they found it at the scene."

"Hmm. But, Anne, do you know how many scrunchies I find in this boatyard after a woman's regatta? They're all over the place." He took her hand and led her towards the bench beside the creek. "Come on. I bet we can find some right now."

"That's OK. I believe you. I've lost a few of my own over the years. But the police were searching everywhere around the launching crane that morning. They could have picked up a scrunchie."

"They did pick something up. I couldn't see what it was. Hmm. I've always thought Petra was the only person mean enough to kill Ruth. And she's strong enough to hook the body onto the boat crane. Have you seen her arms?"

"I have. I was next to her when she lifted her Laser mast onto the boat."

"So she's strong enough. Maybe mean enough." Tim frowned.

"But you've talked to Ruth's husband recently. He sounds … maybe not so much mean as heartless. His wife died and all he can think about is buying a boat."

Anne knew John Neucomb had been thinking about even more than that, but she kept that to herself for now. Instead, she said, "It was very different for me. My husband died fifteen years ago. Sometimes I feel I'm still not over it."

"I've sensed that. Not that you ever talk about him."

"What about you? You told me your wife died when you were in the Philippines."

"Yeah, that was five years ago. I felt lost. I was in the State Department at the time. A couple of days after my wife died, they sent me a notice of transfer back to Washington. I didn't want to leave the place where we'd lived together, so I quit."

"You stayed in the Philippines without a job?"

"I found work on wealthy foreigners' boats. Within a year I met a Saudi who wanted me to bring his boat from Manila to Singapore. That gave me the idea to write about Elcano."

"So you sailed all the way to Spain to get material for your book?"

"No. Just as far as Singapore. It would have been clear sailing from there."

"How long have you been back in the States?"

"About three years. I was offered a government job in D.C., but I wanted time to write my book. I stumbled on this job at the Westport Sailing Club, and it's been perfect. The book's finished and published, but I've settled in here and like it. I've started writing another book."

"What's it about?"

"Die hard sailboat racers."

"What!"

"Just kidding. This one's on the history of U.S. – Philippine maritime treaties."

"Sounds like a page turner."

"Heh-heh."

"I saw you were reading a book about old sailing ships. Like the Pride of Baltimore?"

"Yeah, I've read stories by Conrad and others about sailing on them. I have to admit I'd like to give it a try."

Anne's phone rang. Her mother. "Anne, Sweetie, I heard on the TV there was a murder in Westport. I hope you're all right. I wish you had called."

"I did call, Mom. You might not have heard me clearly. I'm *fine.*"

"Time for what?"

"As soon as I can, I'm going to drive down to visit you and maybe help you sell your house so you can move back here. Like we talked about."

"All right, Dear. Come down and visit me sometime."

"I love you, Mom."

Tim had begun to walk up to the creek to give Anne privacy. He turned. "Something wrong? You look worried."

"My mom has a hard time understanding me on the phone. She refuses to use her hearing aids."

"Maybe you should go talk to her in person."

Anne nodded, and Tim put his arm around her. They stood staring down at the rocks lining the edge of the creek. Tim said, "Stay for a late lunch. Or maybe early dinner. Depends on how long it takes me to make some soup."

"Thanks. Give me a few minutes. I'll run home and get something for dessert."

Real Estate Ron was sitting on Anne's porch in her lattice backed rocking chair when she got home. He stood and looked her over. "You the lady of the house?" He handed her a card. "Ron Whitby. I'm in the real estate business. You have a nice house here."

Anne was repulsed by his presumption and pasty face, both probably the result of spending too much time walking through people's houses and poking into their closets.

"I knocked and didn't get an answer. Your husband's not home?"

"I'm single."

Ron's white cheeks bulged in a grin. "I see. Can we go in? I have someone who's looking for houses in this neighborhood. I might be able to make you a great offer if you're willing to sell."

"I'm not." No way Anne was going to let him know she was just a renter. It was more fun to pretend she owned the house and refused to sell.

"But you haven't heard my offer yet. If I could take a look at the house—"

"No thanks."

Ron shifted his weight to another foot and took a different approach. "Of course. I'm moving too fast. We haven't even gotten to know each other yet." He gave her a thin smile that reminded her of a movie villain contemplating some evil plan. "Are you hungry? Let me take you to the Palais de Paris just over on the Colonial City side. We'll have drinks by the water, a good meal, and talk about possibilities."

"No thanks."

He waved off her refusal with a pallid hand. "Of course, I'm moving too fast again. I meant after you've had a chance to go inside and change."

Anne took umbrage at this. What was wrong with the dark pants and white blouse she had on? She'd had enough of this man. She looked him in the eye. "Sorry. I'm only in the habit of going out with handsome men."

It worked as she expected. Real Estate Ron's self-assured flow of manipulative subterfuge was cut off short. He froze. He blinked.

"But Mr. Ron," she encouraged, "I have a friend whose house you might try to acquire. Ruth Neucomb. I'll give her your card."

13

A transported cuddle

"**Y**ou actually said that?" Tim was stirring his cauliflower and cheese soup when Anne got back with half of an apple pie from her fridge.

"You should have seen his face. I didn't think it could get whiter."

"Let me think about this. If Ruth really was having an affair with Real Estate Ron, as her husband claims, do you think Ron was pursuing her so he could get the house?"

"It sure looks like that was his plan."

"Is he married?"

Anne scoffed. "Somehow I doubt it."

"So you think he planned to marry her after she divorced?"

"Maybe. If he did, he could get her to make him joint owner of the house. And they could turn it into a four-story condo. That was probably his idea to start with."

"I see. But then Ruth was killed, and the house ownership passed to John Neucomb. You lose, Real Estate Ron. Sorry."

"And now Real Estate Ron needs to find another house to buy and convert. I'm sure I won't be the only person he visits and drops his card on."

Tim laughed. "Yeah, I guess he hopes the next person he approaches doesn't mock him by suggesting he get the listing for Ruth's house." Tim tasted the soup. "Not ready yet." He put a plate of thin sesame seed crackers on the desk he also used as a table and poured them mugs of the local Boordy Blush wine. "It's twice as much soup as I usually make, so it takes a bit longer."

"I've got plenty of time. Basically until September." Anne leaned back in the only chair while Tim stood by the stove.

"Not going to Florida? Sorry. I overheard you talking to

your mother."

"I'm planning to drive down to see her sometime this summer. It was my dad's idea to move there, but he died a couple of years ago. My mom's alone there now."

"It's a long drive. There are lots of reduced plane fares in the summer."

"I know, but I want to take my van hoping I can convince her to move back up here."

From the window Anne saw a tall masted ship drift by in the creek. She sighed. "I've always thought it would be fun to sail down the coast to Florida. I know some people who've done that. They said dolphins followed along beside them a good part of the way."

Tim gave her a look that made it hard to guess what he was thinking. As for Anne, she was thinking she'd like to sail down the coast to Florida with Tim. She added, "Of course, I'm still not allowed to go anywhere without notifying the police."

"Me, either. But I'm quite content to stay here for now." Tim refilled their mugs. "Soup's ready, but it's hot. Let's have some more wine and crackers." He opened his little fridge. "There's some smoked salmon and guacamole."

"I'm feeling content here myself."

They finished up the salmon, guacamole, and crackers. By the time they'd eaten the soup and then finished off Anne's apple pie, Anne looked out the little cabin window and couldn't believe it. The sun was beginning to set.

They walked out across the boatyard with Molly and looked out over Town Creek at the lights of Colonial City already making shimmering streaks on the calm, dark water. One of the more brightly lit buildings was the Palais de Paris. Tim turned to her. "Your story about Real Estate Ron made me jealous, you know. I've never asked you to dinner at the Palais de Paris. Instead I've fed you cauliflower soup."

"It was better than any soup they serve over there. I'm sure of that. I had a great time with you today."

"But if I asked you, would you let me take you there sometime?"

The lump in her throat kept her from speaking. She took Tim's hand and nodded yes.

Molly gave a sharp protective bark when Anne touched Tim.

"There, there, Molly. It's OK. Anne's a friend." Tim gave Molly a prolonged cuddle that Anne dared to think he was mentally transporting to her.

"I usually take Molly for a walk in the evening. How about coming along?" Tim put a leash on Molly, who twisted with anticipation at the chance to explore the world beyond the boatyard. They walked a good distance along Tiller Street, Molly sniffing every signpost and streetlamp along the sidewalk and the rosebushes and azaleas in every neatly trimmed yard. They turned onto Windward Street and headed back past the school, past Clyde's Café, Ruth's house, and on towards Anne's house. Molly stopped to sniff a streetlamp on a corner in front of a shingled house with a third-floor turret. Ms. Beatrice's house.

"Hello," Ms. Beatrice called from the rocking chair on her front porch. "Oh, Ms. Anne, is it? I didn't know you had a dog. I'll have to let people know. And it looks like you're with that handsome young man from the boat club. I don't believe I know his name."

"Juan Sebastian Elcano."

"Pardon? My hearing's not what it used to be. Don't forget to clean up after your dog. And I don't know about walking the streets with a young man after dark, Anne."

Tim waited until they were a block away before commenting, "Ms. Beatrice sure tries to keep the whole village in line."

"She was the guidance counselor at Westport Elementary for years. After she retired, she became guidance counselor for all of Westport."

When they stopped in front of Anne's house, Molly seemed confused and pulled at the leash to go on. "Guess we'll say good night here," Tim said. "Think about the Palais de Paris thing."

Anne was too excited to fall asleep for quite some time. When she did, she had weird dreams. First, a big dog like Molly was snoozing next to her in her narrow bed. The dream then shifted to an old woman pulling at her leg as she tried to get into a cruising sailboat. She woke up at eight in the morning tangled in her sheets and bedspread. The phone on her nightstand rang as she was getting out of bed. Sergeant Carrs asked if he could pick her up and bring her in for more questioning.

14

Hating to lose

The police station air conditioning felt even colder than before. The metal chair Anne sat on chilled her legs. Sergeant Carrs hadn't yet given her any hint about what he wanted to ask her. She held her arms close to her body and folded her hands on her lap. If William was no longer a suspect, had the police shifted their focus back to her?

The sergeant looked up from his notebook. "Are you planning to move, Ms. Anne?"

"No, I'm not."

"Because a neighbor reported she'd seen you talking to a real estate agent on the porch of the house you're renting. She says he gave you his card. She wondered if you're planning to move in with John Neucomb now that he has full possession of the house after his wife's death."

"It's the last thing I would do. Believe me."

"All right. She was just giving me a 'tip,' to use her word."

"I'm surprised this 'neighbor' didn't mention also seeing me last night, walking with a friend and his dog."

"With 'that handsome young man from the boat club'? In fact, she did call in later to report that, too. It seemed to confuse her. And she wanted us to understand it gave her some doubts about her earlier suspicion that you and John Neucomb were planning to get married." Sergeant Carrs bit his narrow lip. "We just have to follow up on everything, you understand?"

"So if Ms. Beatrice could see me sitting here talking to you, I suppose she would think the two of us were planning to get married?"

A giggle squeaked out of Ms. Trimble, the sympathetic police clerk at the next desk who had brought Anne a coffee during her previous trip to the station.

A red-faced Sergeant Carrs shot Ms. Trimble an offended look, then turned to Anne. "Let's move on. I have something for you to look at." He reached into a plastic bin on a table beside his desk and pulled out a sealed clear plastic bag, which he held by the very corner as if afraid the contents would infect him. It contained nothing but a wide black hair scrunchie. "Is this, uh, thing—"

"Scrunchie," Ms. Trimble sang out. "It's called a scrunchie, Sergeant."

"Yes, Ms. Trimble. Well, I need to ask you, Ms. Anne, if it's yours."

"No. My hair's too short to use that. It's too wide. It would look silly."

"Just as I told you," Ms. Trimble hummed, bobbing her head.

"I see. So this ... band" —he didn't seem able to make himself use the word 'scrunchie'— "is for a woman with longer hair than yours? Still I need to ask if you recognize the item." He aimed his sharp nose at Anne as if poised to sniff out a lie.

In fact, Anne remembered Petra wearing a black scrunchie like this when they put their boats into the water at the start of the regatta. And Petra was still wearing it afterwards at Blake's Pub. "Where did you find it?" Anne asked.

"I'm asking you the questions."

"At the Westport Sailing Club, most of the women with long hair use scrunchies to keep the hair out of their eyes. So if you found it there, there's no way to be sure who it belonged to."

Sergeant Carrs put the plastic bag on the edge of his desk and pointed with his ballpoint pen. "This one belonged to someone with long blond hair. You can see several strands attached to the, uh ...." He trailed off.

Anne was beginning to suspect that it was indeed Petra's. It was satin and quite wide, which was probably why she remembered Petra wearing it.

Sergeant Carrs took a breath through his nose, waiting for a response. Anne knew that William had told the police he'd gone to the club to meet a friend. He probably hadn't given them Petra's name, aware that the police would question her and the Benzedrine deal might come out.

"Ms. Anne? Does knowing it belonged to a woman with long blond hair help you to know who was wearing it?"

"Let me think." She knew Petra had left the pub about nine thirty and could have been at the boatyard and left before William got there after he got off work at eleven. If one of them killed Ruth, it seemed more likely it was Petra, who had a reason to hate her, rather than William, who didn't know her at all. Identifying Petra as the possible owner of the scrunchie would put Petra in the police crosshairs, where she ought to be. It would also corroborate what William had told the police, that he'd gone to the club to meet somebody.

Anne said, "I do know one of the regatta participants who has long blond hair and wore a black scrunchie. After the regatta, I saw her at Blake's Pub talking to William Jamieson, the cook there."

Sergeant Carrs and Ms. Trimble at the neighboring desk swiveled their chairs in her direction simultaneously. The sergeant opened his notebook. "Did you hear what they said? What is her name?"

"The pub was noisy. But I heard Petra Fields tell William to meet her at the sailing club after he got off work that night."

"Is that all? Did you hear anything else they said?"

This was the question Anne had been dreading. Petra had apparently already received 'bennies," the controlled drug amphetamine, from William without a prescription, and she was to pay him for those and get more from him when they met at the club that night. It seemed that one of the many side jobs William had, in addition to cutting lawns and working on boats, was selling Benzedrine illegally to the few people like Petra who wanted to use the drug as "uppers" to increase their concentration and energy. William's mother, Anne was sure, didn't know this was one of William's sidelines. Anne didn't want to let the police know about it. Rather than do that, she would prefer to encourage Pastor Brown to convince William to abandon that line of work. But she didn't want to lie. She said, "I heard William say that he needed to talk to her." That much was true.

"And they agreed to meet at the boat club later that night?"

"Yes."

"Can you give us contact information for this Petra Fields?"

"You can find it in the regatta entry forms at the Westport Sailing Club." That might give Anne enough time to contact Petra's partner Jessie first. Anne hated to cause Jessie any trouble, knowing she would be embarrassed if her parents found out she and Petra were living together. But more and more it seemed like Petra was the person who murdered Ruth. And the police needed to know that.

Sergeant Carrs dropped her off at her house, warning, "You're still not to leave Westport without notifying us. Do you understand?"

Before even going in, Anne called Jessie as the sergeant was driving away. "Jessie, has Petra come back yet?"

"No. And I don't know who to call."

"How about her family, her parents? Have you contacted them?"

"Petra's estranged from her parents. I don't even know if she has any brothers or sisters. She doesn't like to talk about those things."

"Can I ask you, Jessie? How long have you known Petra?"

"Only a few months. We met on the beach in Ocean City. I tripped and fell against her. I apologized and …." Jessie breathed out a sigh. "Anne, my parents had moved out West. I was alone. Petra saw that, I guess. She put her strong arm around me. And that was that."

"And she's lived with you since then? What else do you know about her?" Anne cleared her throat. "I mean I don't want to sound like your parents."

"She doesn't tell me much about her past. But I know what she's like. I've started wondering if she's disappeared because she didn't do well in the regatta. She expected to come out first. I know Petra hates to lose. How did she do?"

"She wasn't in the first three. I don't know exactly how she placed."

Jessie sucked in a breath. "At least I wasn't there. She couldn't blame me for bringing her bad luck."

"Has she blamed you before?"

"I shouldn't say anything bad about her. She's wonderful."

"Well, Jessie, it's been almost a week. You don't know anybody else to contact? It's probably time to report her missing."

"To the police?"

"I wanted to tell you. The Colonial City police are contacting people who might have information about what they're calling the sailing club murder."

"Oh, I've heard about that. It was terrible. Do they think Petra knows something about it?"

"They're questioning a lot of people. They questioned me. Petra was in the regatta, so they want to question her, too."

"I saw on the news that the police already arrested somebody. The man whose picture they put on the TV."

"They've let him go for now. They're still collecting evidence. Jessie, don't you think it would be good to help the police try to find Petra?"

"Would they put anything about me on TV? That we're living together?"

"You could ask them not to. They might understand."

Jessie was sobbing. "All right. Let people know. Why should I care? I want Petra back."

15

The abandoned boat

Anne went into her house and flopped down on the couch. Where would Petra have run to? Where would Anne herself go if she wanted to disappear? She breathed out a *tisk*, realizing that wherever she might go she'd soon lose courage and come back to admit her guilt. How about Tim? Where would Tim go to disappear? Another *tisk*. Hadn't he already disappeared from the world of the State Department into the little cabin he was living in now?

There was a knock at her door. She looked through the window and saw William Jamieson standing on her porch with something covered by a cloth in his hands.

"Um, come in."

William handed her what he was carrying. She pulled off the cover and saw it was a ten-layer Smith Island chocolate cake.

"From my mother," William explained. He grasped her hand. "The police released me. Thank you, Ms. Anne. You saved my skin."

"Oh, that's wonderful, William. But I can't take credit for it. All I did was tell them I'd seen somebody wearing a scrunchie like the one they found at the boat launch dock."

"They showed it to me, too. I said the woman I was expecting to meet there was wearing something like that. Don't worry. I didn't give them her name. Not much chance they can find her just using that hair band thing."

Anne choked up. "But, William, I did give them Petra's name. I had to. At the pub that night she was drunk and threatened to strangle Ruth. And after that night she disappeared. I think the police need to find and question her."

William's eyes widened. "You think Petra could have killed that woman?"

"I think it's possible."

He bit his lower lip, perhaps wondering how much Anne knew about his connection with Petra.

"William, I know why Petra asked to meet you at the club that night. I heard her asking you to sell her some Benzedrine. But I never mentioned that to the police."

William's eyes fixed on hers.

Anne felt her hands starting to shake. "Believe me. I didn't want them to have an excuse to keep you in custody if it wasn't you who killed Ruth."

"I appreciate it." He closed his eyes and took a breath. "Maybe this is my cue to stop selling people bennies."

"Good idea. Does your mother know you've been selling them? I bet not."

"No. My dad had a prescription when he drove a truck. I'm still managing to use that to make a little extra money now and then. Not many people want bennies these days, but when one comes along …."

"How did Petra know you could get her bennies? She's not even from around here."

"She came to Westport the day before the regatta to practice and get local knowledge of the bay. That's what she told me. She went to Blake's Pub that night. Reggie, the bartender, said she downed a lot of Tequilas. When I brought her some fried shrimp, I heard her tell Reggie, "I need some bennies.""

Anne remembered Reggie telling her emphatically that William didn't "do business" on Sundays and she'd decided not to ask how much Reggie knew about William's benny side-business.

"Anyway," William said, "When she left the pub that night, I went outside and gave her some for the regatta the next day. She said she was low on cash. She'd pay me the next day."

"And the next night, after the regatta, she still hadn't paid you and she wanted more."

"Right. I told her I didn't get off work until eleven when the pub closes. She said she'd meet me at the club and pay me then." William sighed. "But she didn't show up. Don't get me wrong, Ms. Anne. I never worried about the money. I get maybe a dollar more than I pay for each benny. I was worried something might have happened to her." William thanked Anne again and turned to leave.

She said, "See you next Thursday at the church?"

"Oh, right. My mother said you came to help the kids out with their writing. Sure, I'll see you there."

Half of Mrs. Jamieson's Smith Island cake in hand, Anne raced to the boatyard to tell Tim everything. "The police questioned me again. They showed me a scrunchie, and I said it looked like the one Petra was wearing the night Ruth was killed."

"And the police told you they released William?"

"No, he came to my house and told me himself."

A worried frown darkened Tim's face.

"I know what you're thinking, Tim. They let a dope dealer go."

"It's true. I saw William give pills to Petra the morning before the regatta when he helped her carry her boat onto the lot. She called them 'bennies.' I decided to talk to both of them about it myself rather than go to the police. I never got a chance." Tim rubbed his temples. "Maybe I should have told the police, after all, though."

"You mean—"

"Because the bennies might have helped make Petra crazy enough to kill Ruth."

Anne admitted, "I didn't tell the police about the drugs, either. I know how much William's mother depends on him. But William told me the arrest might be a warning for him to stop selling them. I felt he was sincere."

"How about this? If either of us learns he's selling amphetamine again, we'll tell the police."

Anne shook Tim's hand. "It's a deal."

A ring-billed seagull swooped down from the clubhouse roof and landed on the boat rack where club members stored their Lasers after taking off the masts and laying them atop the hull. Anne suddenly thought of something. Only Westport Sailing Club members had a space in the rack to store their Laser after a regatta. Petra wasn't a member. Yet Anne didn't recall Petra getting anyone to help her carry her boat to her van after the regatta. Did Petra disappear without even taking her boat? "Could Petra's boat still be here?" she asked Tim.

Tim clapped his hand to his head. "I never thought about that. Petra could have dismasted and slipped her boat onto a bunk in the temporary rack we have for non-members to use for a day or two after a regatta. The women who came back on Sunday weren't able to get their boats because of all the confusion when Ruth's body was discovered. They trickled back in over the next few days to pick their boats up. But Petra wasn't one of them. Let's take a look."

They lifted the tarp from the small temporary Laser rack which sat next to the permanent one. It was empty except for one boat. "This is a new boat," Anne said. "The same blue color as Petra's. Let's check the hull number."

Sure enough, it was the number Anne and Tim remembered Ruth calling over early in the first race of the regatta. It had been almost a week, and Petra had not come back to pick up her boat. "There must be a serious reason she doesn't want to come back here," Tim figured.

"Right, she would need her boat to practice at her own club in South County for the upcoming Olympics qualifying regatta in Sarasota, Florida. It looks more and more like Petra killed Ruth in a fit of drunken rage that night, then panicked and ran away."

Tim agreed. "Uh-huh. And I saw the police taking fingerprints that morning at the scene. If they find her, they can check the prints against Petra's."

"And I'm sure they're looking. So I called Petra's friend Jessie. I know Jessie didn't want people to know she and Petra live together, but the police will certainly be asking friends and relatives questions. I warned Jessie, and she seemed resigned. I'm sure she has no idea the police might suspect Petra of the murder. She just wants them to find her."

Tim put his hand on Anne's shoulder. "Let's sit over there on our picnic bench and forget about all this for a while."

Anne nodded. "I'll call Clyde's Café and get Pedro to deliver us a pizza. And there's cake."

"And I have wine." He brought out a bottle of Shiraz and the trusty coffee cups.

The sun was starting to set over Town Creek, streaking the sky with orange and painting the water a rippling red. Tim raised his cup. "To watching the sunset together." Anne was watching the sun glow in his light blue eyes.

16

An artificial eulogy

Anne slept deeply the next morning until her phone woke her up with a message from the national weather service. A tropical storm was brewing in the north Caribbean. It was predicted to move slowly in a northwesterly direction towards the east coast of the United States, but it was too early to predict its exact path.

After she finished a bowl of oatmeal and was still in her pajamas, her phone rang with a call from Tim. "Have you heard the forecast? Commodore Dan called me. I think he's being overcautious, but he asked me to call all club members and tell them to make sure their boats are tied down securely."

"Do you need help?"

"I sent out a joint message for everybody I could. I called the few who didn't list cell phones except—"

"Petra? No problem. I wouldn't mind calling Jessie to make sure she's OK. I'll tell her to give Petra the message if she happens to see her."

"Thanks. And Sergeant Carrs called me this afternoon about that scrunchie they found on the launching dock. He said he might come by to show it to me. I told him I'd never recognize it, but he asked me to stay here in case he comes by."

"So I guess you'll be working on your book today?"

"Yeah. How about I call you this evening?"

"Sure."

Jessie was breathing hard when she answered her phone. "Anne, a policeman came here asking all kinds of questions. A lot of which I couldn't answer. Petra never told me where her parents lived. The only friends of hers I knew of were the Laser sailors at her South Bay Racing Club, and they weren't really what you'd call friends. When Sergeant Carr asked me where she worked, all

I could tell him was she was a part time physical trainer at a gym in Breezeville."

"Did the sergeant contact the gym?"

"The owner of the gym called while he was here. Petra hadn't shown up at the gym since before the regatta."

"I'm sorry, Jessie." Anne couldn't help feeling that Jessie would be better off if Petra never came back to her and Jessie found somebody else. "I'll let you know if I hear anything, Jessie. And would you keep me informed, too?"

Anne threw on a T-shirt and shorts. As she was about to slip her phone into her pocket, she got a text. It was a message her principal Lucia sent to all the Westport Elementary teachers: *Late notice. Couldn't be helped. Ruth's husband just told me there will be a memorial service for Ruth TODAY at the Summit Church in Colonial City from three to four. Hope a lot of you can come.*

Late notice, indeed. Ruth's husband had probably decided at the last minute he didn't want to be blamed for not holding any service for her. Anne remembered scolding him for not coming to the little ceremony her school had for Ruth. She felt like she had to go. Lucia would probably feel she hadn't done her duty as Ruth's principal if nobody showed up for a memorial for one of her teachers.

All Anne could think about was what she would wear. She had a black dress, but it was low-cut and might not be appropriate. Black pants and black blouse? Too informal? The Summit church in Colonial City was a historical landmark patronized by old-money elite, ambitious politicians, and aspiring lawyers. Ruth's husband John might have invited some of them to the service. Never mind. The pants and blouse would have to do, she decided.

Anne knew Lucia was afraid to drive across the bridge and "face the traffic" of Colonial City. She texted back, offering to pick up Lucia and any teachers who wanted to go in her minivan, which had three rows of seats.

Stiffly coiffed hair, pearl necklaces, shimmering black dresses, and diamond broaches joined glossy slicked-back hair, fitted black suits, and gold watches at the Summit Church memorial John Neucomb had arranged for his murdered wife Ruth. Anne, her principal Lucia, and two other teachers from Westport Elementary huddled in a pew in the center of the church. Anne saw John in the front row, looking at his phone and noted that Real Estate Ron had not come.

A priest with rather sickly pale skin and frameless glasses stood before a table covered with a gold embroidered cloth that held the purple and white urn with Ruth's ashes. He read from a script. If the long eulogy could be believed, Ruth had been the most beloved wife and teacher the country had ever known. John Neucomb peered into his lap the whole time—possibly following the words on his phone?

Marge Morales, a chatty English as a Second Language teacher married to the owner of a travel agency on Windward Street, whispered, "He got the eulogy from AI, artificial intelligence. He told my husband."

Anne thought that might explain the phrase "ever-loved wife mate," which the priest had briefly stumbled over. As the eulogy went on, Lucia rolled her lens-magnified eyes when the priest read that Ruth was a "fountain of succor" for the children who "thronged to her lap for love."

John Neucomb stood beside the priest at the church door as the "mourners" left. When Anne offered her condolences, he took her hand and held it long enough to embarrass all the women Anne was with. On the way to the car, Lucia chuckled. "Anne, you'd better douse that hand in holy water the next chance you get."

The criticism of John Neucomb continued in Anne's van on the way back to Westport. Marge led the way. "My husband Miguel called him the day of the murder. He said John answered his office phone with a cheery 'Halloo.' Miguel figured maybe John hadn't heard the news yet. He had, though. So Miguel asked if he'd be leaving work and coming back to Westport, but John said he couldn't. He had some important papers to get notarized."

Lucia still hadn't forgiven John for not coming to the ceremony she'd arranged to honor Ruth at the school. "I called him, too. Same answer. He was too busy. Busy with what? I'd like to know." Gloria, the other teacher and band director whom Anne had brought along to the memorial, never participated in gossip. Now, however, she said simply, "I think he did it." The chatter in the van ceased as if she'd voiced what they all were thinking. As for Anne, she still thought Petra's threats and subsequent disappearance made it hard to dismiss her as a suspect.

17

Eviction

Anne parked her minivan in front of her house. She had wanted to ask her colleagues in for coffee, but she remembered feeling ashamed of how it looked when William's mother had stayed with her one night. The walls in the upstairs were peeling and needed painting, a project she'd been saving for the summer break. Her landlord in Washington, D.C., had refused to have it painted, so she'd decided to buy the paint and do the job herself—without complaining. She felt lucky to be renting the house at a reasonable rate. For years, wealthy investors had been buying Westport houses and steadily raising the rent until the poorer renters had to move out, leaving the house available for the more affluent "gentry" to purchase.

She was surprised to see a letter sticking out of the mailbox beside her door. From an office in Washington. She tore it open. *This is a notice that your rental agreement, which expires on September first, cannot be extended. The house is being offered for sale. Please vacate the premises before the first of September, leaving all rooms clean and undamaged as required by the rental contract.*

Anne's heart jumped into her throat. Obviously she couldn't afford to buy the house herself. She was being forced out as many of the less well-off long-time renters in Westport had been. She threw herself on her tattered couch trying to hold back tears.

And then she got angry. This had to be Real Estate Ron's doing. She cursed herself for taunting him, sending him to talk to Ruth as if she didn't know Ruth was dead, pretending she didn't know John Neucomb would never sell their house. Obviously Real Estate Ron had found out Ruth and John Neucomb's house wasn't for sale and had learned that Anne didn't own the house she was living in. He must have contacted the actual owner in Washington and told him he had a client willing to offer a great price for the house.

The first of September was shortly after the school year began. Moving out then would be especially disruptive, even if she'd be able to find a place to go. Any rental in Westport would definitely be too expensive. She'd have to move out of the village and drive quite a distance to school. In spite of her distress, she let out an ironic chuckle. Now parking would be a problem for her like it was for Ruth on days when the Westport Sailing Club was hosting a regatta that she wanted to attend.

Tim called. "Don't get excited. I'm not asking you to dinner tonight at the Palais de Paris. But I made some Filippino adobo. How about joining me here for dinner?"

"You look nice." Tim told her.

"Oh, I've been to a memorial service John Neucomb had for Ruth. But the big news is I'm being evicted." She told him about her lease cancellation.

"How much stuff do you have?" Tim asked.

She looked around his cabin and laughed. "A lot more than you do."

"Because I was thinking. Do you really need a whole house? Maybe you could just rent a room."

"I know. Like you. You seem perfectly content in what amounts to no more than a room with a kitchen and bath. I admire that in you."

"You don't find me lacking in ambition? My father accused me of that when I spent so much time sitting in my room reading books."

"But now you're writing a book, Tim. Your second one. What was it? U.S. – Philippine maritime something or other?"

"Treaties."

"I'm impressed that you can work single mindedly on a project you find fascinating. You remind me of a scientist studying whale songs, or a scholar trying to decode ancient cuneiform tablets."

"Well, I can't say that maritime treaties—"

"They count. If I have school kids who get fascinated by something we've studied, volcanos for example, and start digging more deeply into them than we have time for in class, I tend to let them go, even if that means they're reading about volcanos while I'm teaching the use of the apostrophe."

Tim's jaw dropped. His face turned pink.

"Sorry. I didn't mean to embarrass you."

"No, I'm flattered. And as a matter of fact I'm a little shaky on apostrophes."

"I can teach you in five minutes."

"Maybe not now. Let's talk about what you're going to do when your lease is up. I have another idea. Have you noticed there's an empty house down on Spinnaker Street that's had a *For Rent-Partially Furnished* sign on it forever? It seems strange that nobody's rented it. I wonder if it's in bad shape inside. If that's the reason, and if the rent is low because of that, I could help you fix it up."

"I feel like I'm dumping my problem on you. I didn't mean to do that."

"Not at all. Let me show you the house."

Anne smiled. "For now, I just want to enjoy the dinner you made. Is that all right? I love the vinegary smell. And I want you to show me how to make adobo."

Anne, Tim, and Molly went for a walk after dinner. "It's not quite dark yet. Let me show you the rental house I was talking about," Tim suggested. "It's fifteen minutes away. And Molly needs the exercise."

Spinnaker Street was farther towards Bay Creek than Anne usually walked. There were fewer stores and shops than along Anne's street. Molly sniffed the holly bushes and boxwood hedges, which she seemed to find new and exciting, but Anne noted that the houses looked very much like those on her own street. A block away from the house behind the hardware store, Molly stopped to sniff a flowering hydrangea bush and wouldn't move on.

"Let her enjoy it," Anne entreated when Tim tried to pull Molly on. They stood waiting under the low branch of a sycamore tree that stretched across the sidewalk while Molly continued her investigations.

A white Mercedes Benz silently drifted by and stopped at a house at the end of the block.

"That's the house I was talking about," Tim said. "You can just see the sign from here. *For Rent—Real Estate Ron.*"

The driver's door of the Benz opened, and Anne recognized Real Estate Ron getting out. He opened the passenger door for a woman with streaks of purple hair who looked to be in her twenties. They went into the house together.

"Kind of late to be showing somebody the house," Anne observed. "It's getting dark."

Tim agreed. "Let's just stay here a bit longer. I'm sure Molly won't mind."

A light went on in an upstairs room. No other windows were lit. "I hate to say what this looks like," Tim mumbled.

John Neucomb had told Anne that Real Estate Ron was having an affair with his wife Ruth. Assuming this was true, Anne wondered if their liaisons could have taken place in this vacant house. Maybe Ruth wasn't the only woman Ron had brought here. Where was Ms. Beatrice, the neighborhood sentinel, when you needed her?

"If they don't come out soon," Tim said, "you know what it looks like?"

"What?" Anne asked with mock innocence.

"It looks like Real Estate Ron is using a client's empty house as a trysting place. No wonder it hasn't been rented yet. Ron probably isn't even advertising it. The client who owns the house, I'm willing to bet, doesn't live locally. The sign is there only to fool him if he ever decides to drive by."

"We can check if it's advertised on Zillow." Anne brought up the website on her phone and searched for houses for rent in West-port. There weren't any.

"Judging by the light in the window, he only seems to be show-ing his 'prospective renter' a single room," Tim laughed. "And he's giving her a thorough showing of that room."

Eventually the light in the room went out. There were flickers of light from another window as if from a flashlight. "Here they come," Anne whispered.

"They can't see us behind this tree and hydrangea bush," Tim assured her. "Let's watch."

Ron and the woman came out, the woman straightening her hair with her fingers. They kissed as the woman got in the car. Tim snapped a picture.

Ron turned the car around in the cul-de-sac and headed back past Anne and Tim.

"Duck, just in case," Tim whispered. The white car slipped soundlessly past them.

"That could have been me," Anne gasped. "I mean it couldn't have, of course. I mean I bet that's what that disgusting man—"

"I know what you mean, Anne. I think we should look into this. If Real Estate Ron is doing what we think he is, he should lose his license."

They walked together back up Spinnaker Street and cut through Rosebud Lane, known as Budd's Alley before the Westport com-munity association re-named it, to Windward Street and Anne's house. "Molly seems to want to come in," Anne laughed. "But the place is so messy, I wouldn't—"

"I understand, Anne. Come over to the club tomorrow if you get a chance."

Before she went to bed, Anne walked through her house look-ing for things she really didn't need if she had to move into a single room. If the room didn't have a kitchen attached, she'd need noth-ing in the kitchen, of course. She picked up the mug she had given her father before he died. *World's Greatest Dad.* And the ones her students had given her over the years. There was the griddle her mother had made her waffles on, the punchbowl she'd gotten from her grandmother. Was she ever going to make punch in her life? It didn't matter. She wanted to keep it.

The huge Puerto Rican stoneware vase she and Neil had bought on their honeymoon already took up too much space in her narrow living room. How would she manage to fit it into one all-purpose room? But getting rid of it was out of the question. She plopped onto her bed, holding her hands to her face.

18

Stakeout

The tropical storm had increased to a Category 1 hurricane and was now centered north of Puerto Rico and slowly heading northwest towards the U.S. And besides that, now Anne had something else to worry about. Where was she going to live starting in September? Tim had asked her to come to the sailing club today if she could. She threw on last year's regatta T-shirt and shorts and left.

Tim was watching the weather channel on his little TV. "The hurricane's still far offshore. That's good. We need to find you a place to live."

Anne liked the way he said "we."

Tim told her he had an idea. "I'm assuming Real Estate Ron soon found out you don't own the house he tried to get you to sell."

"Yeah, it wouldn't have taken him long. And he must have found out who the actual D.C. landlord is."

Tim nodded. "And he probably told your landlord he had an offer to buy the house for a ton of money. Just like he told you. But if we can prove Real Estate Ron is cheating one of his clients by using the client's house to meet women in, that's fraud. We can get his license revoked. He won't be able to go through with the deal he made your landlord."

"Then maybe my landlord will let me renew my lease?"

"That's what I'm thinking. At least for another year. He'll need time to find another realtor who can bring him an offer as good as the one Real Estate Ron claimed he could bring him. Up to now, Ron has managed to dominate the Westport real estate business. You don't see any houses sold or rented through any other company."

"But how can we prove Real Estate Ron is using his client's house for a tryst?"

"Tell me what you think of this. I call his office and say I'm looking for a house to rent in Westport. I'll say I'm only free in the evenings. Any night his secretary says he's not available, that might be a night he's set aside for a tryst."

Anne just gazed at Tim with a twisted mouth.

"I'm serious. Let me try it."

Anne bobbed her head noncommittally from side to side. Tim dialed Ron's office. "Hello, this is Juan Sebastian Elcano." He winked as Anne rolled her eyes. "I need an evening appointment with Real Estate Ron to look at a house," Tim told the secretary. "I see. Any weekday evening but tonight and Wednesday? Oh, I'm sorry. Those are the only nights I can make it. I'll have to see if I can change my schedule and get back to you." He quickly ended the call.

Tim was beaming. "Do you have a camera with a telephoto lens?"

"You're kidding? You can't be thinking of—"

"We'll get pictures to prove what he's doing."

"I don't know, Tim. Anyway, I don't have a camera. I just use my phone."

Tim laughed. "Yeah, I guess I'm getting too *secret agent* about this. Our phone cameras will be good enough. Come on. It'll be fun."

"Well …."

"What time was it that Real Estate Ron took the purple haired woman there? About seven o'clock?"

"I guess. I need some time to think about doing this."

"Sure. Anyway, before anything else I need to make sure all the boats are tied down properly before the storm hits. Most of the members came to tie theirs down, but some haven't."

"I'll help."

Even if the hurricane didn't hit Westport directly, any tropical storm or hurricane along the coast made it necessary for Westport Sailing Club members who kept their heavier Snipes, 420s, and

Lightnings on trailers there to tie them down more securely. Anne walked with Tim between rows of trailered boats checking to see if they were tied down securely to rings cemented into the surface of the boatyard. If they weren't, Tim pulled the guy lines tight while Anne re-tied them.

When all the trailered boats in the yard were tied down securely, they needed to add some slack to the lines on the boats tied at the dock so they wouldn't break or pull out the boats' cleats when the hurricane caused the water to rise. There were only two boats tied up to the dock, the Whaler at one side of the landing pier and Bullock's *Knot on Call* at the other. Bullock apparently felt welcome to dock at the club as long as he wanted. Anne held each line attaching the boats to the pier while Tim loosened and re-tied it. They put additional spring lines on both boats to keep them from blowing into the dock.

The club's hefty wrought iron barbecue grill had to be wheeled into a shed. "Let's use it before we put it away," Tim suggested. "I have some sausages we can grill and some corn we can roast."

By the time they'd cooked, eaten, put away the grill, and taken Molly for a long walk, Anne knew she needed to make a decision. Was she really going to stake out the rental house hoping to catch Real Estate Ron using it as a tryst? Tim was studying her silently. "OK," she told him. "I'll do it."

Molly came along, excited to get into Anne's minivan with them. Anne stowed her Laser's daggerboard, rudder, and sailing gloves in a compartment under the floor and folded down both rows of rear seats, making a platform for Molly to lie on. "Your phone all charged?" Tim asked.

"Yes, Tim. Please stop sounding like we're in some spy movie. Anyway, would you take the pictures? I don't feel quite right doing this."

"Sure. And we're going to park with the engine off. How about opening the sun roof to let in some air? It smells kind of briny in here."

"Heh-heh. You noticed that? I guess I'm used to it. What I notice is that it's already starting to smell a little doggy."

"What time do you have?"

"Don't tell me you're going to say we should synchronize our watches? I'm pretty sure both of our phones show the same time."

Tim was silent. Anne figured that's exactly what he'd been about to say.

Anne drove to Cross Street, then turned onto Spinnaker Street. The "tryst house," as they were calling it, was at the end of Spinnaker Street near the cul-de-sac at the bay. "It's not dark yet," Anne noted. "Standing by for instructions, Sir."

"Turn around in the cul-de-sac and park so we'll be heading home."

"Yes, Sir. In case a speedy evacuation is necessary. Is that it, Sir?"

Tim couldn't be shaken from his dead-serious frame of mind. "And park on the side opposite the tryst house. We'll lie in the back to take pictures so the van will look empty."

"How's this?" Anne asked.

"Perfect. Molly, move. We're coming back there."

Before she knew it, Anne was lying on the side of the van nearest the sidewalk with Tim on the other and Molly squeezed in the middle, one paw around her waist. Twilight. Anne closed her eyes and it almost seemed like Tim had his arm around her.

Molly let out a long, shuddering sigh as if resigning to the idea that there was not going to be any more action than this, at least for a while. Anne let out a softer sigh with a similar meaning. With nothing to do but wait, she was almost asleep when Molly sat up, alert. Anne leaned up on an elbow and peeped out the window. A white Mercedes Benz passed by the van and parked in front of the tryst house.

Tim pulled Molly back down. "I got a picture of his car." Real Estate Ron got out of the Benz in a dark gray suit and wearing a red tie. It was Sunday. Anne stifled a laugh, wondering if he'd been to church earlier. He pranced smiling around to open the door for a young woman who looked like she'd been cast in the same mold as the woman on the previous night except that she had bleached blond hair. Tim snapped a picture. The two went into the house as darkness fell. The upstairs light went on. Tim snapped another picture.

Now what. Anne couldn't help imagining what Ron and the woman were doing as she sank back down on the van floor. Tim was lying next to her, but there was a dog between them. Anne sighed, and Molly echoed her. The sighs, Anne was sure, didn't have the same meaning this time.

She didn't know how long she'd been asleep when she felt Tim leaning across her to take another picture. "They're leaving," he whispered. "Don't worry. I got it. Just as he was kissing her."

When she dropped Tim and Molly off at the boat club, Anne said, "Tim, hold off with those pictures until we talk about it some more, will you?"

19

Revenge

Anne slept restlessly that night. In the morning, she checked the weather forecast. The hurricane was growing stronger and had reached the Atlantic but was still a good distance from the U.S. coast.

She was having second thoughts about using the pictures they'd taken the night before to get Real Estate Ron's license revoked. Was it a civic duty to report fraud? Ms. Beatrice certainly would have turned him in if she'd been able to hobble that far down Spinnaker Street and catch him in the act. In a way, though, Anne couldn't help feeling that Real Estate Ron's trysts were his own business.

She was eating a cheese and spinach omelet when someone banged on the door—Real Estate Ron in his usual polo shirt stretched tightly around his hefty midsection and Bermuda shorts ending just above his bony knees. "Hello, Beautiful," he greeted her. "May I come in?"

"We can talk on the porch."

"I should be angry with you. Suggesting I ask Ruth Neucomb to sell me their house when you knew Ruth was dead and John would never sell." He tisked. "And not telling me you were only renting this house. When I found out, I told the landlord what I told you. I have a buyer who will give him an unbelievable amount for the house."

"And then he canceled my lease."

Ron put his sweaty hand on her arm. "But I'm not really angry. I find you quite attractive. There's a clause in the contract allowing me to cancel my deal with your landlord, letting you stay here. All I want is for us to be friends."

A sour taste rose in Anne's mouth. She glared at him.

"The Palais de Paris offer still stands." He gave her a thin-lipped grin. "I'll make sure you can stay in this house as long as we're friends."

Maybe some women Anne's age might be flattered that Real Estate Ron was interested in adding them to his twenty-something harem. What Anne felt was definitely disgust. He seemed to be offering to allow her to stay in her house as long as she became one of his tryst women.

"We'll take it slow," Ron coaxed. "I can introduce you to a more comfortable, luxurious life than you're probably accustomed to. How about it? Palais de Paris tonight? We can start there."

Anne wanted to tell him she'd seen him with two different women at the house on Spinnaker Street, but she thought better of it. Any reservations she'd had about turning him in for real estate fraud had vanished now. She was going to follow Tim's plan, whether it ended up letting her stay in her house or not.

"Anne? Tonight at the Palais de Paris?"

"I'm not your type," she said. "And you're not mine."

Anne walked to Clyde's Café under a clear blue sky, set off by only a few layers of gray stratus clouds and showing no sign that a hurricane was coming. The café was bustling with dockworkers, crabbers, office secretaries, and store clerks chattering about the coming storm. Clyde's graying hair was frazzled, his white apron smeared with grease. A quick glance around showed Anne nobody she knew was here. She took a cup of coffee to a free table by the window and stared into her coffee trying to shake off the chills her encounter with Real Estate Ron had caused to streak along her back.

There was a tap on the window. She looked up. John Neucomb in a baby blue Izod polo shirt stood grinning with his hand over his heart. He pointed to the empty chair across from Anne and pressed his palms together in a pleading gesture. The chills returned, causing Anne to grip her fists. But she had a thought. She waved John Neucomb in.

"This is wonderful," John panted, out of breath from rushing into the café. "I thought you might not want to see me again. Have you thought over my proposal? I'm sure you won't regret joining up with me."

Once again his proposal of marriage sounded more like a business proposition. Anne sipped some coffee to avoid laughing. She said with tongue in cheek, "The memorial you held for Ruth—she would have been touched."

John's face flashed a deep pink. He dropped his gaze to the table.

"I've been thinking about her," Anne continued. "I thought about her when Real Estate Ron approached me recently and he mentioned Ruth."

John twisted a paper napkin into a ball, his mouth tightly shut as if he were gritting his teeth. He looked up. "I see. I see. Ruth is gone and now he has his eye on you. That man needs to be put in his place."

This was the opening Anne had been hoping for. "I've learned that Real Estate Ron is having affairs with more than one woman."

"What? What are you saying?" John's gray eyes darkened with shock.

Anne lowered her voice. "I found out by accident, looking at a house for rent on Spinnaker Street." She gave him a partial report of the trysts she'd observed. "I don't know real estate law, but it seems to me that using a client's house like that is fraud."

John slammed his fist on the table. "I do know the law. I've been trying to get something on that man ever since he started flirting with Ruth. If there is any proof of what you're telling me, I know how to put Mr. Real Estate Ron out of business."

"There are pictures, if that's any help."

Tim was putting the picnic bench into the boatyard shed when Anne brought John Neucomb to see him. Anne said, "Let me help you with that," while John stood impatiently with his hands on his narrow hips.

Tim closed the shed door. "I understand you're interested in buying a sailboat, Mr. Neucomb."

"I am, but I'm here to get the pictures."

Tim lifted a questioning eyebrow to Anne. "I don't understand."

"John's a lawyer," Anne said. "He's very interested in using the pictures we took to get Real Estate Ron's license revoked."

"I already know he's involved in some unlawful deals," John said. "I know exactly what to do. If you let me handle it, I guarantee he'll lose his license and probably be hit with a big fine."

"I don't want us to get involved in this, Tim," Anne urged. "Let's let him do it."

"I won't say where I got your pictures," John promised. "In fact, I'll hire a private investigator to look into this. I'll probably end up using his pictures instead." He held his phone next to Tim's, and Tim air dropped the pictures to him.

When John Neucomb rushed off without a word of thanks, Anne said, "He looks like he's out for revenge."

20

A fingerprint

Anne left the club to straighten up her house and prepare a dinner for Tim. She'd eaten with him at his place several times but had never asked him to hers. She wanted to prepare something special. He liked fish, she knew, and she first went to Harry's Grocery at the end of Windward Street to buy some cuts of bluefish, perch, and croaker, along with mussels, clams, leeks, and tomatoes to make a bouillabaisse. "That's a lot of food for a single lady," Harry joked, his cigar ash nearly dropping onto the white paper he wrapped the fish in. "When are you going to invite me for dinner?"

"As soon as you quit smoking and get a haircut," Anne said for maybe the tenth time.

Harry ignored that. "I guess you're stocking up for the hurricane. Business is great the past few days."

"What's the latest?" Anne asked.

"Still a Category 1. Might not hit the eastern coast directly, but will definitely cause high waves and flooding."

"Give me some milk, too."

"Sorry. We're all out."

"How about coffee?"

"All out of that, too."

Anne was putting the fish into her refrigerator when someone knocked on the door. It was Mrs. Jamieson, William's mother.

"I wanted to thank you personally." William's mother handed her a loaf of lemon bread that was still warm.

"I told William," Anne said, "it really wasn't my doing."

"Yes, yes," Mrs. Jamieson said, obviously assuming Anne was being modest. "I can't come in," she said. "I have a favor to ask. There's a hurricane coming, I'm sure you know. All William's friends are working in the marinas hauling out boats and tying others down to get ready for the storm. He wants to give the little dinghy he made a water trial before the hurricane makes it impossible to launch it." Mrs. Jamieson took a breath. "I was wondering—"

"It's not too heavy, is it? I can help him carry it down to the creek at the end of your street."

"God bless you," William's mother crooned.

Anne lifted the bow of the eight-foot cypress dingy while William took the stern. They managed to carry it half a block to the creek and slide it into the water. It floated. "Mind getting in," William asked her, "While I hold on to the painter?"

Anne took off her shoes, waded out to the boat, and sat on the helm seat, studying the inside of the hull. "No leaks that I can see," she called to William. She rocked the dinghy to one side then to the other. "Topsides aren't leaking, either."

William tied the boat to a piling on the shore. "I'll just get in with you to add some more weight." He sat on the center seat plank. They rocked again from side to side. "Looks sound," he said. "Don't you think?"

Anne gave him a high-five.

"After the storm, I'll take you for a ride on its maiden voyage. We'll catch some crabs with bait lines. My mother's really good at steaming them."

A police siren gave out a single loud squawk. They looked up. A cop was getting out of his car—Sergeant Carrs. "William Jamieson, you are under arrest," he called out, and began pulling the dinghy into the shore.

"What? Why?" William asked. "I don't understand."

"The lab confirms a match of a fingerprint on the launching crane control button with yours. Put your hands behind your back." Sergeant Carrs handcuffed William. "You have the right to remain silent ...."

Anne held her hands over her ears, unwilling to hear any more.

"He's innocent," she called out as the sergeant put William into the police car and drove away, leaving Anne standing beside the beached dinghy.

She sat on a flat rock beside the creek looking out over the water. William's fingerprint on the crane's control button? He'd told her he waited there for Petra until he heard a dog bark, then ran away. He never said anything about touching the crane.

The dingy sat abandoned on the muddy shore. Anne called Tim for help to carry it back to William's house. William's mother was sweeping out the shed when they got there. "Oh, no. My poor boy. Is he drowned? What happened?"

Anne's throat swelled and her words were hoarse. "William's been arrested again, Mrs. Jamieson. Something about a fingerprint. He's going to need a lawyer."

"Oh, dear. Oh, dear. Mercy me."

Dinner with Tim at her house wasn't as joyful an occasion as Anne had planned. Tim gushed over the bouillabaisse, claiming it the best he'd ever tasted. And then they sat side by side on her couch drinking the pinot grigio he'd brought. But the conversation centered on whether William would be granted bail—probably not—and whether he would have to use a public defender—probably. On her phone Anne found the location of the county detention center, about five miles from Colonial City. The website listed visiting hours, for family members only. Tim kept going back to "If his fingerprint was on the switch, it looks like he operated the crane."

They turned on the evening TV news. Weather men and women were jumping with barely disguised delight at having something significant to point out, an actual meteorological event for their watchers to worry about. The weather announcers on the various networks, "meter-ologists," as the broadcasters often referred to them, seemed to be competing for viewer ratings by outdoing each other in dramatic, repetitive descriptions of each pressure system, front, and air mass contributing to the progress of the coming hurricane.

Squeezed in between ongoing reports of the weather, a news flash appeared. "Colonial City police have obtained new evidence and arrested a man previously released in their investigation of the boat club murder. No further information is available at this time."

"I want to believe William didn't do it," Anne sighed.

"Are you sure he didn't know Ruth?"

"He said he didn't. Ruth never went to Blake's Pub, so she couldn't have met him there. She didn't have any reason to go to Miller's Marina, where he sometimes worked during the day."

"And she never mentioned him, right?"

"She didn't. And he never mentioned her."

Tim frowned. "There are still a lot of details about the murder we don't know. Time of death, for example. The police said the medical examiner placed her death somewhere between nine and midnight, but we don't know the exact time."

"And I saw red marks on her neck. Was she strangled? Was she asphyxiated with that plastic bag?"

"Assuming William is arraigned, he'll probably be assigned a public defender," Tim reasoned. "The prosecutor will have to give his evidence to his attorney. And if his attorney will talk to us, maybe we can get some answers."

Anne agreed. "Since I told the police I heard William agree to meet Petra at the club, they'll probably name me as a witness, and William's attorney will probably want to talk to me. Maybe to you, too."

"That's good, I guess." Tim leaned back on the couch and closed his eyes.

Anne did the same. "William's poor mother. I wish I could tell her something to comfort her. But there's nothing I could say."

Tim remained silent, his eyes still closed as if he'd drifted into a faraway world. Anne studied the expressionless contour of his face, his stoic mouth and handsome chiseled chin. What was he thinking? She hesitated to interrupt. There was so much about him that she didn't know.

Tim soon shook off his reverie. "Sorry. I kind of spaced out for a minute."

"Where were you?"

"It's this hurricane. I was thinking of another hurricane in the past. A typhoon, actually."

Anne made a guess. "In the Philippines?"

Tim looked at her. "Yes."

"You don't have to tell me about it if you don't want to."

He took a breath. "My wife was killed when a typhoon blew the tin roof off a neighbor's house into ours. I wasn't home. I was safe in a concrete government building where I worked."

Anne felt the blood drain from her face. "Oh, Tim. How awful." She took his hand in both of hers. He shifted as if to get up, but Anne held on tight. "Don't go right after telling me that, Tim. I'll be miserable all night. Stay a little longer."

"I was also thinking about you, Anne. You'll be in this house when the hurricane hits. I'll be in my cabin. I don't want—"

"No, Tim. Let's promise to be together in the storm."

He stood and shook her hand. "That's what I want. And Molly, too." He gave Anne a hug. "Which reminds me. I have to go back and give her some dinner."

21

Hurricane party

Lily called the next morning. "Anne, this hurricane is getting closer. They've posted a hurricane watch for the Mid-Atlantic. I'm afraid the storm surge might break my oyster cages loose and wash them away. Can you help me?"

At the Harvey's Marina dock on Town Creek, Lily was putting wire cutters, pliers, and rope into her power boat when Anne got there. "Oh, thanks," Lily gushed. "Jorge would have helped me but he's busy hauling out boats before the storm comes."

The ride to Greenthumb Point was bouncy and wet as Lily splashed through choppy waves churned up by sailboats and motor yachts racing to tie up at marinas to ride out the coming storm. Anne had to hold on to keep from flying out of the little boat. As soon as Lily cut the engine and they drifted into the inlet, the wind picked up. "Don't worry, guys," Lily sang out. "We won't leave you here in the storm." Anne held onto a fallen branch to steady the boat while Lily cut the cage loose from the wire tying it to a tree. Together they lifted the cage and set it gently on the sole of the boat.

Lily backed the boat out of the inlet. "I'm not only worried the cage will be blown away," she explained. "If the storm makes landfall south of here and comes from the west, it'll blow fresh water into the bay from its tributary rivers. The salt level will decrease, and the oysters won't survive. I want to tie this cage to my dock on Town Creek. I'll take it back to Greenthumb after the bay salinity has gone back to normal."

They bounced over choppy waves and both of them were soaking wet when they passed the Westport Sailing Club and turned into Town Creek. Lily noted Bullock's sailboat still docked at the club. "That man," she scoffed. "Do you know what he's done now?

He's contacted every member of the Board of Trustees of Severn Heights College individually and leaned on them to support his application for the presidency. My dad says Bullock promised the businessmen on the board to throw college purchases their way and offered the lawyers, like my dad, to retain them for college legal advice."

"Did it work?"

"He's lost my dad's vote. But my dad is afraid the other trustees will insist on hiring Bullock."

When they were tying up Lily's boat, Lily asked Anne to dinner at her house.

"I'd like to," Anne told her, "but I'm having dinner with Tim Griffin tonight in his cabin at the club."

"Oh. I see." Lily's grin went from ear to ear. "You've known him a couple of years. Has something changed?"

Anne felt her face flush. "It seems that trying to find out who killed my colleague on the property he manages has brought us closer. I have to admit I'm happy it has."

"Me, too, Anne."

After Anne helped Lily hang the oyster cage from her dock, she needed to buy candles and kerosene for her lantern in preparation for the hurricane. Harbor Hardware on Independence Street stocked items that both longtime and newer Westport residents shopped for. Howie sold dustmops as well as robovacs, oil lamps and smart bulbs, doorknobs and keyless Wi-Fi locks. A bell attached to the door jingled when Anne walked in, and at the same time a recorded woman's voice crooned "Welcome" from a hidden speaker.

Immediately behind Anne, Tim came in with Molly on a leash. Molly excitedly nuzzled Anne while Tim glanced around, possibly to be sure Ms. Beatrice didn't happen to be in the unusually crowded store. Howie, the owner, was busy ringing up candles, matches, lamp oil, kerosene, screws, nails, and lots of duct tape.

Westport was preparing for the storm. Tim called out, "Still have plywood?" Howie yelled, "In the back."

Anne got her candles and kerosene and stood in line to pay. Howie was out of bags and wrapped the candles in a piece of newspaper. Anne carried them and a can of kerosene around to the back of the shop to join Tim as George, the lumber guy, tied two window-sized sheets of plywood together. Tim hooked Molly's leash to his belt, and the three of them walked awkwardly to Anne's house to drop off her things, then to the boat club.

Tim's wooden cabin had been damaged by a hurricane in the past, so he wanted to be sure it would survive this one. Anne helped him nail the plywood over its only two windows. "Will that be good enough?" she wondered.

The cawing of seagulls had ceased, leaving an eerie silence. "Let's see what category the hurricane is now." Tim checked his phone. "Still Category 1. But getting stronger. And it's moved closer." Tim winked. "If it hits really hard, I guess Molly and I could flee to your house."

Anne nodded, wishing she had scraped and painted the upstairs walls during the past winter break. They walked out into the boatyard with Molly, and Tim scanned the sky. "Nothing yet. The calm before the storm?"

"Let it storm," Anne said, taking his arm. "We'll have a hurricane party."

They pulled two chairs out of the shed. "When I was little," Anne mused, "my mother and father used to love hurricanes. We'd sit out on the lawn with kerosene lamps watching the wind start to pick up, my parents drinking Tom Collins while I drank lemonade. My father had a good voice and sang Irish songs. Those are some of my happiest memories."

Without notice, Tim launched into a rendition of "Molly Malone" in a lilting voice that took Anne's breath away. She sat stiff, afraid the slightest motion would embarrass him and make him stop.

The last strains of Tim's song were joined by a low moaning of wind streaming through the masts of the trailered sailboats. "Here it comes." Anne checked her phone. "Now they've changed from hurricane watch to hurricane warning. It's approaching the mid-Atlantic states."

"In the last hurricane, there was a foot of water over the whole boatyard," Tim recalled. "Deeper by the launching dock, where the yard slopes closer to water level."

Anne remembered, too. "One of the big Solings was blown halfway off its trailer. The landing pier by the crane was under a yard of water."

Just then a dilapidated flatbed truck beeped and pulled into the boatyard loaded with sandbags. Lily and Jorge got out. Anne had never seen Lily in such shabby shorts and T-shirt. Lily called out, "Storm prep crew is here. I remember Tim sweeping water out of his cabin after the last storm. And this one's going to be bigger." Jorge took a wheelbarrow down from the truck he'd borrowed from Miller's Marina. He smiled at Anne. "Good to see we have plenty of help."

With each of them holding a corner, they loaded the sandbags one by one onto the wheelbarrow, then lifted them out to form a low barricade around Tim's cabin while Molly supervised. When the job was done, Anne and Lily giggled, displaying their dirty shirts to each other. Anne thanked both her and Jorge with a hug.

Tim patted Jorge on the back. "I don't know where you got these sandbags when all of Westport is looking for them."

Jorge grinned. "The marina had some 'extra' bags sitting around. Lily couldn't let her sailing club dockmaster be flooded out."

"Drinks are on me," Tim announced. "Beer, that is. I stocked some in for the storm." He murmured to Anne, "No Tom Collins, but I do have lemonade."

"That's all right. I'd love a beer."

They dragged two more chairs out of the shed and sat in a half circle facing Town Creek with Molly and a cooler of beer in the middle. The sky was getting darker. Anne pulled her sweaty shirt away from her body, happy to let the chillier air cool her off. She badly wanted Tim to sing another song but, not wanting to embarrass him, took a long sip of beer and began herself to sing one of her father's old favorites. "Don't know why there's no sun up in the sky, stormy weather." It was a sad song, but she was thrilled when Tim joined in. Lily knew the tune and hummed along. Jorge nodded, smiling, then took a harmonica from his pocket and played along in harmony.

They sang and laughed until the wind moaning through the masts and rigging had turned to a high pitched whistle. Lily thought she should go home. "Me, too," Jorge agreed.

"Stay out here a little longer?" Tim suggested to Anne when Lily and Jorge left.

"Or we could go to my house," Anne said.

Tim looked out over the whitecaps now sending flecks of foam into the air over Town Creek. "The Westport Sailing Club needs me to stay here and keep the damage down as much as I can. I was only kidding about staying at your house. Let's put the chairs away again, and I'll walk you home."

"No."

Tim looked into her eyes.

"I'll stay here with you," Anne said simply. And definitively.

22

Purple shorts

The wooden walls of the cabin shook. Anne clung to Tim's arm, sitting beside him on the narrow bed. Rain pounded the roof and clattered against the wood panels covering the windows. The electricity was out. Even the candle Tim had set on his desk flickered in the wind that somehow managed to stream in through unseen crevices. Tim's weather radio announced ten-foot waves in the ocean and four- to six-foot floods along the coast of the bay.

A crash sounded out in the boatyard. Tim jumped up and peered out through a slit he'd left in one of the boarded windows. "There goes one of the Snipes, blown loose on its trailer and tipped onto the boat next to it. The wind indicators on the top of lots of masts have blown off and are flying through the air. I can hear the water rushing across the boatyard in waves, but I can't tell how deep it is."

"Do you think the sandbags will hold?" Anne leaned down to pet Molly, who was trembling.

"I'm going to risk taking a look." Tim cracked open the door. "The water's almost to the top of the bags." Tim used his knee to re-shut the door. "That means down at the launching dock it will be much higher. I wouldn't be surprised if it's under a good bit of water already. That part of the yard is more open to the bay."

There was a long screeching sound. Tim looked from the window slit again. "Not sure, but I think the trailer of one of the Lightning boats just tore loose from its tie-down ring and was blown up against the one next to it."

Anne was quivering, whether from cold or fear she couldn't tell. "Tim, I think you should get away from the window. Come sit next to me, would you?"

Something banged against the cabin wall. Tim said, "Just let me look… that was a shingle torn from the clubhouse. All right, Anne. Here, I'll hold your hand."

Anne felt calmed immediately. She said, "I wonder how the rest of Westport is holding up? What about William's mother alone in her house? I'm going to try to call her." The phone connected after a short delay. "Mrs. Jamieson, this is Anne. Are you OK?"

"I am, Dear. My house is rattling, but I poured myself a little glass of sherry. I've lived here through lots of storms and hurricanes. And Reggie from Blake's Pub came to check on me and bring me some candles and a pot of hot soup."

"I'm glad to hear that. After this hurricane passes, I'd like to get back to you and see if we can make sure William has an attorney. I'll call you again soon."

The wind was now a constant high-pitched wail. Anne hoped old Ms. Beatrice was safely ensconced in her third-floor turret, keeping an eye on the storm. She leaned closer to Tim. "What if Ms. Beatrice could see us now?"

"You're cold. Lie down, and I'll get you a blanket."

Anne slipped off her sneakers. "I won't be able to fall asleep, I know." The sound of the rain hitting the low roof reminded her of sleeping in a tent during the rain with her girl scout troop. Then and now, the experience of lying dry and protected with the rain sounding just above her head gave her an unanticipated feeling of contentment.

She awoke the next morning, wondering for a moment where she was. Tim wasn't there. The rain still sounded on the roof, but the wind had settled a bit. She opened the door to see Tim in a poncho and rubber boots picking up branches in the boatyard. "Don't come out yet," he called. "I'll get you some sailing boots and a foul weather jacket from the lost and found bin in the clubhouse." Anne only nodded. Tim gave no hint of how their night together had gone. The last thing Anne remembered was thinking about sleeping in a tent when she was a girl scout. She studied Tim's face when he brought her the rain gear. Nothing except bright blue eyes.

She pulled on the boots and jacket and sloshed out into the boatyard. Tim had already picked up most of the sticks and brush and piled them out by the sidewalk. She helped him find the wind indicators that had blown off the top of several masts and pick up a few boat covers that had torn off. Tim pointed to a Snipe that was leaning against the boat next to it. "I don't know if you—"

"I can help you tilt it back up." They worked together, Tim heaving up the low end of the hull with his shoulder while Anne tugged in the other direction on the main halyard that had come loose. It worked. Tim gave her a high five, the second one since the regatta. She didn't know why that pleased her so much.

"Still have energy left? Let's push that Lightning trailer back into its place. Lightnings aren't that much heavier boats than Snipes." But both are a lot heavier than Lasers, Anne thought when they re-positioned the trailer. She was glad her own boat and the other Lasers were stored unrigged in racks with their masts tied flat across the hulls.

"Now to check the twenty-six foot Solings," Tim said. "If one of those got dismasted or blown off the trailer, the owner will have to get a mobile crane to deal with it. Let's hope those big boats rode out the storm."

They waded through the flooded boatyard to the line of Solings in front of the boat launch dock. Tim checked carefully, and none seemed to have suffered any damage. "Let's check the launching dock behind these boats."

The water got deeper as they approached the boat launch crane. Anne's boots were shorter than Tim's. "Get on my back," he said. "I'm just curious to see how deep it is over there." He carried her towards the crane at the edge of the dock, then stopped short. "What the …?" They both looked down. Still half-covered in flood water, a human body lay washed up by the hurricane onto the dock. Anne gasped. Truthfully it was more like a scream.

"It's a woman." Tim leaned down to look, and Anne slid off his back.

"Did she drown in the hurricane?" Anne wondered. They took a few tentative steps closer, Anne's short boots filling with water. "Ugh," she moaned. "I can't look. This person's been in the water a long time."

"Oh no," Tim gasped.

"What?"

"I think it's Petra."

"What?" Anne held her arms to her chest and dared another look. The face was barely recognizable, but the long blond hair undulated loosely in the water. No scrunchie. And the purple shorts with the SBRC logo were a giveaway. They were the South Bay Racing Club shorts Petra had worn in the regatta. Anne covered her mouth. "I think I'm going to be sick."

"There are scrapes on her arms," Tim noted. "And both hands. Like she was grasping something when she fell in. Her shirt's torn in front. And she's missing a shoe."

"She scraped herself on the edge of the dock, probably. We know she was drunk the night after the regatta."

"If Petra was really evil enough to murder Ruth," Tim said, "she could have fallen in while hoisting her up on the boat crane hook. And then she might have been too drunk to climb back onto the dock."

Anne had another thought. "Could Petra have been pushed in?"

"You mean murdered? Hmm. She doesn't have a plastic bag over her head like Ruth. No marks on her neck that can still be made out. Who knows? In any case, Petra had no inflatable life jacket to float her up immediately. That's why her body didn't wash up until the hurricane."

The police in translucent raincoats, hat protectors, and boots sloshed through the flooded yard taking pictures and setting up a yellow barrier tape in the same area once again. Anne and Tim watched from the top step of the club as Petra's body was photographed, lifted by forensics technicians, photographed again, and wheeled to the waiting ambulance.

Sergeant Carrs waved them down from the steps. "You can come down now. I'll need to ask you some questions about *this* body." He hunched over his notebook. "From your call to the police, I understand both of you found the body this time? And you've both identified the deceased as Petra Fields? Ms. Anne, is this the person you say you heard asking William Jamieson to meet her here at the dock the night Ruth Neucomb was found dead?"

"Yes."

"What exactly was their relationship?" Sergeant Carrs looked first at Anne, then at Tim.

Tim said, "William helped Petra and some others carry their boats into the yard for the regatta. He does that at Laser regattas. Some of them give him tips."

Sergeant Carrs rubbed a finger alongside his nose. "Did Petra give William a tip?"

"I didn't notice."

"No argument between them?"

"No. He helped carry her boat. He helped some others, too."

"OK, do you know of anybody who might have wanted to harm Petra Fields?"

Tim said, "No." And so did Anne. Although Petra was an aggressive sailboat racer and annoyed some people, including herself, Anne couldn't imagine anyone actually wanting to kill her.

Sergeant Carrs put his notebook back into his pocket. "No one is to enter the taped off area until the flood has subsided and we've finished examining the area." He signaled to the police car, and the woman whose desk was next to his in the office got out, pulling on a raincoat and hat. "Ms. Trimble from our department will watch over the area to see that it remains secure."

Ms. Trimble, the police clerk who had teased Sergeant Carrs

about being reluctant to use the word "scrunchie," gave him a raised-eyebrows look. "Right. I'll just stand here in the rain until the flood recedes."

The sergeant bit his lip. "Well …."

"The clubhouse has a glass door at the top of these stairs," Tim offered. "We can set up a chair inside giving Ms. Trimble a view of the yard."

"That will be—" Sergeant Carrs broke off as Ms. Trimble had already headed up the steps. Tim followed and unlocked the glass door to take her in.

The sergeant asked Anne if she would recognize Petra's van.

"No. I talked to her roommate in South County, and she said it was a large white van, but she didn't know the model or license plate number. It wasn't parked at their house. Now I think we can guess why. She never went home."

The sergeant checked his notebook. "You say it was a night eleven days ago that you heard Petra Fields say she was coming back to this club from the pub? The condition of the body suggests you might be right."

Anne said she didn't know what Petra's van looked like, but she was sure it was big enough to hold a Laser in the back. "Probably a utility-type van," she told the sergeant. "I've kept an eye out as I walked around the neighborhood, hoping to see a van with the SBRC logo on it, but I haven't found one. There are lots of white utility vans in Westport near the club. Boat equipment vans, sail-makers' vans, grocery vans—"

"I get the idea. The police have looked, too. We couldn't run the plates on every white van in Westport. Besides, "white?" Is light gray white? Or light silver? If we recover her driver's license from the body, we'll be able to find the van."

Anne reasoned, "And if it's parked somewhere near here—"

"We'll know for sure she never went home."

23

A desirable disqualification

Anne climbed up to the clubhouse after the police left. Ms. Trimble and Tim, in armchairs pulled next to each other, were chatting about books they'd read. "Don't mean to interrupt your book club," Anne quipped, "but a bloated body has just been hauled away from this boatyard."

Ms. Trimble shook her head slowly. "If the autopsy report finds that the woman was murdered before she fell into the water, I'm afraid it's going to look even worse for William Jamieson."

"So you think he killed Petra, too? But Petra might have slipped in and drowned, right? I know she was drunk."

"But you've got the fingerprint on the crane and two women killed the same night in the same place. That's all I'm saying."

"But why would William kill them?"

"I guess the police are trying to figure that out now."

Anne stood looking out at the splashing of the rain in the flooded boatyard. She wondered if Jessie had been notified yet of Petra's death.

"They called that friend of the dead woman," Ms. Trimble told her. "Said they'd notify her if the driver's license confirms it was her."

"Poor thing, I should call Jessie myself."

Jessie answered in a croaky voice. "Anne, the police said they found a drowned person at your club they think is Petra. I can't believe it. Why won't they let me come and see her?"

Anne didn't know how to answer.

"They asked if Petra had any enemies. I couldn't think of anybody."

"Do you have someone to talk to, Jessie? Your mother, maybe?"

"I can't face telling my mother about Petra right now."

"Well, when the hurricane damage has cleared, you could come here to the club and I'll help you pick up Petra's boat and find her van. We can talk then."

The rain had stopped and the boatyard flood was beginning to seep back into the surrounding creeks. A few club members came to inspect their boats, competing with each other in stories about trees and branches fallen in their yards—and peppering Tim and Anne with questions about the taped-off launching dock. All Anne and Tim told them was, "Some drowned person floated up onto the dock in the hurricane."

Anne and Tim were picking up branches around the cabin when Ms. Trimble came down from the clubhouse and handed Tim back the book about whales he'd lent her. "Just got a call," she said. "Captain Blunt and the forensics team have determined there's no more evidence we can collect from the flooded dock. I'm going to take down the tape, and they'll send somebody to pick me up."

"No more evidence to collect?" Anne asked. "So that means the medical examiner has already ruled the death an accidental drowning?"

"No. They don't have the autopsy report yet. All I know is what I told you."

After a cop Anne didn't recognize drove Ms. Trimble away, the light in Tim's cabin came on. An electric company repair truck roared past the club, probably on to the next place where trees and branches had hit the wires. Anne thought she should call some people to be sure they were OK.

Mrs. Jamieson, William's mother, had lost electricity but had a gas stove and she'd managed to cook a strawberry pie. "Still half of it left," she chuckled. "Come see me and we can finish the rest."

"I can't come now," Anne apologized.

"Not sure any will be left if you wait. But I'll bake another one. What's your favorite? I have apples."

"I love apple pie. I'll drop by as soon as I can."

Mrs. Jamieson told her she'd received a text from Pastor Brown. "The children's workshop at the church is canceled tomorrow. The electricity at the church is out."

Anne called Lily next. Lily had lost electricity, and a tree had fallen in her back yard. Her husband had already called a tree company to take care of that, and she had a whole-house backup generator—of course, Anne thought. Lily's husband spent most of his time at the Colonial City automobile dealership he took over from Lily's father. He had plenty of money to spend on making their house up to date and comfortable.

Anne's principal lived near Anne's house. "No lights until just now," Lucia told her. "My basement flooded and I had to keep mopping it up and dumping it into the toilet. The sump pump will take care of it now. How's your house?"

Anne realized she hadn't thought about it until now. Not wanting to mention where she'd spent the night, she said, "The same."

Anne's electricity had come back on, and Tim helped her mop and sweep water into her basement sump. "Westport's nice," he commented. "But it's close to sea level, so you have to have a good drainage system. I'll help you install a battery backup to your sump pump."

"I'm losing my lease, remember?"

"That's right. Strike that idea."

Anne held her shirt out from her body. "Look at me. I've carried sandbags—sorry about your bed—walked in blowing rain, sloshed in smelly creek overflow and basement water. I want to take a shower and change."

When she came back down into the living room in a yellow V-neck and clean white shorts, Tim and Molly were waiting, and a good smell was in the air. "I found two cans of beef stew in your cabinet and heated them up," Tim said. "Hope you don't mind."

"See if there's anything in there Molly could eat."

Molly perked up at her name. Tim said he'd already found something.

They checked the TV news. So far, the only reports were about the hurricane aftermath, nothing about another body being found at the Westport Sailing Club. When they'd all three eaten—Molly was finished in three seconds—Tim suggested going for a walk, another word that made Molly's head shoot up.

The sky was still gray, but the wind and rain had left the air with a fresh, clean smell. Road crews were picking up leaves and tree branches that littered the street, and Westport residents were just beginning to come out and cut up branches in their yards. They waved to Anne and Tim, and most of them seemed to know Molly's name, even if they didn't know Anne's or Tim's. The sound of chain saws punctuated the otherwise silent evening.

For some reason comprehensible only to the canine mind, Molly wanted to turn off Windward Street into a shrub lined alley, or rather "lane," and sniff along the boxwood. With no destination of their own in mind, they let her lead them to the entryway of a marine gas and diesel fuel station on Town Creek. A white van was parked on a plot of grass beside the drive. Anne saw a note under its windshield wiper. She carefully unfolded the drenched paper and read the blurred ballpoint pen message: *Please don't park on our grass.*

"This has to be Petra's van," Anne smirked. "Rules didn't apply to Petra. It's been here for some time. I'm surprised they didn't call the police."

"I know Fred," Tim said, "the owner of this station. It's where I bring the club's boat for fuel. Fred likes the club and probably knows the van belongs to a racer. I'm guessing the request not to park there is as far as he's been willing to go so far."

"Let's look in the windows." Anne peeped in the driver's side window. "There's something on the passenger seat."

"A letter," said Tim, who was looking through the window on that side. "I can read it. Let me see." He wiped rain spatter from the window with his elbow. "It's from the ILCA, the International Laser Class Association of North America. To Petra Fields."

"Can you see what it says?"

Tim took a picture of it, read it, and told Anne, "The association says there's been a complaint that she's been using an unlicensed sail in regattas. It warns her that using a sail made by an unlicensed loft invalidates her score in the regatta. It says she will be disqualified from the Westport Sailing Club regatta unless she lets them examine the sail she's used and verify that it was made by a licensed loft."

"Rob Green didn't want her to use it," Anne recalled. "He insisted it was a prototype, a demo sail to be used in races that don't count for anything. Not in an Olympics qualifying regatta like this one."

"I'm sure she had a licensed sail she could show the ILCA," Tim ventured. "She probably figured she could show that to the association instead, claiming that's the one she'd used."

"But it turned out that Petra didn't win or place in our regatta. Maybe she preferred not to have her poor score count in her overall record. All she'd have to do would be turn in Rob's sail to the ILCA and let herself be disqualified. It would be as if she hadn't sailed in our regatta at all."

"You're right. And if she turned in the sail Rob made, he'd be in trouble. He'd never get his loft authorized to produce Laser sails." Tim frowned. "I wonder if Rob knew about this letter."

"He did. I heard him mention it when she was rigging her boat next to mine."

"He knew? Then he realized it would be to Petra's advantage to turn in his unlicensed sail if she wanted to nullify her poor performance in the regatta."

Anne couldn't keep a sardonic tone from her reply. "Lucky for him she died before she could do that."

24

No sail

Anne lay in her own bed that night, kept awake by trying to reason things out. John Neucomb, Petra, and Rob Green had motives for killing Ruth. William didn't, as far as she knew, and yet it was his fingerprint that was on the lifting crane. And now it seemed that Rob Green might have a reason to want both Ruth and Petra out of the way. Anne must have fallen asleep eventually because she woke up the next morning to the sound of a tree cutter on her street.

And then her mother called. "I wanted to warn you, Annie, a hurricane is coming your way. I heard it on the news. I think you should stay out of that little boat of yours during the hurricane."

"I will. I mean I did. The hurricane has passed, Mom, and I'm fine."

"Well, that's good," her mother said. "Let me know …." She clicked off. Probably hit the End Call button by mistake.

Anne sat stirring a bowl of leftover beef stew. She sprinkled a bit of paprika into it to improve the flavor.

She picked up her phone when it rang again, "Hi, Mom. Seems like we got cut off."

"It's Jessie." Petra's partner sighed. "I wish I could talk to my own mother, but I can't face that yet. You're lucky you have a mom you can talk to."

"Uh-yeah. How are you doing, Jessie?"

"The police told me they can't yet rule Petra's death an accidental drowning. They're still waiting for the autopsy report. But who would want to kill her, Anne? I know she could be abrasive. She didn't want anything to stand in the way of her campaign to earn a gold medal in the next women's sailing Olympics. But do you kill her for that?"

"I wouldn't think so, Jessie. When we found her on the dock, we saw scrapes on her hands and arms and her shirt was torn a little. Did the police say anything about that?"

"They did. And they said they're waiting for a report on a cut they found in her stomach. The scrapes might have been from grasping at the dock when she fell in. But they couldn't say yet whether she was pushed or just slipped." Jessie sighed. "They asked me if Petra could swim. I said she was a great swimmer. One of my happiest memories was when I met her on the beach at Ocean City. I can't understand why she drowned, even if she fell in."

Anne had an idea about what might have inhibited Petra's swimming that night but only asked, "You've been with her since Ocean City?"

"Yes. Petra had her boat there for a regatta on the Assawoman Bay and she brought it to my house in her van. That was last summer. I mean she travels a lot going up and down the east coast to regattas, but she's always come back here."

"Did you look around for any letters or papers that might show where her parents or family live?"

"The police did. There were certificates and trophies, receipts for sailing equipment, but nothing else that would—" Jessie stopped. "Sergeant Carrs is calling me again. I'm going to take his call."

"Tell him Tim and I found Petra's van," Anne quickly put in.

Tim was hosing dirt and leaves from the boatyard when Anne got there. "I'm still thinking about Petra's sail," he said. "Did you notice any sail either rolled or folded in her boat when we found it in the temporary rack?"

Anne hadn't, and they checked again. "No sail," Tim said. "The daggerboard is here, the rudder and tiller are here, but the sail is missing."

"But I'm sure Petra went straight to Blake's after the regatta. She didn't even change her clothes. She'd been there quite a while when I got to the pub. She wouldn't have had time to take her sail all the way to where her van was parked."

"Besides, why would she take just the sail?" Tim noted. "You said she told you she was planning to sleep in her van that night. Then she would probably plan to drive it back here the next day and load the Laser and all its equipment into the van at once."

Anne voiced what they were both probably thinking. "While Petra was in the pub, maybe Rob Green took the unlicensed sail he'd made so that Petra couldn't give it to the ILCA."

Tim nodded. "But of course she could still admit to the ILCA she'd used an unlicensed sail that Rob had made for her. That alone would have thrown out the regatta from her record."

Anne bit her lip. "Unless Rob decided to make sure she didn't tell them."

A police car turned into the yard.

"You say you found the van?" Sergeant Carrs asked Anne. "Mind taking me to it?"

Tim stayed to finish cleaning up the boatyard. Anne rode in the sergeant's car with a forensics woman, who put on blue latex gloves when they got to the van and circled it twice before reporting it was useless to look for fingerprints after the hurricane. Sergeant Carrs drew on gloves of his own, tried the doors, took pictures of the van, and even photographed through its windows. Anne watched as he read the letter on the seat. "Can you explain what this means?" he asked her.

Anne gave the sergeant a quick rundown on sail regulations for competitive events.

"Who is the nonregulation sailmaker this letter refers to?"

"Rob Green of Green Sails."

"Did Petra Fields give them that sail and tell them Green Sails made it?"

Anne said she didn't know. She stopped short of suggesting Rob might have pushed Petra off the dock before she had a chance to do that. Anne figured the police now had all the facts she had. If there were any conclusions to be drawn, she'd prefer that the police do that themselves.

Sergeant Carrs wrote down the license plate number and called his office to confirm the van was Petra's, then called for the van to be towed to the county forensic services. Anne thought that might be best for Jessie. The fewer reminders of Petra that Jessie had to go through, the better.

"Was Petra's identification on her?" Anne asked the sergeant. "Nobody seems to know who her relatives are or where she's originally from."

"This is an on—"

"Ongoing investigation, I get it. You can't say. It's just that Petra's friend Jessie doesn't know who to notify of her death."

"If we find any next of kin, we'll notify them ourselves."

Anne walked back to the club when the sergeant and forensics woman drove away. A tow truck passed her on the way. When she got to the club, a small red car was in one of the club parking spots and Tim was talking to a pretty, fragile-looking woman in her late thirties or early forties with rosy cheeks and light brown curls. "Anne, this is Jessie Belinski, Petra's partner." Tim looked relieved to have help in sympathizing with the teary eyed woman.

"We're so sorry," Anne told Jessie, taking her delicate hand. "This has been a shock to all of us."

"I couldn't talk to anybody at the gym who knew her. It's still closed because of the hurricane. I needed to come and talk to somebody who knew her."

"Are you going to be all right?" Anne asked. Meeting Jessie in person made her even angrier that Petra had brought this sensitive woman under her control.

Jessie held her hands to her cheeks. "I've never been good at reaching out to make friends. Petra saw me and liked me and the next day we were living together."

"Was Petra your only …."

"I know what you mean. I was actually married once. For three weeks. The guy ran off. I was too boring, he said." Tears were dribbling down Jessie's cheeks, and Anne didn't want to ask any more personal questions for now. Jessie wiped her eyes with a lace trimmed handkerchief. "Can you show me where you found Petra?"

Anne gave Tim a glance to relieve him of this duty. He nodded and said he'd be in his cabin.

Jessie wavered as they approached the launching dock, and Anne took her hand. "Petra's body was found here on the dock."

"What's that scary looking thing?" Jessie's voice was quavering.

"It's a crane we use to lift boats into and out of the water." Anne didn't mention that Ruth's body had been found hanging on the crane's hook.

Jessie pointed to the narrow landing pier extending from the dock near the crane. "Do you think Petra was walking on that and fell in?"

"I guess she could have been. It's for people to board racing sailboats like Solings, Lightnings, or Snipes that are launched by the crane. The race committee boat ties up to it briefly during a regatta. Sometimes the club allows big boats to dock temporarily on the other side of it."

Jessie looked down at her feet. "Right here? This is where you found her?"

"Um-hum. Jessie, how about coming to my house? We can talk there for a while."

"**I** love the way you knew people and talked to them as we walked here," Jessie remarked. "I know hardly anybody's name in my apartment building. We pass by each other in the hallway and nod. Your neighborhood is so friendly."

"You're right. Westport is a nice place to live. You probably noticed people helping their neighbors clear out their yards after the hurricane."

"I wish I could live here. There's a medical lab nearby that I was thinking of transferring to." Jessie dropped her head. "But Petra liked the South Bay Racing Club better."

"You say you met Petra in Ocean City. Did she know you lived near the South Bay club?"

Jessie's face reddened. "Yes. I couldn't believe how quickly she wanted to move in with me. I guess I have to admit that was partly the reason."

"But she stayed with you since last summer?"

"I mean, she traveled to regattas. When she went to Ontario, she stayed there a few weeks. She stayed a few weeks in Oyster Bay, New York. And of course when she went to St. Petersburg and Sarasota in Florida, she stayed almost a month in each place."

"That's a lot of time away from your apartment in Breezeville."

"She was set to go to Long Beach in California right after the regatta here. I always felt lonely when she was away."

To Anne it was beginning to look like Jessie wasn't so much Petra's "partner," whatever that meant, as she was the provider of a crash pad for Petra to stay at when she was in the vicinity. "Did Petra pay half of your rent?" Anne asked.

"Oh, no. Even if she offered, I wouldn't let her."

Anne suggested Jessie have a glass of wine.

"No, thank you. I have to drive back to Breezeville. That policeman told me I have to let him know if I 'leave town.' That's the way he put it." Jessie gripped her hands together. "Do you think that means he suspects me of something?"

"It's not that, I'm sure. Until the police decide whether her death was an accident or not, they probably want to keep in touch with you. They told me the same thing. About Ruth, I mean."

"That woman who was killed? I can't understand how a woman could have been murdered in a nice place like Westport."

Possibly two women, Anne thought. But she only said, "I can't either."

25

Observing an observer

Anne walked Jessie back to her car and gave her a goodbye hug. Tim called from his cabin door. "Anne, come take a look. The networks finally got word of Petra's death." There was no picture, of course. The TV report only said the body of a drowned woman had been found at the Westport Sailing Club at the same location that Ruth Neucomb was found murdered. "Police have identified the woman as Petra Fields and for now are treating her death as an accidental drowning until they get the autopsy report. They say no further information will be released until the investigation is complete."

Tim said he hoped it was just an accident. "Rob Green's been trying to get his company certified to make one-design sails. That would really increase his business. But I can't picture him killing anybody to get the certification."

"You know him better than I do," Anne conceded.

The squeal of car wheels at the club entrance startled them as a long black sedan swung into the yard. The door flew open, and a powerfully built man in a tight-fitting gaberdine suit ducked out. "Mr. Bullock," Tim said. "I guess you've come to check on your boat after the hurricane?"

Bullock gave Tim a stare.

"Doctor Bullock, I should say," Tim apologized. But Bullock was sizing up Anne. "Hello, young lady," he said in an exaggerated tone of pleasure. "I don't believe we've met. I'm the soon-to-be president of Severn Heights College, Doctor Bullock." He held onto Anne's hand too long for her comfort.

"We took care of *Knot on Call* for you," Tim assured Bullock. "Let me show you."

At the landing pier beside Bullock's boat, Tim pointed out the lines he and Anne had loosened before the hurricane. "The rise in water level would have pulled your cleats out otherwise," Tim explained. "The boat probably would have been blown away." He added, "As soon as the water level drops to normal level, we'll re-tie the lines."

Bullock didn't seem impressed. He was looking over at the launching dock. "I just heard the news in my car on the way here. Is that where the drowned woman was found? What a shame. You can't help wondering what a drunken woman was doing poking around here late at night." Bullock turned back to Tim. "I'm looking for help selling this boat. With my new duties at the college, I'm not going to have much time for leisure activity other than golfing. No inquiries yet to the notice you put up?"

"None yet," Tim said. "But we might have a lead. I'll get in touch with him and show him your boat if you want."

"Perfect. And the Laser awards ceremony was canceled, but I'm still on for supplying steamed crabs if your club ever gets its act together enough to hold its traditional Fourth of July feast. I'm told some bigwigs often attend. A college president always has to network and schmooze for donations and support."

When Bullock drove off, Tim shook his head. "I wish somebody would buy that guy's boat and get it out of here." He asked Anne if she'd heard from John Neucomb since they'd sent him off in pursuit of Real Estate Ron. "Neucomb's the only person who seems interested in the boat so far."

Anne said she hadn't seen him lately. She had her own private reason for not wanting to contact John Neucomb—his marriage proposal.

"He can help you by getting Real Estate Ron's license taken away and the offer on your house rescinded. Besides, I would love to have that boat gone." Tim took out his phone. "I have John Neucomb's number. I'm going to call him."

Anne was sure the Real Estate Ron thing hadn't been taken care of yet. If it had, John Neucomb probably would have contacted her. "Let's not press Neucomb about the real estate license," she entreated Tim. "Just call him about the boat, if that's OK."

Tim put the call on speaker phone. John Neucomb's office secretary answered. "Mr. Neucomb is away with an inquiry agent." Tim told the secretary he knew of a boat Mr. Neucomb might be interested in. "He can call me at this number."

"Did the secretary mean he's away with an 'inquiry agent' right now?" Anne wondered.

"She said *is* away. What are you thinking?"

"I'm thinking 'inquiry agent' might mean private detective."

Tim's blue eyes brightened. "You think he's showing the detective where that scumbag's tryst house is right now? It might be fun to drive by and see."

"Too risky," Anne warned. "It's on a street that dead ends at the bay. They'd see us."

Tim bit his lip. "You're right."

"Oh, well."

"So let's take the Whaler."

Anne un-cleated the lines and held onto the landing pier while Tim started the engine, and they motored out of the creek into the bay. Tim cut the engine to idle while they drifted just offshore from the spot at the end of Spinnaker Street where the house Real Estate Ron used as a tryst stood.

"There's the house." Tim looked through binoculars. "No cars parked near it."

"The sun's gone down," Anne worried. "It's getting dark."

"There's a street lamp. Let's stay a little longer."

"Just to see John Neucomb show his detective where the house is? I shouldn't have mentioned this."

"Hold on. A car's coming." Tim adjusted his binoculars. "A white Mercedes Benz. That's Real Estate Ron's car. Yep, he's getting out. I can't tell if this is the purple hair or the bleached blond."

"Or somebody different?"

"Could be. Wait till they get under the street lamp." Tim handed

Anne the binoculars. "Maybe you can see better."

"Another car is pulling up," Anne exclaimed. "John Neucomb is driving and a guy with a bald patch on the top of his head holding a camera."

A series of white light flashes shot out from the car window. "That must be Neucomb and his detective," Tim figured. "The detective's taking pictures."

Anne adjusted the binoculars. "Ron and the woman are on the porch now. They're going in."

"More flashing from the car," Tim noticed. "I assume they're using a telephoto lens."

The detective's car turned around in the cul-de-sac and parked on the tryst house side. More flashes shot out towards the upstairs window. Anne said, "If they're going to wait like we did until Ron and the woman come out again, they won't have to wait long. Real Estate Ron does quick work, we found out." She gave the binoculars back to Tim. "Looks like they've caught the 'scumbag,' to use your word."

"Uh-huh, we caught John catching Ron. Let's hope something comes of it." Tim started the engine. "It's been a long day. I'm hungry. How about you?"

"Starving."

"Let's motor around to the Town Creek Grill."

Anne checked what she was wearing. V-neck top and shorts. "But I don't have—"

"My treat," Tim said. He might have noticed she was looking him over. "Yeah, same clothes I was wearing when I hosed off the yard. We'll eat outside on the dock. It's dark enough."

They motored back around the club into Town Creek. The "Grill," as the locals called the dockside restaurant, was on the Westport side of the creek. A thin line of smoke streamed up from its chimney. They tied up at the landing pier. Tim helped her out. "You can smell that food from here. Pork chops, I bet. It's their specialty."

They ordered inside but ate braised chops, spinach soufflé, and Hasselback potatoes at a table on the dock. "The only thing to drink with this meal is beer," Tim insisted as he ordered two pints of Loose Cannon. The post-hurricane air was fresh and cool, and they were the only customers eating outside. Two large boats, their sails furled, slowed and circled in the creek in front of the drawbridge, waiting for the bell signaling it was about to rise. When the bridge opened, they motored to their moorings on the other side.

"They must have hauled out their boats at some marina like Miller's to ride out the hurricane," Anne figured. "Now they're bringing them back."

"You'd like to have a big sailboat, wouldn't you, Anne? Why don't you buy Doctor Bullock's?"

"For one thing, it would cost about five years of my salary."

"And another thing? Because I guess you could take out a loan."

"I should probably buy a house first."

"Or find a cabin to live in for free like me."

"Don't you see yourself moving out of there someday?"

"Sure. Right now I have a contract to finish writing this book on maritime treaties. Until recently, the little Westport Sailing Club cabin has been a perfect place to work on it."

"You weren't expecting any murders?"

"No, I wasn't."

"I hope me hanging around so much recently hasn't disturbed your peace and quiet."

"Anne, having you around is what keeps reminding me that I was right to settle down here in Westport for a while."

26

Swimming ladies

Anne's only response to Tim's compliment had been to blush. She had, in fact, been wondering if she was being a pest by hanging around the boatyard so much lately. Tim had never referred to the night she'd spent in his cabin, on his bed. He acted as if there was nothing to it. And in a way there wasn't. She'd woken up in the same spot and in the same clothes she'd fallen asleep in. Nothing had happened. Had Tim slept next to her in that narrow bed or had he slept on the floor? It absolutely didn't matter. Yet she wanted to know. And she had to admit why. If he'd slept next to her when she wasn't aware, she wanted to picture that in her mind now.

She tossed in her bed wondering if she'd ever have the nerve to invite Tim to stay over at her house. Probably not. Even though it wasn't Tim's actual job, he seemed to feel it was his duty to be a kind of watchman at the boat club. He'd told her he felt guilty for not checking more carefully the night he saw William running out of the yard.

The next morning she woke up with nothing urgent to do. Go to the library? No, she'd get a summer read later. Why kid herself? She knew where she was going to go. She gulped down some corn flakes and headed for the Westport Sailing Club.

Jessie called her before she got to Tiller Street. "Sorry to bother you, Anne. The police asked me where Petra's boat is. They want to take some fingerprints. I said the boat must still be at your club."

"It is." Anne realized there must be plenty of fingerprints on it. Petra's, William's, Rob Green's, and even hers and Tim's.

"Would it be all right if I came over? I'd like to have a last look at it myself before the police take it away, if that's what they plan to do."

"Sure, Jessie. I'll meet you there."

The police hadn't arrived yet when Anne found Tim finally taking down the plywood they'd put over his windows before the hurricane. "Ugh," she groaned. "The police are coming back again."

Tim laughed. "Another body, I presume. I thought I heard something last night. This is getting old."

"No, not another body. Not yet, at least."

Sergeant Carrs pulled into the yard with his forensics crew. Anne told Tim they wanted to fingerprint Petra's Laser. He said, "Good luck with that."

The sergeant with two women wearing blue gloves asked where Petra's boat was. "We figure it's here since it wasn't in her van."

Tim and Anne threw off the tarp covering it in the rack. "Have at it," Tim said.

Anne noticed the same shaking of their heads she'd seen when the forensics crew tried to get fingerprints from the van that had been washed by the hurricane. Then the shorter woman said, "Here. I can get one off this handle." Meaning tiller, Anne saw. Fine, she thought. You now have a fingerprint of Petra, probably of her thumb.

"Can't get any from this gray surface," the taller woman said, moving a finger along the rough non-skid surface of the deck. They brushed dust everywhere else and picked up a few more prints from the rudder, daggerboard, and the black metal grabrails.

Tim asked what they hoped to use the fingerprints for. Sergeant Carrs only said, "We need to be thorough."

Minutes after the police drove away, Jessie's little red car pulled onto the lot. Anne and Tim were just starting to drag the tarp back over Petra's Laser. They called to her.

Jessie stared at the boat and gave out a long sigh. "I took off from work. I was afraid the police would take it before I got here. Are they going to?"

"They didn't say. I don't think so," Anne told her. "It looks like the fingerprints were all they wanted."

"What's going to happen to it?"

Tim said, "We'll keep it here for now. They're looking for Petra's next of kin. If they don't find any, I'd say the boat is yours."

"I don't have any use for it. Your club can keep it. I only wanted to look at it one last time. I need to move on. I've already donated the clothes Petra left in my apartment to Goodwill."

"I think that's good, Jessie."

A loud truck roared into the boatyard and stopped next to Jessie's car. Jorge got out and took down a wheelbarrow from its flatbed before noticing Tim and the women standing by the Lasers. "Thought I'd pick up the sandbags," he called to Tim. "Take them back to Miller's."

The sand was damp and the bags were heavier than before the storm. The four of them lifted each bag together into the wheelbarrow, Tim and Anne at one end and Jorge and Jessie on the other. Jorge kept saying, "Careful. Watch your fingernails, Jessie. I can handle this end," but Jessie insisted on helping. In fact, she did end up with a couple of broken polished nails.

When the truck was loaded, Anne mentioned to Jorge that Jessie was a friend of Petra. His persistent smile left his face. "I'm so sorry," he told Jessie. "I talked to her in Blake's Pub the night of the Laser regatta."

"Anne told me Petra didn't win that regatta," Jessie said. "Did you notice how she was she feeling about that?"

Jorge squirmed uncomfortably. Anne knew he'd overheard Petra cursing Ruth for calling her over early. "Well," Jorge answered, "it's hard on anybody to lose. I bought her a drink to make her feel better."

Jessie seemed entranced by Jorge's deep brown eyes. "That was very nice of you."

Anne was hoping Jessie wouldn't ask her for more details about how Petra was feeling—or what Petra said—that night. Luckily, Jorge changed the subject and asked Jessie if she was a Laser sailor, too. "Oh, no." Jessie waved her hand. "I don't know how to sail. I've watched Petra in some regattas and practice sessions at the South Bay Racing Club. The only activity I do myself is swimming at my apartment complex pool."

Anne remembered Lily teasing Jorge about liking "sailing ladies." She wondered if he also liked swimming ladies. In fact, Jorge's smile had returned. "I don't sail, either. I work on sailboats, haul and launch them, repair their engines, but my own boat is a Key West powerboat."

There was a pause. Neither Jessie nor Jorge seemed to know what to say next. Anne stepped in. "Have you heard when the next children's workshop is scheduled for, Jorge? Is the church electricity back on?"

"The lights are back. You should get on Pastor Brown's phone text list. They're having it today instead." Jorge looked at his watch. "Plenty of time to get these sandbags back to Miller's before going to the workshop."

Jessie asked what the children's workshop was. "It sounds interesting. A few years ago I visited an elementary school to give them a little demonstration. It was fun."

"What kind of demonstration?" Jorge asked.

"There's this goop you put on their hands and desks that has fake bacteria in it. You have them wash their hands and wipe their desks clean. Then you shine a special light on their hands and desks. If they didn't wash all the 'bacteria' off, it shows up an ugly green. The giggles are what I remember the most."

"Fantastic," Jorge said. "We could definitely use something like that at the children's workshop."

Jessie blushed. "Really?"

"Is there any chance you could do a demonstration like that for us? It's usually Thursdays at noon."

"I live about forty-five minutes from here. Maybe next Thursday I could come."

"If Ms. Anne is coming today, she could show you where the church is. And you could sit in and watch."

"I am coming," Anne said. She hadn't planned to, but Jessie and Jorge seemed to be getting along well, and that seemed to be a good thing. She eyed Tim. "Maybe all of us could go?"

"I'd like to," he said, "but I need to finish this book I'm working on. The publisher wants me to bring it to New York for a peer review when it's done."

Jorge drove the truck back saying he'd meet them at the church.

Pastor Brown welcomed Jessie to the workshop. "I'll have you sit between Anne's table and Jorge's table. You'll get an idea of what we do here."

Anne worried as she put nothing but paper and pens on her table while Jorge set up tubes of water, funnels, and basins on his. She knew which table the kids would be more attracted to. A side glance showed that Jessie was also more interested in Jorge's project. Jorge asked her what line of work she was in. "I work in a medical lab, analyzing specimens," she told him. Jorge seemed pleased. "That's sort of what my project is."

By passing around her phone to let each kid add to a story, Anne managed to hold her kids' interest. But if Jessie brought her goop and glow light to the next workshop, Anne would have to jazz up her project or make sure they sat at distant tables. For now she was surprised and pleased to hear Jessie and Jorge laughing together as if they were old friends.

When the workshop was over, Jorge took Anne and Jessie to Pastor Brown and suggested he add them to his workshop phone message chain. Anne noticed Jessie and Jorge glance at each other as he did. A first impression might suggest that the petite, pale Jessie in her yellow capri shorts and the powerful, tattooed Jorge in his sleeveless black shirt were an odd couple of friends. But they chattered together about bacteria levels in water and the causes of hurricanes all the way back to the Westport Boat Club.

27

Partners

As soon as Anne stepped onto her porch, her phone rang with a call from the *Office of the Public Defender.* "Ms. Anne Bateman?" a young sounding woman said. "This is Terry Sullivan from the county public defender's office. Mr. William Jamieson is being held in the county detention center without bail. I've been assigned to his defense. It was his mother who asked me to contact you for a character reference. Are you able to answer a few questions?"

"Definitely."

"Thank you. My office is in the county courthouse, but I'm at William's mother's house now because she doesn't drive. I understand you live nearby. If you're free now, I'd like to stop by and talk to you."

Terry Sullivan was a tall, thin woman with a pink nose and red-frame reading glasses hanging from a red strap around her neck. "I love these quaint Westport houses," she gushed as Anne led her into the living room. "Someday I'd like to move to Westport myself. Thank you for being willing to talk to me. William claims he didn't kill Ruth Neucomb. I'm hoping to find information that will support that."

"He didn't even know her. I'm sure he's telling the truth."

Ms. Sullivan unzipped a black portfolio, slipped out a leather notebook, and pulled on her glasses. "William claims he left Blake's Pub when he got off work at eleven o'clock. The toxicology report on Ruth Neucomb's body—excuse me for speaking so plainly—shows that she died between about nine and midnight the night of the regatta. They go by amount of water in the lungs—sorry again—well, by things like that."

Anne said, "So Ruth could have died when William was there, or she could have died a couple of hours before he got there."

"Yes, but they found his fingerprint on—"

"I know the police found his fingerprint on our boat launching crane. And I imagine it was hard for William to explain that."

"He tried. The police say he changed his story when they re-arrested him." Ms. Sullivan met Anne's eyes. "That doesn't look good, of course. This time he told the police he had come to your club to meet Petra and saw the other woman, Ruth, floating in the water beside the dock. He lowered the"—she checked her notes—"boat launching hook, put it through her life jacket strap, and lifted her out of the water with the crane. He says he was checking to see if she was alive when a dog barked and he ran." Ms. Sullivan looked at Anne over her red glasses. "Sergeant Carrs and Captain Blunt are skeptical of that explanation."

"It's the first I've heard it," Anne said. "He didn't tell me that."

"I see. Before I go, I should ask if you know of anyone else who could have killed Ruth Neucomb."

Anne wondered if she should mention Petra as a possibility. Petra actually had a motive.

Ms. Sullivan said, "It looks like you are thinking of somebody. It might help William's case if you tell me."

No more harm could be done to Petra now, Anne thought. She told Ms. Sullivan why Petra was infuriated with Ruth, carefully explaining the over-early penalty. Should she mention what she'd heard Petra say in the pub?

Ms. Sullivan took off her glasses. "There's something else, isn't there?"

"Yes. Petra said she could strangle Ruth. I didn't think she meant it literally, of course."

"And yet Ruth Neucomb was strangled," Ms. Sullivan pointed out. "The medical examiner found that she died by a combination of strangulation followed by asphyxiation from a plastic bag being tied over her head."

Anne held her hands over her face.

After writing down the names of Jorge as well as Reggie, the Blake's Pub bartender, who also might have heard Petra say she could strangle Ruth, Ms. Sullivan gave Anne her card and got up to leave. "Thank you very much. May I call you Anne? What you've told me could be very helpful. I've been given the name and number of Mr. Tim Griffin at your boat club. I'm going to finish some work in my office and call him tomorrow."

As soon as the public defender left, Anne rushed out to tell Tim everything. William's mother stopped her on the sidewalk, out of breath.

"Ms. Anne, may I talk to you," she gasped. "William has a lawyer now. I gave her your name as a reference for William."

Anne took her arm. "Don't get too excited, Mrs. Jamieson. Remember your heart."

"She asked me more about that woman William went to the sailing club to meet. How well did he know her? Was she his girlfriend or what?" Mrs. Jamieson stifled a grin. "I told her that woman must have been twice his age. I shouldn't laugh, though. The poor thing is now dead herself."

"Petra was her name. Did William tell you much about her?"

"No. After the police let him go at first, I did ask him. He said he helped her carry her boat from her van. I asked why he went to meet her that night. He said she told him she'd give him a tip after she got her wallet from her van."

Close enough to the truth, Anne thought. She didn't feel the need to tell William's mother about the bennies.

"His lawyer tells me William changed his story about that night. He says he saw that teacher floating …. It's all so sad."

Anne said she couldn't imagine any reason William might have wanted to kill Ruth. "They're going to have to keep investigating. I'm sure of that. The best way to prove William's innocence is to find who actually did it."

Anne walked Mrs. Jamieson all the way back to her house but refused her offer to come in for dinner. Anne gave her a hug. "Call me any time, especially if you hear any more from William's lawyer."

Tim opened his cabin door. "You seem out of breath."

Anne blurted out everything she'd learned from William's public defender. "She said William changed his story after the fingerprint was found. She said she was going to call you, too, tomorrow."

Tim touched her arm. "You seem upset. We'll talk about this. But it's late. Let's eat first. That always settles me down. How about walking down to Clyde's for a crabcake?"

Pedro brought them each a huge Maryland lump-meat crabcake, green beans stewed with bacon and garlic, and an ear of silver queen corn. Anne was starting to relax. "We have to stop eating like this," Anne joked.

Tim winked. "Fine. Tomorrow night I'll make us some tuna fish sandwiches."

Tomorrow night. That sounded like of course they would have dinner together again tomorrow. Last night they'd had dinner on Town Creek, and afterwards, like two neighborhood friends, she went home to her house and Tim went back to his dog Molly in his cabin. Tonight would be the same. Would this routine continue? As long as it did, as long as she could presume he liked being with her this often, she was happy. It seemed risky to want to change things.

And so they walked back to Anne's house after dinner and sat for a while on her porch, Tim in the straight backed lattice chair and Anne in the rocking chair. They talked about the thing that neither could totally push from their mind for very long. Who killed Ruth Neucomb?

"Will we ever find out?" Tim wondered.

Anne held her head as if to think more clearly. "The police strongly suspect William because of the fingerprint. And they might also find his fingerprint on Petra's boat since he helped her carry it into the boatyard before the regatta."

"But they also seemed to suspect Petra might have killed Ruth,"

Tim pointed out. "I don't know if they've backed off that theory now that Petra's dead, too."

"And John Neucomb is on their list of suspects," Anne said. "And me! Rob Green is the only person who doesn't seem to be on their radar." Anne began restlessly rocking in her chair. "This whole thing has hurt our sailing club."

"Definitely," Tim agreed. "Do you realize the Snipe fleet has moved its regatta to the South Bay Racing Club?"

"I heard. And sailors are usually coming onto the club grounds to take their boats for a test ride or work on them. It's almost like they're afraid to do that anymore."

"Of course the hurricane shut us down for a couple of days. But I was surprised at how few people came in to check on their boats."

"And the Soling boat guys used to have informal races on Wednesday evenings. They've missed two since Ruth was found hanging from the boat crane hook they use to launch their boats."

Tim's light blue eyes twinkled. "You might say it's dead around the club."

Anne gave him a light punch on the shoulder. "Let's talk about something more upbeat. Jessie and Jorge, did you notice anything?"

"They seemed to like each other. Were you surprised?"

"A little. I guess I shouldn't have been. Jessie told me things about Petra that made me think Petra was just using her. It seems Petra found Jessie's apartment a convenient home base because it was near the South Bay Racing Club. But she left Jessie there for months at a time when she traveled to other Olympic qualifying regattas."

Tim drew some air through his lips. "I'm kind of out of my element here."

"The 'partner' thing?"

Tim nodded.

"All I know is what Jessie told me. She was lonely and Petra saw her on the beach, found out she lived near her favorite racing club, and moved in with her. I think Jessie was flattered."

Tim cocked his head. "'Partner' seems to imply more than that."

"Maybe. I worry about Jessie. I don't know Jorge very well."

"I do. I can't imagine him hurting Jessie. I mean if that's what you're worried about."

"Good. Anyway I'm probably getting ahead of things. So far they're nothing more than friends." As soon as Anne had said that, she wondered if the same was true of herself and Tim. Why had she rushed to Tim's cabin to tell him about the public defender? The fact was she was starting to feel that they belonged together. He seemed to feel that way, too, but was she imagining it? He hadn't said any more about going to New York. She wondered when that would be. And how long he'd be there.

Tim sighed. "I hate to leave, but I'm afraid Molly's been waiting too long for me to feed her." He gave Anne's hand a squeeze. "Good-bye, partner."

28

Initiations

Anne hadn't given Terry Sullivan the name of Ruth's husband as a possible suspect. The police already had him on their radar. The other person she could have named was Rob Green, who, when Ruth said she was going to report in the *Westport Voice* the race committee's suspicion that Petra used an unauthorized sail in the regatta, had muttered that somebody needed to teach her to mind her own business. If Anne found any more reason to suspect Rob killed Ruth, she'd call the defender. And if the police eventually determined that Petra was also murdered, she'd definitely implicate Rob.

But what to make of William's revised story? Ruth could have died as much as a couple of hours before William got to the club according to the medical examiner. So it was possible that he found her dead, floating with her inflatable life jacket still on, just as he now claimed. If this is what happened, why didn't he explain it to the police from the start? Was he afraid the police would suspect him if he admitted that he'd even touched Ruth? Did he fit a profile that automatically attracted suspicion?

Anne walked to Clyde's Café to get one of their flaky croissants and a cup of coffee. As she passed the schoolyard, she waved to Tonya, the girl who had made her a good luck bracelet. Tonya was big for a ten-year-old and was kicking a soccer ball around the yard with a group of neighborhood kids a little older than her. Some of them waved back, too. Anne had taught them before they moved on to middle school.

Tonya came over to the chain link fence to talk. "It's terrible what happened at the boat club, Ms. Anne." She looked at the bracelet Anne was still wearing. "I was sure you'd be OK. Did you win that boat race?"

"No, but it was fun. You told me you'd never been in a boat, Tonya. Can you swim?"

"Pretty good. I go swimming at Sandy Beach on the bay when my mother takes me there."

"I could take you for a sail sometime if you want."

"For real?"

"Not now, but is there a way I can call you?"

"I don't have a phone, but you can usually find me here."

Pedro brought Anne the large croissant and coffee. Clyde's wasn't very crowded and she found a table towards the back of the café. Talking to Tonya had given her an idea. Anne had always thought it wasn't right that kids whose parents couldn't buy them a boat were excluded from the fun of sailing. Tonya was athletic and would learn fast if she had the chance. If the police didn't confiscate Petra's boat and if Jessie didn't want it, maybe she could use it to teach Tonya how sail.

Anne sat facing the café wall, hoping John Neucomb wouldn't see her if he happened to come in. She'd only taken one sip of coffee when she heard a familiar voice behind her. "Ms. Anne, I'm happy to find you here. Is it possible I could sit with you?" She turned to see a large man with a short black hair sticking up straight and an eagle tattoo on his muscled arm.

"Hi, Jorge. Sure. Good to see you again." Anne laughed to herself imagining what Ms. Beatrice might think if she came by and saw her with yet another man.

"Your friend Jessie is very nice," Jorge began. "Do you think she might really come to the children's workshop next Thursday?"

"She'd probably have to take some time off work, but she seemed seriously interested."

"I hope she comes. I'd like to see her bacteria demonstration myself."

"Ah, so it's scientific curiosity? That's why you hope she comes?"

Jorge blushed through his olive skin. It took a moment before he went on. "She's so sad about losing Petra. Her *mejor amiga*, it seems."

"Her best friend. Yes, Jessie was close to Petra."

"I only met Petra that night at Blake's Pub. She was *atractiva*, yes. Long blond hair. But not pleasant. Very different from Jessie."

"Mm. I know what you mean."

"They lived together, yes? This means Jessie's not married?"

"That's right. She told me she was married once but only for three weeks. I think that was a long time ago."

Jorge stared down at the table murmuring, "Only three weeks. And she's been with Petra ever since that?"

"No. Only for the past year."

Jorge stroked his chin with a calloused finger. "Jessie's my age, she told me."

"Oh. I only met her recently. I don't know anything about her life before she met Petra."

Jorge smiled. "It doesn't matter. I like her. I want to see her again."

Anne insisted Jorge take half of her large croissant. "It's too big. I can't eat it all." Pedro came by and Jorge ordered a cup of coffee for himself.

"William has a public defender now," Anne told Jorge.

"That's great. I'll never believe he would hurt Ruth. Or anybody."

"Her name is Terry Sullivan. She seems to be gathering information that might help William's case, like who else might have done it. I told her that in Blake's Pub I heard Petra say she could strangle Ruth. I gave her your name. I thought you might have heard that, too."

"I can't say I heard that, but I could tell the public defender how angry Petra was at Ruth."

"Here," Anne said. "Ms. Sullivan gave me her card. Maybe you can call her."

As she was handing him the card, she heard it. Ms. Beatrice's dreaded tap of the cane. Anne looked up. The neighborhood sentinel had caught her with a third man in only a couple of weeks.

Tim was working on revisions to his book when Anne stopped by his cabin. The desk was scattered with papers, some typed, some handwritten, and many with passages crossed out. A pile of reference books sat next to his laptop. "There," he said. "I think I'm ready to take my book to the peer review committee in New York. I got a call today. I have to fly up there tomorrow."

"Oh."

"I don't know how long I'll need to stay there."

Anne tried to ignore the lump in her throat. "Well, I guess it's a good time for you to go. As you said, the club is 'dead' these days anyway."

"Yeah. I notified Commodore Dan. He agreed it would be a good time. The upcoming regatta's been canceled. I'll put a note on my door for anybody to call the commodore if there's an emergency." Tim took a breath and looked at Anne.

She asked, "What about Molly?"

"Um …."

"I'll take care of her. She can stay with me at my house."

"Really?"

"Sure." Anne smiled. "She'll be like a security deposit guaranteeing you'll come back."

Tim didn't seem to know how to respond to that. He cleared his throat.

Anne asked him if William's public defender had called to ask him any questions.

"She did. When I talked to her, the topic of Benzedrine never came up."

"It didn't come up when she questioned me, either."

"She asked me if Petra had ever threatened to hurt Ruth. I told her how angry Petra was about the regatta penalty. She asked if I'd heard Petra use the word 'strangle.' I said no but you did."

"Did she tell you William's explanation for how his fingerprint got on the boat launch crane?"

"Yeah. I guess what he says is possible."

Anne told Tim that the sailmaker Rob Green's name didn't come up when Ms. Sullivan questioned her.

"Not with me, either," Tim said. "Or Ruth's husband. So I didn't mention them to her. The thing is, I'm still leaning towards Petra as Ruth's killer."

"Me, too. With Ruth's husband maybe a close second."

Tim closed his laptop and stacked the papers into a pile. "Let's clear our heads. Want to take Molly for a walk?"

"Sure. As long as it's not past Ms. Beatrice's house."

They let Molly lead them down Tiller Street towards the dockside lane that led to the drawbridge. An early rising moon in the deep blue sky cast a bright silver path across the creek to the Colonial City side, where rows of modern high rise apartments lined the waterfront. Doctor Bullock lived in one of these luxury "monstrosities," as Westporters called them. Anne was always amazed that wealthy people seemed to prefer looking at boats from their balconies to actually sailing them.

The water level in the creek hadn't completely subsided after the hurricane, but the water was no longer murky, and the health department had announced that it was again safe to swim in. Tim unleashed Molly and let her jump into the creek from the dock. He and Anne sat on the dock and watched Molly paddle after the rippling streaks of moonlight as if she was trying to catch them. "Do you ever think our life is like that?" Tim asked Anne.

"Yeah. Sometimes. But maybe it doesn't matter as long as we're having fun."

"Clearly Molly would agree."

Anne asked Tim if he thought the Westport Sailing Club commodore and board would agree to an idea she had. "If we can't find anybody who wants Petra's boat, why don't we keep it at the club and use it to train kids who are too big for the little

Optimist dinghies?"

"Train them? We have a program to train kids from eight years old to fourteen. You went through that whole program yourself, didn't you?"

"Yes, but the kids in that program have to have their own boats. I'm talking about kids who can't afford to buy a boat, like most of the kids in my school. They see the parents of wealthier kids from Colonial City and the county driving their kids to the Westport Sailing Club to sail their little boats and know they'll never be able to join them. I'd like to teach them how to sail, too, if they're interested. If any of them like it and end up being good at it, they could crew on two- or three-man boats in regattas without needing a boat of their own."

"Sounds great. I'll take the idea to the board first thing tomorrow morning before I leave for New York."

"Thanks." Anne was getting a little hungry. "You mentioned a tuna fish sandwich?"

Tim called Molly and she jumped back onto the dock and shook herself dry, getting Tim and Anne wet. "She gets me every time," Tim complained. "And now you're initiated, too."

Anne somehow liked the idea of being initiated.

After sandwiches and riesling, Tim gave Anne a spare key to his cabin. She thought it might be a good idea for him to bring Molly into her house for a while so she'd get used to it before he left for New York the next day. Molly rushed around the first floor as soon as they went in. Anne and Tim sat on the couch, and Molly, still a little damp, squeezed between them. In minutes she had her head on Anne's lap. "Let's see what happens when you get up," Anne suggested. Molly rolled her eyes towards Tim but didn't budge. "OK," Anne said. "I think she's initiated."

29

Not what it looks like

The next morning Anne drove her minivan to the club. Tim told her he'd called Commodore Dan and convinced him to take her idea of free lessons for kids who couldn't afford to pay to the next board meeting. "Also, the commodore wanted me to list another contact person for non-emergencies. I was thinking of you."

"Me?"

"I trust you. You live nearby."

"I know, but—"

"And you're not like most of the other members avoiding the club because of Ruth's murder."

Anne didn't want to throw a wrench in Tim's plans at this late stage. "If you think—"

"I think you'll be fine." Tim showed Anne the main electrical and water shutoffs for the boatyard and gave her a key to the clubhouse door. He had packed everything including his laptop into a duffel bag which they put into her minivan, along with Molly's food and water bowls. They were off to the airport.

With Molly in the car, Anne could only let Tim out at the curb and wave goodbye. "It's all right, Molly. We're going to have fun at my house." Molly wasn't so sure as they drove away, but she settled down after Anne brought her inside and filled her bowl. Anne had lived alone for a long time and had become used to it. For the first time since she was a child she started to think it might be nice to have a dog.

While Molly was eating her dog chow, Anne made herself a spinach quiche, thinking about the recently deserted boat club. Now even Tim was gone. There was no reason members couldn't come and work on their boats or take them for a sail like they used to do. But the club seemed to have suffered by association with Ruth's murder. As Tim said, it would only get worse if the police determined that Petra was murdered at the club, too.

A loud rap sounded on the door. Molly barked. Anne peeped out the window to see John Neucomb looking in at her. She held Molly's collar and opened the door.

"Hello, Gorgeous. Ah, that's right. Ms. Beatrice told me you had a dog now."

"What is it, John?" Anne crossed her fingers hoping he was coming to tell her he'd already managed to have Real Estate Ron's license revoked.

"I'm ready to buy us a boat. There was a cash transfer I needed to make, and that's taken care of. The Westport Sailing Club looked abandoned when I went there. A message on the cabin door said to contact you. What a pleasant surprise."

"The last time I saw you, you were thinking more about Real Estate Ron than buying a boat."

"Heh-heh. Don't worry. I'm going to make sure he won't be dealing in real estate any more. The process has started. These things take some time, but it won't be long before you stop seeing his name on signs and ads plastered all over Westport." John put his hand on Anne's shoulder. Molly growled. He took it off. "Anyway, you and the dockmaster said you know a boat for sale that I might like. Come on and show it to me."

Anne unlocked Tim's cabin and went in to look for the key to Bullock's boat in case Bullock had come back and given it to Tim. First Molly, then John Neucomb followed her in. "Pitiful little hovel," John commented. "Wait till you see how I fix up the house that's all mine now. I'm thinking you might like a jacuzzi, marble floors in the bath, granite kitchen counters."

"Wait outside, would you?"

Molly ran out, but John pulled Anne towards him. "I want you as my wife, Anne. We're a perfect match, you have to admit." He locked his arms around her. Anne struggled, puffing. She looked over his shoulder through the open door and saw a figure approaching. It was Sergeant Carrs.

"Ms. Anne, is it? Ah, and Mr. Neucomb."

Anne twisted herself free of Neucomb. "This isn't what it looks like."

Sergeant Carrs stood blinking a moment before he said, "It looks like you two are romantically involved. That's what it looks like to me. Which both of you previously denied." He signaled to a young cop waiting beside his car to come join him.

"What if we are?" John Neucomb retorted.

"But we're not," Anne cried.

John put his hands on his hips. "What are you here for, Officer?"

The sergeant, one hand on his waist near his handcuffs, said, "I've come with a warning. William Jamieson's attorney insists on pointing out something that, of course, we're quite aware of. There are people who had a more obvious reason to murder Ruth Neucomb than William. We haven't scheduled the preliminary hearing on William's case until three weeks from tomorrow so that we can investigate the possibility that William was hired to kill Ruth Neucomb."

"Believe me." Anne's voice was choked with anger. "John Neucomb and I are not romantically involved. I want to make that clear. This man would *like* to have a relationship with me. He's been harassing me about it. But there is nothing between us."

The sergeant gave no indication whether he believed her or not. He said, "If you are in a relationship and you lied about it previously—"

"You already have the murderer," John Neucomb shouted. "The guy in the security camera footage."

The sergeant beckoned for the young cop to move closer to John Neucomb. "Let me be clear. This investigation is not over. Anyone who might have a motive for killing Ruth Neucomb is subject to further questioning." He wrote something in his notebook. "I'll have to remind both of you not to leave the neighborhood without notifying the police."

John Neucomb's hands were gripped into fists. "Then I'm giving you notice now. I'm buying a boat and Anne and I are going to sail to the Caribbean together."

"Not possible," Sergeant Carrs snapped. "Since you threaten to leave the country, I'll have to take you into custody now." He told the young cop to put John Neucomb into the car.

Anne's voice came out rather shrill. "Please, we're not going anywhere. At least I'm not. I give you my word. You're not going to arrest me, are you?"

"I'll just caution you for now," Sergeant Carrs agreed. "As for John Neucomb, his temper problem when we first questioned him and again now has to be taken into account."

Anne had seen his temper, too. Without saying so, she agreed that John Neucomb's temper made it more likely that he could have murdered the wife who seemed to be conspiring to leave him for Real Estate Ron.

Sergeant Carrs eyed Anne closely. "I want to ask you something. I understand you gave some interesting information to Ms. Terry Sullivan, the public defender in William Jamieson's case. She reported to us that you heard Petra Fields say she could strangle Ruth Neucomb. Is this true? Did you hear her say that?"

"Yes. And it's possible the bartender at Blake's Pub heard it, too."

The sergeant scribbled in his notebook and squinted, tapping his pen on the paper. He'd obviously come knowing it was possible that Petra might have murdered Ruth, which was supported now when Anne confirmed she heard Petra threaten to strangle her. But, regardless of Anne's attempt to explain it, he'd accidentally stumbled on Anne gasping in John Neucomb's arms, and he'd witnessed Neucomb's propensity to fly into a rage. The sergeant's initial suspicion of John Neucomb, and of Anne, must have been unexpectedly revived.

As Sergeant Carrs returned to his car and drove off with Neucomb, Anne's knees felt shaky. She tottered back into Tim's cottage and sank down onto the bed. Her throat tightened at the sight of the empty chair at Tim's desk. His desk was cleared. Molly came and sat by her feet looking up at her. Anne knew she wanted to go for a walk.

As she reached for the leash, Ms. Sullivan, William's public defender called. "I wanted to update you on some things, Anne. As you suggested, I talked to the bartender at Blake's Pub. He remembered Petra Fields being angry and drunk that night, but he didn't remember her making any actual threat against anybody."

"He did remember she was angry, though? That's something, isn't it?" As soon as she said this, Anne felt a tightness in her chest. Now that she had gotten to know Petra's partner Jessie better, she'd begun at least to hope that Petra wasn't the killer. If she was, that would probably devastate Jessie.

Ms. Sullivan went on. "And you gave me the name of Jorge Martinez. He called me. He believes William is innocent. But he admitted he didn't hear Petra make a direct threat against Ruth, only that Petra seemed angry with her."

Good enough, Anne thought. Jorge wouldn't have to testify to anything more damning than that against Petra in some possible public trial. He and Jessie were close now, and the relationship seemed good for both of them. Jessie would never believe her partner Petra had been a person capable of murder, and if Jorge gave evidence against her, that might ruin their relationship.

"And there's something else, Anne. I understand Sergeant Carrs told you they're investigating the possibility that William was hired by someone to kill Ruth. In other words, his motive could have simply been money. To give the police more time to investigate this, the prosecutor has delayed William's preliminary hearing."

"No! I'm sure William isn't capable of that." Anne felt her throat tighten. "Who do they think might have hired him?"

"Well, I have to tell you, the police think you and John Neucomb had a reason to want Ruth killed."

Anne cringed at remembering Sergeant Carrs finding her in Tim's cabin with John's arms around her. "You mean they suspect we paid William to kill Ruth?"

"I'm just letting you know what the police said. Sergeant Carrs claims he saw you congratulating William with a high-five down at the creek just before they arrested him again."

"What! Oh, I was congratulating him that his dinghy didn't leak."

Ms. Sullivan chuckled. "I'll pass that on if they bring it up again. Just so you know, I believe you, Anne."

30

A hard deal to close

When Anne finally left to take Molly for a walk, Lucia's car was in the principal's parking spot at Westport Elementary when she walked by. Lucia was said to be a workaholic, but Anne had never known her to go into the school on a Sunday. She took Molly to the door and tried it. The door opened with a creak. Lucia peeped into the hallway from the teachers' room. "Lord, you scared me." She clasped her heavy breast with both hands. "Come in, Anne. There's something you can help me with. I don't know about that dog, though."

Anne slipped the loop of Molly's leash over the outside door handle and followed Lucia into the teacher's room. "A temporary teacher has been assigned for the fall to replace Ruth," Lucia explained. "I need to clear out Ruth's desk for her to use. I called Ruth's husband, asked him to come pick up her things, but he said he didn't want them. Just throw them away. Now me, I'd want to look through them to see if there was anything of sentimental value," Lucia scoffed. "Obviously not. Or anything important. So I was checking."

Lucia pulled open the top drawer and pulled out a stack of papers. "Good grief," she gasped, shuffling through them. "Unmarked student papers and tests. They go back as far as last Christmas. Oh my goodness. If I had known about this …."

"I could go through them, see if they might have affected the students' final grades, if you want."

"That's all right, Anne. Ruth always gave high grades. That's how she avoided complaints. Any changes would be to lower the grades. We're not doing that." Lucia gathered the papers and dropped them into the trash bag she'd brought into the room. "Let sleeping dogs lie."

The second drawer was filled with items Ruth had confiscated from her students. Anne lined them up on the desk. Water guns, yo-yos, a rubber snake, lipstick, a glamor magazine, and a Rubik's cube, which Anne knew belonged to Jorge's nephew Roberto because she'd let him show her class how to solve it. "I'll give this one back to Roberto," Anne offered.

"Teachers are supposed to give these things back to the kids after school," Lucia muttered indignantly, and swept them into a cardboard box. "I'll put the box in the schoolyard, where the kids still come to play in the summer."

Anne pulled out the center drawer. These papers were more personal. She stacked them on the desk and started leafing through them. Ruth's updated résumé, website printouts on how to "ace" a job interview and on the definition of plagiarism, a contractor's estimate for turning her house into a four-story condo, and a business card from Real Estate Ron with "Call me" written on it.

The résumé and suggestions for conducting a good job interview jibed with her husband's saying she considered her job beneath her now that she had an Ed.D. The construction estimate confirmed his claim that she wanted to turn her house into a condo. The business card from Real Estate Ron didn't prove she was having an affair with him, but it had said "Call me" and Ruth had kept it. All in all, the papers from Ruth's desk confirmed what John Neucomb had told Anne about his wife. And it strengthened the suspicion that he might have wanted to do away with her.

"These things," Anne said uncertainly, "since Ruth's husband doesn't want them, I think should be turned over to the police while they investigate Ruth's death. When Sergeant Carrs questioned me, he asked for any information I had, no matter how unimportant it seemed."

Lucia's attention was fixed on the résumé. "I know Ruth didn't seem very happy here, but she never told me she might be looking for another job." Lucia glanced at the other papers. "I don't see how any of this could help find her murderer, but I'll turn them over to the police, as you suggest." Lucia's hands were trembling. "I mean I'll call the police to come get them. The idea of going into a police station frightens me."

Anne said she couldn't keep Molly tied to the school door any longer. Back in her house, she called Tim, but the call went to voicemail. She didn't leave a message. He was probably busy. She called her friend Lily.

"Vince and I are sitting out back on the patio listening to the Orioles game and sipping Tom Collins," Lily giggled. "Come over and join us, Anne."

"OK if I bring Tim's dog Molly? I'm dog sitting while he's in New York."

A scarlet sun tinted the lush green of Lily and Vince's lawn, and the tips of the thin cedars forming a privacy border swayed gently in the cool evening air. Lily knew Molly. "Go ahead and sniff my roses, Molly. And I have a snack here for you."

Lily's husband Vince, a thin lipped man with round frameless glasses and slicked-down hair, handed Anne a tall cold drink with a slice of lemon stabbed onto the rim. "Ninth inning. Orioles ahead two to one." He led her to a white Adirondack chair on the sandstone and red patio. "Lily's been telling me she knows the second woman who was found dead at the Westport Sailing Club. Unbelievable. Washed up onto your dock from the bay, Lily says."

Anne nodded, sipping her drink. "Mm-hum. Petra. We both knew her. She sailed in our regatta. The police are still waiting for the autopsy report to determine whether she drowned or was murdered."

Vince said, "No plastic bag over her head, Lily tells me. Probably just drowned, right?" Vince spoke like a man accustomed to getting all the facts on the table from the start, a habit Anne imagined he'd found useful in closing a deal on a car in the showroom. He offered his initial suggestion. "Different modus operandi, so two different killers if the second woman was murdered."

Anne felt like she was expected to give a counter offer. "Or maybe the second woman killed the first woman and then fell in herself and drowned while hanging her up on the hook?"

"Can't rule that out," Vince responded.

"And yet," Lily interjected, "John Neucomb had a reason to kill his wife. She was having an affair, they were getting a divorce, and he wanted her house."

Vince eyed Lily, Anne imagined, like a car dealer who now had to settle the wife's objections before the deal could be closed. "So you're saying he suffocates his wife, hangs her up to dry, and leaves. And then this other woman falls in somewhere and happens to wash up later at the same place?"

"Isn't that possible?"

Vince massaged his temple with a finger. "Seems like it. You might be right about John Neucomb. The day after his wife's murder he comes into the showroom and starts looking at top-of-the-line Range Rovers. Any idea whether he had life insurance on his wife?"

Anne said, "I'm sure the police have checked into that. But they've found a fingerprint on the boat launching crane that Ruth's body was hanging from—belonging to a cook at Blake's Pub, William Jamieson."

Vince took off his glasses and cleaned them on the tablecloth next to his chair. "Uh-huh. Lily tells me you don't think William did it, Anne. But let's say he did. Was the second woman's death related?"

Orioles win, two to one!

Vince turned up the radio. All thoughts of the dead women seemed to have vanished from his mind as he listened to a recap of the last inning. Lily refilled Anne's glass from a Waterford pitcher, saying, "So, Anne, Jorge keeps asking me about Petra's friend Jessie. I'd love to see him finally find a woman who'd treat him well. What do you think?"

"It would be good for Jessie to find somebody, too."

"You sound like there's a *but*."

Anne couldn't decide what to tell Lily about Jessie's relationship with Petra. In fact, she didn't really know what it was except that it had been one-sided. All Anne said was, "Jessie told me she loved Petra. Petra came into her life when she was feeling very alone."

Lily tapped Anne's knee. "I know all that. Jessie told Jorge, and Jorge told me."

"Jessie told him everything there is to tell? Good. I hope it works out for them."

Vince shut off the radio. "By the way, Anne. Did Lily fill you in on the latest about your Westport Sailing Club donor?"

"Donor?"

"Lawrence Bullock. At least he claims he's going to get his Fellowship Club to make a big donation. Lily's dad says the rest of the Board of Trustees of Severn Heights College overrode the faculty recommendation along with his own vote and approved the appointment of Bullock as the president of the college."

"Lily told me she thought they would."

"But have you heard the latest? Bullock says if he accepts the position, he'll need a membership to the Colonial City Golf Club. For schmoozing with the County Council to get more funds for the college, he claims."

Lily added, "And he wants the Board of Trustees to pressure the college into buying him that membership. Do you know how expensive that is?"

"It's about half my annual income," Vince told Anne.

Lily shook her head. "Doctor Bullock pointed me out at the start of the regatta and asked me to put in a good word for him with Dad. I just hope when the college sees what kind of man Bullock is, people don't think I had anything to do with him getting that position."

Vince put his arm around Lily. "Don't worry, Honey. Most people already knew what kind of person he was long before the regatta."

Molly gave Anne a bored stare and sigh, and Anne sipped the last inch of her drink. "Molly says it's time to go. This has been fun. The club's been deserted these days, Lily. Let's go for a fun sail sometime soon."

"Sure. But come with us. We're going to the Palais de Paris to eat some Coq au Vin."

"I wish I could. I have to stop by the Harry's Grocery to pick up some doggie bits before they close."

31

No call or message

Anne finished the leftover spinach quiche for dinner while Molly ate her doggie bits. Almost seven o'clock. Tim hadn't called her back. She'd assumed discussions about his book wouldn't take place on a Sunday. Even if they did, wouldn't they be over by this time?

To occupy her mind she thought about the papers she'd found in Ruth's desk. The printout of a Wikipedia article on plagiarism puzzled her. Ruth had underlined several of the various definitions as well as the typical punishments and sanctions involved. In Anne's experience even in the upper grades it had been rare that a teacher received a paper that seemed copied. In fact, Anne could only recall a single incident. That student freely admitted her mother had written it for her.

Maybe the reason Ruth had been so interested in plagiarism could be found on Ruth's school laptop. But the principal hadn't mentioned Ruth's laptop when they cleaned out her desk. Ruth had probably taken it home. Maybe the police had confiscated it.

Molly woke Anne up the next morning, hungry. She fed Molly and checked her phone. No call or message from Tim since he'd left the previous morning. She dialed his number. The "call could not be completed." She told herself not to worry. They were just friends, after all, even though it had begun to seem like more than that. In fact, she had declined Lily's invitation to have Coq au Vin at the Palais de Paris mainly because she wanted to save that experience to have it with Tim. Never mind. He'd call when he had a chance.

She fed Molly a can of Big Flavor Protein Delight that she'd brought over from Tim's cabin. There were only four more cans left. She fed herself a bowl of cinnamon raisin oatmeal. When she took Molly out for a walk, Molly pulled in the direction of the boat club. She missed Tim, too. She scratched at the door to Tim's cabin.

"He's not here," Anne warned, opening the door. Molly ran to the miniature kitchen, then to the bathroom. No Tim. "He'll be back soon," Anne said, speaking to herself as much as to Molly. She checked Tim's mini-fridge to see if anything was going bad. It was pretty much empty. She sat on Tim's bed, and she and Molly emitted a mutual sigh.

Her phone rang. She and Molly did a simultaneous jump. It was Commodore Dan. "Glad Tim gave me your number. I convinced the Westport Sailing Club Board that we should give your idea a try, Anne. Some of us have always thought we should have some program to reach out to our neighbors. Can we meet at the club?"

Anne sat at a table upstairs in the clubroom with Commodore Dan to give him some ideas. Her main point was that not every kid has to have his own boat if he or she could be trained on small club-owned boats. "Then, when they get older, they can sail in the Snipe fleet, Lightning fleet, Soling fleet—all the fleets are always looking for crew."

"I know." Dan sailed a Soling, and needed a crew of two in addition to himself, one to handle the jib and one to handle the spinnaker. "And I think you're right to start them young. We can buy a few Optimist dinghies for the smallest kids. Our treasury can't afford the bigger boats right now. So for the bigger kids, your idea of teaching them on a Laser could work. Just make sure they can pass our swimming test, and get their parents' permission."

When Commodore Dan drove home, Anne put Molly's leash on to take her back to her house, but Molly didn't want to go. She wouldn't leave Tim's cabin. "OK, girl. You can stay here until I come back." Anne filled her water bowl and left the door ajar.

No kids had been in the schoolyard on Sunday, but they were back to playing soccer there again today. Anne had brought the

Rubik's cube with her. Sure enough, Roberto was there. He called, "Time out," and he and Tonya ran up to her. Anne returned the cube to Roberto. "Those things in the box by the school wall," she told the kids, "are what Ms. Ruth was meaning to return to all of you." A little stretching of the truth wouldn't hurt. "You can take back whatever's yours."

Roberto wanted to get back to the soccer game. He put the Rubik's cube in a sack hanging from his bike's handlebars and ran onto the field. Tonya bent down to rub the muscle of her mahogany calf. "Twisted it a minute ago."

"Tonya, I wonder if you'd like to go for a sail. I don't want to take you away from the game. I mean sometime."

"I'm ready right now. I asked my mother and she said OK."

Anne used her own phone to call Tonya's home to double check. Her mother was excited. "Tonya says you're her favorite teacher. Of course, you can take her. Don't worry. She's a great swimmer. Good at pretty much every sport she tries."

Anne told Tonya, "I still have to see you swim the length of the little course we use at the club to test kids before we let them sail. Since you don't have a bathing suit with you, maybe we could do this tomorrow."

Tonya gave a scornful glance down at her jeans shorts with their rips and frayed hems. "No problem. I'll just go in these. They'll dry off before I get home."

Anne laughed. "You sound like me when I was your age. Where do you live, Tonya?" Anne knew that the majority of her students didn't live in the village of Westport proper, which over many years had been undergoing a slow gentrification. Anne's students mostly came from the western stretches of the Westport school district where the housing prices were lower.

"I live in an apartment over in the Heights. I usually take a bus to school, but when school's out I ride my bike."

Anne checked the leaves blowing at the top of an oak tree along the sidewalk. Enough wind, but not too much. "OK, Tonya.

Let's go. Bring your bike."

Molly rushed out of the cabin to greet them at the club, and Tonya ruffled the dog's neck. "I wish we could have dogs in our apartment."

Anne led Tonya to the sloping Laser platform. "Jump in here and swim to the end of the dock and back."

Tonya didn't jump. She dove in and emerged with a grin, water streaming down her springy hair. She did an Australian crawl at racing speed to the end of the dock, flipped, and did a backstroke back to Anne. "Come on in," Tonya called.

Anne checked her pockets, put her phone and keys on the dock, and dove in. Swimming wasn't allowed at the club except for swimming tests, but the club was deserted these days. The cool water washed away any concerns from Anne's mind. They raced to the end of the dock, and Tonya won. "But not by much, Anne laughed." This must be what it's like to have a daughter, she thought. Tonya was ten. She could easily have had a daughter her age.

Molly, who'd been watching too long from the dock, finally jumped in and paddled towards them. They splashed her, splashed each other. Anne's endorphins were surging. "One more race," she yelled. "I'm warmed up now." Of course, Molly joined them, but she was last. This time Anne beat Tonya, but she suspected Tonya had let her win.

They climbed onto the platform, water from their T-shirts and shorts trickling down their legs, while Molly shook herself dry and went into Tim's cabin. Anne followed with her phone and keys, then retrieved two life jackets from the club storage room. Tonya helped her to rig and launch her Laser. "It's really a one-person boat," Anne explained. "But we can both fit on it. Sit right across from me and watch what I do. The main thing is always to know what direction the wind is coming from. Watch the sail and keep your eye on the little wind indicator on the front of the mast."

Tonya caught on fast to trimming the sail to windward. Now the tack. "See how low the boom is, Tonya? You're going to have to duck down really far when it swings across. Ready?"

"Ouff!"

"Grazed your life jacket. You have to bend lower. Ready? We'll tack back the other way."

Tonya's face showed a deeper concentration than Anne had ever noticed in class. After a few more tacks, Anne let her control the sail with the mainsheet. Then the tiller. Then both. In no time they were out in the bay. They had to sail downwind to get back to the club. "Ease the sail all the way out, Tonya. Now keep turning, duck, and the wind will blow the boom all the way to the other side of the boat, really fast." Anne jerked the mainsheet to keep it from catching on the stern.

"Woah!"

"See what I mean? That was a jibe. We'll practice that another day."

"I'm not tired," Tonya sang out.

"But I am."

As they were sliding the boat back into its rack, Anne saw John Neucomb coming into the boatyard in a yellow polo shirt tucked into maroon shorts. She saw him pull open the cabin door and look in. "Hey!" Anne yelled.

John jumped and turned to see Anne and Tonya sloshing towards him in their wet sneakers. His mouth drew a large O. He rubbed a finger across each eye. "Anne? What happened?" As if whatever had befallen them might be catching, he took a half-step back as Anne and Tonya neared him.

Anne muttered, "I see the cops let you go," then said, "John Neucomb, this is my friend Tonya. We've been going for a sail."

"A sail? But you're all wet."

"That's part of the experience."

"You're kidding. Ah, you mean in those little boats."

"That's where you start learning." Anne stifled a grin, remembering John had proposed she teach him how to sail.

"I plan to learn on a big boat. That's what I came here to talk about." John gave Tonya a squinty glance.

Tonya shifted on her feet. "I should be going home, Ms. Anne." Anne gave her a wet hug, and Tonya, nodding to John Neucomb, got on her bike and rode off.

32

No playing with dolls

John's eyes followed Tonya until she was out of sight. "I thought this was an exclusive club," he commented.

"Don't worry. I won't report you for being on the grounds."

"You laugh now, but I'm going to have enough money to buy an ocean cruiser and dock it at whichever Westport marina I want. I won't need this club."

"Going to?"

"Huh? Oh, I have plenty of money now, but I'm going to have even more soon."

"When the life insurance pays off?"

John's face turned almost the color of his maroon shorts. "Was it you who told the police about that? They subpoenaed the company and found I had a policy on Ruth's life." John squeezed his hands into his pockets and shrugged. "They think I have a motive to kill Ruth, but they have no evidence. They couldn't hold me. I know the law."

"Did you kill her?"

"How can you ask me that? I told you I have enough money already. I didn't need the house or the insurance money. All I wanted was to divorce her."

"So you convinced the police you were only kidding about us sailing off to the Caribbean?"

"Yes. But, Anne, I wasn't really kidding. My offer still stands." A tight-mouthed grin spread across his face. "You're soaking wet and have eelgrass in your hair, but in that wet T-shirt you look very sexy."

"Don't touch me. If you continue to harass me, I'll report you to the police."

When he gripped her arms, she stomped hard on the toes of his sockless foot. He uttered a canine yelp, which was followed by a bark from Molly, rushing from the cabin. John Neucomb paled and, with a slight limp, hurried out of the boatyard.

Anne raked the seaweed from her hair with her fingernails. "Come on, Molly. I need to clean myself up." She gathered her keys and phone from the cabin and saw she had a text from Tim: *Sorry, I've had my phone off. Long story, but the police located Petra's mother. Her mother, outraged, called Commodore Dan. Dan gave her my number, asked me to handle it. Her mother wouldn't stop talking. When she finally hung up, I shut off my phone. Book appraisal going well. I might have to fly to Boston.*

An open jeep drove into the yard. Commodore Dan rolled his eyes over Anne, registering her appearance without any reaction. After all, Anne thought, he'd often seen her soaked and dripping ever since she was a pre-teen learning to sail. "Anne," he said, out of breath. "Something's come up."

"Petra's mother? Tim texted me."

"She's going to sue the club for negligence."

"What? Petra is 'estranged from her parents,' according to Petra's friend."

Dan didn't seem interested in hearing about Petra's family relations. "You and Tim found Petra's body after the hurricane. Can you talk to her mother? She's totally hysterical."

Anne dialed the number Dan gave her and put it on speaker phone. Petra's mother answered in an old lady smoker's voice.

"Mrs. Fields? This is Anne Bateman from the Westport Sailing Club."

"The police called us to say our daughter Petra drowned on your club grounds. They're still awaiting the result of an autopsy, but I know nobody would want to harm Petra. She slipped, that's all. What kind of place doesn't put up guard rails to keep people from falling in? You'd better have more information than your club chief could give me. He says you found our poor daughter's body."

"Yes, Ma'am. It was a shock. We're very sorry."

"If you knew how we devoted our lives to coaching her, keeping her focused on the goal of growing up to be the top woman sailor in the country and even in the world. While other girls were playing with dolls, we put Petra in a little sailing dinghy and arranged for her to practice long hours every day. My husband had been on track to becoming a sailing star himself when he was injured. We placed all our hopes on Petra."

"Um, may I ask, Mrs. Fields, when was the last time you spoke to Petra?"

"I don't know what Petra told you. We haven't spoken since she went away to college and let the drinking and partying set distract her from her goal. But she was a star on the college sailing team, and we've followed reports of her victories ever since. And we've wired money into her account every month."

"What did the police tell you, Mrs. Fields?" Anne wondered if they'd mentioned the possibility that Petra might have killed Ruth.

Mrs. Fields let out a throaty sigh. "Something about a toxicology report. They hinted she might have been inebriated or whatever when she landed in the water. They said they'd call us when the forensic tests are complete and asked what we wanted to do with her body, send it to a funeral home up here in Rhode Island or …." She couldn't go on.

"I'm so sorry, Mrs. Fields."

"Can you imagine what our friends will think? The police are implying Petra was too drunk or whatever to swim. We've bragged about her accomplishments, and now this."

Anne got the idea Petra's parents wanted to lay the blame on the club rather than on Petra's drinking "or whatever" by suing the club for negligence.

"Her reputation will be tarnished," Mrs. Fields rasped.

"Did the police say anything about another person losing her life after the same regatta?"

"They did. They said they might have more information about this other woman later. Why they thought I'd be interested I don't know."

Anne pursed her lips and thought a second. "Mrs. Fields, Petra is known at our club as a first-class sailor. Her unexpected death will never change that. I have an idea how you and our club could perpetuate her memory. Would you possibly be willing to set up an endowment in her name at our Westport Sailing Club? We could use it to support local kids who can't afford club membership." Of course, Anne thought, assuming Petra isn't found to be a murderer.

Mrs. Fields, breathing hard, called to her husband. "They want to set up a Petra Fields Memorial Endowment." He came onto the phone. "Now that might be something we'd be interested in. Get back to us with the details." He hung up.

Anne looked at Commodore Dan and shrugged. He gave her a powerful bear hug. "Way to go, Annie. You amaze me."

"But you realize we can't have a Petra Fields Memorial Endowment if she turns out to be a murderer."

"Uh-huh. But we can at least delay the lawsuit by keeping the negotiations going until the old lady and her husband...."

"Die?"

"You didn't hear me say that."

Anne had barely finished showering, washing her hair, and wrapping herself in a towel when Jessie called. "I hate to keep bothering you, Anne, but I have to ask you something. It's about Jorge. I like him. But he's your friend, so I don't know."

"He seems to be a good person. I'm glad you two seem to be hitting it off."

"I mean, if you like him ...."

"He's not my boyfriend, if that's what you mean."

"Yeah, Lily said he wasn't. I just thought I should check with you. I'm thinking of inviting him to come for a swim at my apartment complex pool. He told me he likes swimming, and that's the only activity I ...."

"Great idea, Jessie." Anne tried to decide whether to tell Jessie she'd talked to Petra's parents.

"You could come, too, Anne. It's a beautiful pool. Petra never wanted to go and I don't like to go there by myself."

"I'll come sometime. The police located Petra's parents, by the way. Her mother called our sailing club. She hadn't talked to Petra since she went away to college."

After a silence Jessie mumbled, "So they didn't know about me. Maybe I should write them a letter of condolence."

"Sure. I don't know their address, but if I get it, I'll tell you." Thinking like Commodore Dan, Anne reckoned such a letter might help dissuade Petra's parents from suing the Westport Sailing Club, and of course make Jessie feel better.

Jessie said, "Something else I was wondering about. I guess Jorge realizes I was pretty close to Petra. Has he ever asked you anything about that?"

"No. To me he seems like the kind of guy who would take that in stride."

"I know. He only cares about the present. Me and him." Jessie gave an embarrassed titter. "That came out too melodramatic."

"I'm happy to see you moving on, Jessie. Let's promise to stay friends."

Ms. Sullivan called as Anne was getting ready for bed. "I'm afraid I have some bad news, Anne. The police have now ruled Petra's death a murder."

Anne's heart started racing.

"The police say you and Tim Griffin found Petra's body. Can you give me a description of what you saw?"

Anne swallowed and resolved to do her best. "How detailed should I ...."

"The medical examiner found marks of struggle on her hands and arms. Did you notice those?"

"Yes. We thought they might be from trying to climb back onto the dock."

"And you didn't notice any other sign of injury?"

"No. I mean we didn't, like, examine her."

"The autopsy report indicates there was a small rip in her shirt and a deep puncture wound in her upper abdomen under the rib cage. She was dead before she fell into the water."

"We saw the rip but couldn't …. I mean her clothes and body were all …."

"I understand. And you told the police you had heard William agree to meet Petra at the boat club?"

"Yes. To meet her there when he got off work at eleven o'clock." Anne swallowed. "They're not accusing William of murdering Petra, too, are they?"

"I'm afraid they are."

Anne tried to think. "Did the medical examiner determine the time of Petra's death?"

Ms. Sullivan took a moment. "The bay water is brackish, the report says. Which may have helped preserve the body long enough to estimate that she was in the water at least ten to twelve days before the body was found."

"Let me see." Anne counted on her fingers. "It couldn't have been more than ten days. She was alive ten days before we found her."

"Correct. Which means she was killed the night William was to meet her."

"But what time that night?"

"The medical examiner couldn't be sure of that."

"Do the police have a motive for William wanting to kill Petra?"

Ms. Sullivan hesitated a moment. "They're still investigating the possibility that it was a murder for hire."

"You mean that somebody wanted both of them dead? And paid William to kill them? Who could have done that?"

"The police told me they're looking for people who knew both Ruth and Petra. Who might have something against both of them."

33

Pretend wife (1)

Molly slept on the floor next to Anne's bed. On their walk the next morning, Anne let her lead the way down Windward Street. In front of Ruth's house was a sign: *Yard Sale—Two Days Only.* Tables and chairs covered with household items and books filled the small front lawn. John Neucomb came out of the door carrying an open cardboard box filled with women's clothes, dropping it on the grass beside three other boxes of women's clothes, all of which Molly thoroughly sniffed.

John looked up at Anne as if he'd been caught doing something naughty. "Ah, Anne. Just cleaning some things up. A contractor's coming soon to give me an estimate on some interior remodeling." He shifted uneasily on his feet. When Anne stood silently looking over the boxes of Ruth's clothes, John said, "Anything you want you can have. Just take it."

Anne looked through the books. *Elementary Geography, Fun with Arithmetic, Beginning Grammar,* and the thick red psychology textbook she'd seen Ruth shove into her bag to take home from school. Anne had thought it strange that Ruth would be interested in a book like this. She picked it up and saw it had a Library of Congress catalogue number on it. It was a loan from the Severn Heights College library.

John noticed her looking at the book. "You can have it, Anne. Not something I'd ever read."

"This should be returned to the library," Anne snipped, hand on hip. "Never mind. I'll do it." She tucked the book under her arm and started to walk away.

"Anne, is that your dog? How cute." It was Marge Morales, one of the Westport Elementary teachers who had gone with Anne to Ruth's memorial ceremony. Marge glared at John Neucomb, now pulling blouses out of a box to pile onto a table. She raised her voice. "Isn't this all so sad, Anne?"

"Oh, hi, Marge," John called out huskily. "Any friends of Ruth's can have whatever you want for free. There's more inside, ladies. You're welcome to go in and look around."

Marge tapped Anne's arm. "I'd like to do that if you'll come with me."

Anne brought the dog along. The house was laid out very much like Anne's but was dark and musty. Clearly John hadn't moved back in yet. There was a table by the front window with a framed picture of a boy about eight years old standing in front of a rather ramshackle house with a blue cub scout cap on his head. Marge picked the picture up. "That's John Neucomb. My husband went to elementary school with him. Poor John. There's a story about that cap. John's father died when John was young, and his mother struggled to get by. John wanted to be a cub scout, but they couldn't afford the uniform and he couldn't join. So John bought just the cap and pretended he was a cub scout. Miguel says John wore it to school every day, not just on days when there was a cub scout meeting."

The story brought a lump to Anne's throat. Suddenly she saw John Neucomb in a new light. In a way, he was still that little boy pretending to be something he couldn't be. Now he was trying to be a salty Maritime Republic of Westport sailor. That picture of the little boy in the cap was going to haunt her for a while. Could you feel sorry for a man who might have murdered his wife?

Neither Anne nor Marge wanted to go upstairs. On the front lawn again, Anne asked John if he'd found Ruth's laptop. "I was wondering because it belonged to the school. They lend them to the teachers."

"The cops took that." John wrinkled his nose.

Marge picked up a purple vase from one of the tables. "I'll take this for Miguel's travel agency, John. We were sorry to hear you canceled plans for a trip to Antigua."

"Yes." John Neucomb raised an eyebrow at Anne. "Now I'm hoping to sail there in a boat of my own. Don't worry. I'll still use Miguel to make the onshore arrangements."

On the way home Anne got a call from her friend Lily. "The Natural Resources rehabilitation sanctuary says the baby eagle's wing has healed. They want to set it free in the same place we found it. Jorge's going to take us all in his big boat."

"All?"

"Yeah. A Natural Resources guy is in charge of setting the eagle free. They have their procedures. But they're allowing me, Jorge, and Jessie to watch how they do it. Want to go?"

"Sure. When?"

"Right now. We're in Jorge's boat and heading for the club. We can pick you up there."

Jorge's twenty-foot Key West fishing boat pulled up to the sailing club dock soon after Anne left Molly in the cabin with a bowl of food. The three women sat together on the transom seat, Jessie in the middle clinging to Lily's arm on one side and Anne's on the other. Fred, the Natural Resources man, sat with Jorge. The engine throbbed slowly out of the creek until the boat reached the open bay. Jorge grinned, "Hold on." Jessie's grip on Anne tightened. The engine rumble switched to a whining roar as the bow of the boat shot up. There was too much noise and wind to talk. Anne held on to the slippery life rail, lifting her head to let the wind and briny smell of the bay clear her mind of everything but the thrill of being out on the water.

In no time they reached Greenthumb Point and slowed to turn into the cove and tie up to a tree that had blown down in the hurricane. Jorge opened the cuddy behind the boat's wheel and Fred took out a cage with the peeping baby eagle. Jorge pointed to the top of the cell tower where the huge eagle's nest had been. The hurricane had blown most of it away, but a new one was already under construction. While they were looking, an eagle flew in and landed atop the nest with another stick in its claws.

When Fred opened the baby eagle's cage, Jorge said, "Your bad times are over, little guy. You're free to fly away now."

The eagle peered out of the cage opening, at first seeming to be afraid to go out. Then it took one, two steps, and as soon as it was out, flew high and disappeared into the trees. Jorge slowly nodded in satisfaction. Jessie stood holding her hand over her mouth, and Jorge put his arm around her. "See? Easy as that," he said.

Anne, Lily, Jessie, and Jorge met Lily's husband Vince at Clyde's for dinner. The special was herb-crusted fillet of catfish, which Pedro said had been caught in the bay that morning. Vince was interested when Anne said there was some information in Ruth's school desk that the principal had turned over to the police. "Anything to incriminate one of our suspects?"

"Not exactly, but a couple of things tend to back up John Neucomb's claim that she was having an affair with Real Estate Ron. I don't think that's been proven yet."

Lily laughed. "Tell that to Ms. Beatrice, our neighborhood sentry."

Anne added, "Also there was a contractor's estimate on turning the Neucomb house into a condo."

"So double motive," Vince observed. "John Neucomb punishes her for the affair and keeps her from turning the house into a condo." Vince looked like he wanted to shake somebody's hand on the conclusion of a deal. Anne wanted to end the conversation there, too, before the idea that Petra might have killed Ruth came up, which Anne was sure would shock and embarrass Jessie.

Jessie nibbled at her fish, glancing now and then at Jorge in a way that made Anne think of the eaglet hesitating at the open door of its cage. Neither of them said much during the dinner.

Lily said she had taken the oysters she was raising back to the inlet at Greenthumb Point. "The water's returned to its normal salinity, so they'll be able to thrive there."

"When can we eat them?" Vince joked.

"Never," Lily scoffed. "You know that. I'm going to put them on an artificial reef the Natural Resources Department has built where they can spawn. If we bring back enough oysters in the bay, they'll return it to its once sparkling water someday."

Jorge, his mouth full of fish, nodded approval. "Mm. Mm." Jessie gave a little clap of applause. Jorge's plate was clean, and Jessie had had enough. "I should be getting home," Jessie said. Jorge said he'd walk her to her car.

When they left, Vince observed, "They make a good couple, what do you think?" as if ready to seal the deal.

Molly followed Anne up to the bedroom. Anne showered and slipped on the silk nightgown her mother had given her for her birthday many years ago but which she seldom wore. She lay in bed, her phone in her hand. No calls or texts from Tim. His phone must still be turned off to prevent Petra's mother from bothering him. His last text was from the previous afternoon. She hadn't been able to tell him she'd given Petra's mother the idea of starting a Petra Fields Memorial Endowment and that the club's commodore liked the idea—unless Petra turned out to be Ruth's murderer, of course.

Her phone rang and she jumped. Tim? Ugh, it was John Neucomb. She let it go to voicemail. The thought of that man selling and giving away all of Ruth's clothes and possessions so soon after her death gave Anne a chill. Of course, Ruth had been unfaithful, that was true. The fatherless boy pretending to be a cub scout had grown up to marry a wife who left him for a shady real estate tycoon. He must have been hurt even though it was simply anger that he showed. Anne took a look at the voicemail transcription rather than listen to his voice. *Anne, I'm resigning myself to the idea that you won't marry me. It's sad, but I can bear it. I have another proposal. I buy that boat at your club dock and we sail to Antigua together as if we were married, maybe even tell people we're married. When we get back to Westport, you'll be free to walk away and*

I'll have the memory to hold onto.

"A pretend wife," Anne cried out loud. "The boy who had to pretend to be a cub scout is now resigned to pretending to have a wife." She felt tears of sorrow welling in her eyes. Was this the kind of man who would murder someone? It didn't seem so. But maybe it was. Who could say?

Anne tossed in bed trying to go to sleep yet fearing what kind of dreams she might have. She must have fallen asleep because she woke up in the middle of the night thinking she heard the loud roar of a lion or bear. It took a moment before she realized it was Molly moaning in her sleep. Molly, not Anne, was having the nightmare. "Wake up, Molly," she called. "Come up here on the bed and sleep next to me."

34

Pretend wife (2)

Anne's phone woke her up early the next morning. Was it Tim? No. It was someone named Vivian Witherspoon.

"Anne Bateman? I understand you are in charge of the Westport Sailing Club grounds temporarily. Sorry to bother you, but I'm at my wit's end. A man named John Neucomb found a number my husband put on your bulletin board with a notice that our boat *Knot on Call* is for sale."

"Ah, your husband is—"

"Lawrence Bullock. We don't share the same last name. For some reason my husband thought it was acceptable to put our home number on a *For Sale* notice and then go on an extended trip to Hilton Head, South Carolina, to play golf."

"I'm sorry to hear that. I'll be glad to take the notice down until he gets back."

"I'm afraid it's too late. This John Neucomb is quite persistent. He keeps calling to ask if I can come and show him the boat."

"I see. I know Mr. Neucomb. I'll contact him and tell him to stop calling you."

"You say you know him? Hm. If you could be with us at the boat club, I might be willing to show him the boat. I'm the actual owner. I'm the one who bought it and named it. My husband and I both want to sell it."

"If you tell me when, Mrs. Witherspoon, I can meet you at the club."

"Let me see. Unless there's an emergency at the hospital, I'm free today and next Monday. Could you arrange something?"

Anne said she could meet her that morning.

"Wonderful. Will you call Mr. Neucomb for me? And call me back if he can come at about nine thirty?"

A yellow sports car slipped into the sailing club lot, and a long-legged woman in a black pants suit climbed out. Vivian Witherspoon was tall, with black hair done in a chin-length layered bob—and was a good bit younger than her late-sixties husband. Dark eyebrows and long eyelashes enhanced her office-pale face.

"I feel like I've seen you before," Anne said, shaking her hand. Then she remembered. Doctor Witherspoon's picture and profile had been in the *Colonial City Magazine*, which featured page after page of restaurant ads showing rich specialty dishes alongside ads offering services that wealthy women might need after eating all that food: liposuction and "body sculpting", plastic surgery, cosmetic dental work, and family law. Local professionals who bought these advertisements were given picture profile articles in the magazine.

"Probably that magazine," Vivian Witherspoon suggested. "I'm an anesthesiologist for a plastic surgery practice, and they put my picture standing alongside the surgeons in the last issue."

John Neucomb dashed into the boat yard, breathing hard. "Hope I'm not late." He stood staring, or more accurately gawking, at the trim, comely figure dressed in black who was just a bit taller than himself. He stuttered, "I … I recognize you, Doctor Witherspoon. From the *Colonial City Magazine*."

Vivian Witherspoon smiled. "After publication of that issue, I suppose it would be impossible for me to commit a crime without being recognized."

"I've always wished they'd put my picture and profile in that magazine. I'm a Colonial City lawyer, but I guess its readers aren't interested in corporate law."

"No," Vivian agreed with a half-stifled grin. "The readers are mostly women who let their husbands worry about that kind of thing."

"The article said you live on the Colonial City side of the creek in a high rise apartment overlooking the waterfront."

"I do. My husband's choice. I'd really prefer to live in one of these charming Westport houses. I realize they're probably quite spartan inside, but I'm sure they could be made quite comfortable to live in."

"My idea exactly." John Neucomb stepped closer to her. "We haven't shaken hands yet. I'm very glad to meet you."

Anne interrupted their shared moment. "The actual dockmaster is away, and I'm just substituting. Unfortunately, if Doctor Bullock ever gave Tim the key, he hid it somewhere and I can't find it. We can go look at the boat and walk on the deck, though. *Knot on Call* is a beautiful Beneteau 38 in like-new condition."

Vivian Witherspoon scoffed. "It sure is. My husband doesn't know how to sail it. I bought it thinking we'd sail together, but he's afraid of boats, I found out too late. I'm the one who brought it over here to the club."

Anne led them to the corner of the yard where the boat was docked. "If we walk out on the landing pier, we can step onto the deck," she said. "Hold onto the life rail when you do."

Vivian hopped onto the deck with ease, but John stood hesitating. "I can see it pretty well from here."

"Here, take my hand," Vivian called. "You can do it."

Anne enjoyed watching this little scene. John managed to get on the boat but wouldn't let go of Vivian's hand until she'd led him down into the cockpit to sit behind the wheel. "You just steer it like a car," Vivian told him. John's face looked a little pale. Vivian asked, "Are you sure you want to buy this boat?"

"I do," he said. "But I'd need somebody to show me how to sail it."

"Well, that's better than my husband," Vivian responded. "He's never even cared to learn."

"I don't suppose a few lessons might be included with the sale," John ventured.

"Heh-heh. *After* the sale, you mean? Hm, that might be fun."

"All right, I'll buy it," John said. He hadn't asked the price.

Vivian rattled the padlock on the hatch boards covering the companionway. "The registration and documentation are inside. Looks like we'll have to wait till the dockmaster gets back before we can finalize the sale. That OK with you?"

"Sure." John looked like his main worry was how he was going to get back off the boat onto the pier. Vivian might have noticed this. She jumped off and held out her hand again, helping John crawl back onto the landing pier.

"I wonder if this suggestion would be out of line?" Vivian asked John. "I have today off, and you said you have a house here in Westport. I've never been inside of one. Do you think it would be possible to have a look at your house?"

John looked like a kid who'd been given an eagle scout award. "Come along," he urged. "It's walking distance from here. I'll appreciate any suggestions you can give me for fixing it up."

Anne couldn't stop smiling as she watched John and Vivian walk out of the boatyard together. Let Vivian Witherspoon be his pretend wife for a while, she thought. I need the break.

While Anne was taking Molly for a walk, public defender Terry Sullivan phoned. "Couple of things, Anne. Thank you for encouraging your principal to send Ruth Neucomb's papers to the police. And I wanted to ask if you've thought of anything else that might help William's case."

"Well, there are some things that have puzzled me from the start. First of all, Ruth didn't go to Blake's Pub after the regatta with almost everybody else. We'd all left the boatyard by about six o'clock. Ruth's husband says he went to their house about the same time, six o'clock, with some papers for Ruth to sign, and she wasn't there. He says he waited there from six until after midnight and she still hadn't come back. So where was Ruth between six and nine o'clock? That's what I wonder. If she was wandering around the club for three hours, somebody would have noticed."

"Why nine o'clock?"

"That's the earliest she could have been killed according to the police. And the latest was about midnight. So if she was killed as late as midnight, where was she between six and midnight? That's *six* hours she was missing."

"The time of death is only an estimate, of course," Ms. Sullivan noted.

"I realize that. If she was killed any time before 11:15, William couldn't have killed Ruth because he didn't leave the pub until eleven, when he got off work. He wasn't caught on the security camera entering the boatyard until 11:15. And it caught him leaving at 11:25."

Ms. Sullivan seemed to be scribbling some notes. "All right. Ruth Neucomb's location not known for three to six hours before her murder."

"Right. I don't think she was sitting on the dock dangling her feet in the water all that time."

"Any thoughts on what she might have been doing?"

"I'd like to know. What about her phone? Was it in her pocket? Is it still operable?"

"It wasn't on her. They assume it fell into the water."

"Ruth's husband told me the police took her laptop."

"Yes, they told me they have it. They're working on cracking the password."

"If they get any information from the laptop, will they show it to you, Ms. Sullivan?"

"Yes, if they're going to use it as evidence." Ms. Sullivan went silent a minute, then asked, "Is there some reason you think the contents of the laptop might throw a light on this case?"

"It could tell us more about what Ruth was up to before she was killed. For example, I'd like to know why she printed out a definition of plagiarism. Maybe I'm just being too curious."

"All right, I'll ask the police if there's anything on her laptop they're going to use as evidence." Ms. Sullivan paused as if to jot down a note. Then she cleared her throat. "But the other thing I need to tell you is that the police have listed you as someone who knew both Ruth and Petra."

A lump constricted Anne's throat. She managed to say, "I'm not a murderer, Ms. Sullivan."

"I believe you. So let's say we eliminate you as a suspect. And the same for William. Let's say he's not capable of murder for hire. How viable as a suspect do you think Ruth's husband is? He says he was in their house between six and midnight. But no one can confirm that."

Anne said, "He has a motive for wanting Ruth dead. That's for sure. Ruth was having an affair. That might be enough. And also he wanted sole possession of their house, which she wouldn't agree to in a divorce."

"You still sound doubtful."

"Well, first of all, I don't think he even knew Petra."

"But what about his wife?"

"I guess you saw the pictures of Ruth with a plastic bag tied around her head, dangling over the water from the boat launching crane? John Neucomb might've wanted his wife out of the way, but I don't think he has the guts to do something like that. Earlier today he came to the club to look at a boat for sale, and he was afraid to walk on the pier. The woman selling the boat had to hold his hand."

Ms. Sullivan laughed. "You know the police clerk, Ms. Trimble, who sits next to Sergeant Carrs? She wasn't hesitant to give me her opinion on whether John Neucomb committed the murder. According to her, he's 'too much of a wuss.'"

35

Bad battery

The next day Anne let Molly lead her down the street towards Ruth's house again. Ruth's front yard was still littered with most of the things from a couple days ago. John Neucomb must have left them there the whole time. Anne figured a layer of dew had settled on them each night. Most or all of these things were probably destined for the dump. She thought she might take another look at the books in case there were others that needed to be returned to the library.

The house door opened a crack and John Neucomb peeped out. "Just take whatever you want."

Strange not to even greet her, Anne thought. But then the door opened and Vivian Witherspoon, Doctor Bullock's wife and owner of the boat John said he would buy, walked out, her pale face showing reddish signs of embarrassment. "Oh, hello again," Vivian said. "Mr. Neucomb was asking me for advice on some interior improvements to his house."

John followed Vivian out into the yard. "Are you here about the boat, Anne? Did you find the key? Vivian was telling me she's a member of the Colonial City Yacht Club, which I've always wished I could join. She said she would sponsor me. The only requisite is you have to have a sailboat."

"Actually, I was looking to see if there were any more library books that needed to be returned."

John screwed up his face in annoyance. Vivian reached to shake his hand good-bye. "Don't leave yet," he urged Vivian. "I was going to order delivery from the Palais de Paris. Anne won't take long looking though the books, right?"

"I've already looked at these. Are there any more in the house?" Anne asked.

"No. They're all out here."

"Sorry, then," she told John and Vivian as she left. "Enjoy your meal."

Molly pranced up onto Anne's porch as if she lived there. She was getting used to staying with Anne. Did Tim's dog miss him? Of course. And so did Anne. She looked on her phone calendar. Tim had been gone four days. She'd tried to call him once, but the call couldn't be completed. Then she got his long text message explaining about Petra's mother nagging him and saying he was going to shut his phone off. That was three days ago. And the problem with Petra's mother had been taken care of, hadn't it? Anne had convinced the woman to wait for details about setting up an endowment in Petra's name. But of course Anne hadn't been able to tell that to Tim. His phone was off.

She tried dialing him again. The call couldn't be completed. Was his phone still shut off? Tim's text had said he might have to fly to Boston. Maybe he was on the plane to or from Boston now and his phone was in airplane mode. That was possible ....

No. Something was wrong. She checked the contacts on her phone. Commodore Dan's number was there. She called him.

"Hello, Annie. What's up?"

"I was wondering if the Westport Sailing Club board has made any decision about setting up an endowment in Petra Fields' name?"

"They have. We called Mrs. Fields and gave her some tentative plans." Commodore Dan laughed. "The ball's in her court now. She has to come up with the money. I think I hinted to you, we're going to slow-walk this until we see if Petra is determined to be Ruth Neucomb's murderer or not."

"Right. Have you contacted Tim Griffin? He texted me that Petra's mother kept calling him with threats to sue our club."

"I did call him, but his phone was off the hook. We'll fill him in when he gets back."

Anne thanked the commodore. She'd been worrying that Tim

was "ghosting" her, as the kids say nowadays. Now she also had to worry that something might have happened to him. It wasn't as if Tim had a father or mother or wife or son or daughter she could call. For the first time it hit her what a solitary life he led. He was a person unconnected to others like Petra had been with Jessie. Anne gave Molly some food and walked up to Blake's Pub.

"Get you something to eat?" Reggie asked when she ordered a beer at the bar. "Fish tacos," she said.

"Sorry. The new cook can't make those. They were William's specialties. The new guy's OK with hamburgers."

"Fine. I'll have a hamburger. With fries?"

"Yeah, he can do those, too."

Anne took a long swig of her beer, and when she put her mug down, a suntanned young man with short blond hair wearing an Eastern Sails polo shirt plopped down next to her. "Buy you a shot of Tequila to go with that?"

"Uh, why not?"

Reggie poured them each a shot. They clinked their glasses. "Cheers." Anne had to wash her Tequila down with a mouthful of beer. She smiled, looking at his shirt. "I guess you're a sailmaker."

"I am. Let me see. I guess you're …."

Don't say movie star, she thought. I've heard that line before.

"A Laser racer," he said.

"What makes you think—"

"I saw you in here after the women's regatta back before the hurricane. My name's Tom."

"I'm Anne. My day job is fifth-grade teacher."

The new cook, who looked like this might be his first job, put a huge hamburger and plateful of fries on the counter. Anne would be embarrassed to eat all this in front of Tom while he watched. She asked for another plate, cut the burger in half, and offered half to him. "I can't eat all these fries, either."

He tilted his head in thanks and picked up the half burger. The awkward need for small talk diminished while they ate. Tom, with a mouth half full, muttered something like, "Wrspr-emry?"

"Pardon?"

He swallowed. "Westport Elementary? My cousin goes there. Clarence Witt."

"Um-hum." She swallowed. "Yea, I know him. He'll probably be in my class next fall."

Tom only nodded a response, his mouth now full of fries. For a few minutes, there was a mutual truce on talking. Anne was hungry and managed to finish her half burger just when he finished his. Picking at their fries, they resumed talking. Tom said, "I might not have offered you a shot if I'd known you were a teacher. I'm a little afraid of teachers."

"I get that a lot. I won't bite."

"Or correct my grammar? Or expect me to know who wrote the Declaration of Independence?"

"You don't know who wrote the Declaration of Independence?"

He flushed. "Um, it was Thomas Jefferson, wasn't it?"

"Correct. You may have another beer. On me."

Anne had come to Blake's Pub after almost every women's Laser regatta, but she'd always socialized with the other women in the race. She couldn't remember how long it had been since she'd talked to a strange man in a bar. She was having fun.

"Thank you, Ma'am," Tom said.

"Welcome. Now finish your fries. There are starving children in India."

Tom laughed. "This isn't fair. I assume you're not afraid of sailmakers."

"Actually, I'm afraid they're going to ask me if the leech of my sail flutters when I go to windward or the roach sags in light air."

"You sail with a floppy roach? You don't know how to fix that?"

"Um, stiffer battens, right?"

"Correct. We may continue to talk."

And they did. By the time Anne had finished most of her

second beer, she'd forgotten to worry about whether Tim was ghosting her. It was fun joking with a stranger at a bar. She hadn't done this in years.

She finished her beer. "It's been nice talking to you, Tom. Do you come here often?"

"Not that often. Usually after I've finished a sail and delivered it to a customer."

"So should I congratulate you?"

"Yeah, I sold a reaching genoa to a guy with a J/65." He grinned. "Translation for women who are afraid of sailmakers: a big sail to a guy with a big boat."

"Great. Well, I need to go home now. *Adiós*. Translation for men who are afraid of teachers: Bye-bye."

Walking home, Anne wondered if she'd gone too far with that young man. She hoped he didn't think she was flirting with him. Well, she was, of course, but it was just for fun. Leading a man on whom she couldn't be serious about was something Anne never wanted to do. But really, it was presumptuous to think he might be interested in her in the first place. He'd seen her in the pub the night of the women's regatta and assumed she was a sailor. He just wanted to share with somebody his excitement about making a commission on an expensive sail and bought her a drink.

As she neared the Small Boat Tackle Shop on Tiller Street, she glanced down the narrow passage that led into the Westport Sailing Club. It occurred to her that this was the route Petra must have taken when she left the pub that night and went to meet William. What if somebody from Blake's Pub had followed Petra when she left? What if she'd been killed by some person she'd been talking to in the pub? A sharp twinge of fear suddenly shot through Anne's breast and she turned to look behind her. She sped up and raced quickly onto Windward Street.

When she reached her house, Tim was sitting on her porch in the rocking chair, asleep.

"Tim, you're home! I've been worried."

He shook himself awake and stood to hug her. "Anne, I missed you."

"How did you get here? Why didn't you call me? I would've picked you up at the airport."

"I took an Uber. Your number's on my phone, but the battery died. I didn't have your number memorized." He took his phone from his pocket. "Look. The battery overheated and swelled up. I didn't have time to find an Apple store to replace it."

"I'm so glad you're back."

There was a scratching at the window. Tim laughed. "Molly and I have been talking through the glass. I told her I don't have the key and we'd have to wait till you get back."

Anne unlocked the door. Tim followed her in with his duffel bag. Molly went crazy, jumping all over him until Anne pulled her away. "That's enough, Molly. Tim must be tired. He's coming into the kitchen, and I'm going to make him a cup of coffee. Or do you want something else, Tim? You must be hungry. I'll fix you something to eat. Is a chicken salad sandwich good enough?" Anne knew she was chattering on but couldn't help it. "Sit here, Tim. Would you like some wine?"

"Before anything, I'd like to use your bathroom."

"Of course. It's upstairs. I'll show you."

Molly followed them up. "It's right there," Anne told Tim. "I guess that's obvious." She told herself she needed to calm down. "Let's go, Molly. We'll wait downstairs."

Making Tim a sandwich calmed Anne down a little. She told Molly, "Broken battery. That's all it was. He came back."

Tim finished his sandwich and looked like he was about to fall asleep in his chair.

"I have a spare bed you can rest in before you go back, Tim."

He nodded groggily and followed her upstairs. "Yeah, didn't get much sleep on the trip." He thew himself onto the bed William's mother had slept in, and Molly jumped in beside him. Anne took off Tim's shoes and pulled a light blanket over him.

36

A fake button

Anne was already up and making a cheese and broccoli omelet for breakfast when Tim, his light brown hair in a tangle, came downstairs rubbing his eyes and holding his shoes. "Sorry. I guess I …."

"…got a good night's sleep. You and the dog were snoring in harmony."

"Before I forget. Tell me your phone number, Anne. I need to memorize it."

They sat at Anne's small maple table covered with a cloth her mother had embroidered years ago. "How did the peer review of your book go?" Anne asked.

"They liked it. With only a few suggestions of things I should add, which I did. Then I took it to a naval historian in Boston. He read it and is going to recommend his university publish it."

"Fantastic. So you're going to be rich."

"Heh-heh. It's not the kind of book many people want to read. A couple of university libraries might buy it. That's all."

"I'll read it."

After breakfast Tim asked Anne if he could leave Molly with her a little longer so he could go to an Apple store in Colonial City to get a new cell phone.

Alone again with Molly, Anne washed the dishes and threw some dirty clothes into the washer, all the while imagining what it would be like if she and Tim lived together. How would Tim feel living in a regular house with another person instead of being the master of his own little 'mansion'? Rather than tie her brain in knots with thoughts like these, she took Molly for a walk to sniff the tea roses in the front yards along Windward Street.

When they got back, Anne realized that the children's workshop at the church was scheduled for today. She wanted to spend the time with Tim and sent Pastor Brown a message that she couldn't come. As soon as she pressed Send, her phone rang.

"Calling you on my new phone. Dialed you from memory. The iPhone guys said the battery was defective and gave me a whole new phone."

"Great, Tim. That was fast."

"Uh-huh. I'm pulling into the club now. If you bring Molly over, I can take her off your hands."

Tim was brewing them tea in his cabin when Terry Sullivan, William's public defender, called Anne again. She sounded flustered. "Anne, I've been trying to answer your question about Ruth Neucomb's whereabouts between the end of the regatta and the time she was murdered. I've tried to get in touch with the dockmaster, Mr. Tim Griffin. But I haven't been able to get hold of him. I'm told he was on the committee with her."

"Oh, he's with me now. His phone was dead for a few days. I'll put him on." She switched to speaker phone and handed it to Tim.

Tim told Ms. Sullivan, "The race committee met in the clubhouse after the regatta. Ruth sat there with the rest of us. She just listened while we went over the results. Then we all left the clubhouse. Some of the committee went to Blake's Pub, but I had to help set up tables in the yard for the crab feast we planned to have the next day. I didn't see where Ruth went. She might have gone home. Anne says Ruth didn't go to the pub."

"Her husband says Ruth wasn't at her house between six and after midnight."

"As far as I know," Tim told the attorney, "she wasn't here at the club between about six, when everybody left for the pub, and eight thirty, when I walked Anne home. I was back by nine and didn't see her then, either."

"Thank you, Mr. Griffin. May I speak with Anne again?"

Anne said, "I'm sorry, Ms. Sullivan. Nobody I've talked to saw Ruth after she came out of the clubhouse with the race committee at about six o'clock."

"This is strange. I contacted the club commodore. He hadn't seen her. He gave me the names of the other members of the race committee. I contacted them, and they didn't notice where Ruth went after their meeting. A few of them mentioned an argument, they called it, between Ruth and a sail maker on the committee boat."

"Ah, I'll let you talk to Tim again. He was there."

"Rob Green. Yes, I know him," Tim told her. "He made a practice sail for one of the Laser sailors, Petra Fields. Yes, there was a discussion on the committee boat about whether she'd used an unlicensed sail in the regatta. Rob Green asked Ruth not to mention the discussion in her report to the *Westport Voice*, but she wouldn't agree."

"Why didn't he want that mentioned?"

"We all thought he meant that bringing it up would put the regatta in a bad light." Tim seemed reluctant to go on but added, "I've learned since that he's the one who made the sail and had asked Petra not to use it. Having a customer use an unapproved sail in an Olympic qualifying regatta could hurt Rob Green's career."

"The committee members say Rob Green muttered that somebody needs to teach Ruth Neucomb to mind her own business. Do you remember him saying that?"

Tim hesitated. "I do. I'm not sure he meant it in a threatening way."

"I'm sure you understand, the more we can show that there are other suspects, the less certain the police can be that my client William Jamieson committed the murder."

"The murder, you say. I assume that means the police have decided not to charge him with the murder of Petra Fields, as well?"

"No. Unfortunately he's still being charged with both murders. And he admits he knew Petra Fields."

Tim ran his fingers through his hair, closing his eyes. Finally he said, "And so did Rob Green."

"I don't understand. What are you saying?"

"It's a little complicated. Maybe I shouldn't have brought it up."

"Mr. Griffin, I believe an innocent man is being charged with two murders. Anything you can tell me to—"

"I understand, Ms. Sullivan. All right. Anne and I were the first to find Petra's van after she died. We were able to read a letter to her on the passenger seat. I can send you a photo I took of it through the window. It was from the organization that authorizes sail lofts to make sails for Lasers to use in a regatta. They asked Petra to show them the sail she used in our regatta to prove it was legitimate. But it wasn't legitimate. It was made by Rob Green's unauthorized loft. If she showed the unauthorized sail she'd used, this would have damaged Rob Green's career."

"And did she show her sail to the organization?"

"Immediately after the regatta, Petra left her boat at the club and went to Blake's Pub. She stayed there until a least nine o'clock that night. So, no. She couldn't have taken the sail to the Laser association that day. And after that she was missing. Until her body washed up in the hurricane."

"How about her sail?"

"We looked in her Laser. The sail was gone."

"The sail was gone? How do you know she didn't take it to the Laser association?"

"First of all, the association doesn't have the sail. I called. Also, according to Anne, the medical examiner's report shows that Petra must have died the night she left the pub. Is that right?"

"Yes. The examiner said she'd been dead ten to twelve days when you found her body. And she was alive and in the pub ten days before that. So she had to have died the night she left the pub. I see what you mean. She had no opportunity to take the sail to the Laser association."

"That's right. She died before she had a chance."

"Then how did the illegal sail come to be missing from her boat?"

"I'm thinking it's possible somebody took it from her boat to make sure she couldn't give it to the association."

"The sailmaker, you're implying? The man whose career would be ruined if she took them the sail."

"That seems possible," Tim replied tactfully. "That's all I can say."

Ms. Sullivan asked to talk to Anne again. "I wanted to tell you. The police haven't been able to get into Ruth Neucomb's laptop yet. If there's anything on it we can use, I hope they get it before William's preliminary hearing."

When the public defender ended the call, Tim held his head in his hands. Anne knew how he felt. He said, "I can't really imagine Rob Green murdering anybody. You don't kill people just because they hurt your business."

"It's been done, I suppose," Anne commented. "And Rob's reputation as a sailmaker was at stake, too."

Tim raised an eyebrow. "He's the only person we know of who had motive and opportunity to kill both Ruth and Petra."

"Or to hire somebody to kill them." Anne added. She shuddered. "Of course, I knew both Ruth and Petra, too."

"The police can't possibly—"

"They think I had a reason to kill Ruth." She trembled to recall Sergeant Carrs finding her in this very cabin with John Neucomb's arms around her. "Maybe they'll try to find something I held against Petra, as well."

"You seem worried. Did the police bother you with more questions while I was away?"

"No. I think they see me now as John Neucomb's motivation more than they see me as the actual killer. Although I can't be sure. It could be the other way around."

"I can't be sure what they think of me, either," Tim echoed. "I was the first to discover both Ruth's and Petra's bodies."

Anne breathed out a sigh. Tim took her hand. "Let's go sit by the dock and forget all this for a while."

Out in the creek, two kayakers drifted quietly by. A flock of gulls circled and dove for fish into a silvery ripple in the water. A cooling breeze brought the familiar brackish smell of the bay onshore, and Anne leaned close to Tim, soothed by the silence. They sat without talking as if listening to the wordless voice of nature.

In the distance, the bell of the drawbridge to the city across the creek rang out, signaling the bridge was about to open. Cars on the bridge stopped to let a tall-masted cruising ship pass from its anchorage into the open creek on adventures that it thrilled Anne to imagine.

"I don't have any food in my mansion," Tim said.

"My cupboard is pretty bare, too."

"My publisher gave me some money for the trip to New York. I didn't spend it all. Let's take the Whaler around to Bay Creek and get some of the Sea Shanty's crab casserole."

Mallards streamed out of the way, trailing little wakes behind them. Along the shore, silver perch jumped as the boat puttered by, and a blue heron was startled from its perch in the cordgrass. Tim let Anne steer as they slowly made their way into Bay Creek. A blue light on the shore lit the entrance to the Sea Shanty's dock. Anne cut the engine, and they drifted into a slip alongside a vintage wooden two-masted yawl.

The restaurant sat on stilts above the high water line. Anne ran her fingers through the thick waves of her hair and brushed some pollen from her black jeans as they climbed the stairs.

"You look great," Tim told her. She knew it was a lie, but this wasn't a place to worry about a dress code. Anne had only been here a few times, always with a group of teachers or sailors. Fishermen, crabbers, and dockworkers sat in their work jeans drinking at a heavy oak bar or eating at bare plank tables in booths padded with cracked red vinyl cushions. The low ceiling, supported by exposed beams, seemed to echo the lively chatter of the customers, mostly men. The Shanty didn't have to worry about its décor. Everyone in

Westport knew its crab casserole was the best in the county.

They sat at the only booth available, which was big enough for four people. Tim ordered two pints of Loose Cannon. "Casserole is fresh," the dusky skinned waiter suggested. Tim nodded.

They were sipping their beers when Anne looked up to see Rob Green come in accompanied by a pretty woman with long, straight black hair. The waiter asked if Tim and Anne minded if they joined them in the booth. "Very crowded. Sorry."

"Thanks," Rob said, beaming. "This is my wife, Kim. She's also my manager and translator at the loft. Most of the seamstresses are from Korea."

Kim's dark eyes and pretty smile sent an immediate twinge of guilt through Anne. She suddenly saw Rob Green more as a proud husband than as an aggressive businessman.

"So nice to meet you," Kim said. "Rob has told me Mr. Tim runs the best regattas on the east coast."

"Oh, that's uh …." Tim mumbled. Like Anne, he might be feeling that they'd heaped suspicion of two murders on Rob too precipitously simply because they wanted to show William's public defender that William wasn't the most likely suspect.

"Beer and casserole?" the waiter asked Rob.

"Beer for me, and just water for Kim. And, yes, crab casserole, please." Rob was holding Kim's hand under the table. Anne noticed that Kim was pregnant.

Anne shot a glance at Tim. Like her, Tim must be wondering if the public defender had already told the police that they had hinted Rob could have murdered Ruth to keep her from reporting the rumors that Petra had used an unauthorized sail. And murdered Petra to keep her from confirming this. Anne gripped her hands together in her lap. What if the police had already contacted Rob?

"Rob told me about the woman who was killed," Kim said. "How terrible."

Anne and Tim looked down at the table.

"Her name was Ruth Neucomb," Rob said. "I saw her in the

boatyard after the race committee meeting. Everybody had put their boats away and left the yard, and Ruth Neucomb was still standing around. I asked if she was going to go up to Blake's Pub. She said no. She had something to do."

Anne gripped her napkin.

Rob went on. "I convinced her not to put anything in the *Westport Voice* suggesting Petra possibly used an unauthorized sail."

Tim's eyes widened. "How did you do that?"

"I took her to Petra's boat and pointed out the red ILCA button on the sail." Rob's face reddened. "I told her that proved her sail was legitimate."

Now Kim's face turned pink. "Even though it didn't. It was a fake button that Petra made."

"Yeah," Rob admitted. "I lied to Ruth. The sail wasn't legitimate. I'd asked Petra not to use that sail in the regatta, but she used it anyway. If she'd won the regatta with it, I would have had to admit it wasn't an authorized sail. But when she was called over early, I knew she wouldn't even place in the regatta. It didn't matter what sail she used."

"Rob was afraid people would think using it was his idea," Kim explained.

Anne, her heart beating fast, asked Rob, "Were you afraid Petra would tell the ILCA she'd used it?"

"I thought about that. Maybe she could have had her low score for that regatta nullified if she admitted the sail wasn't legitimate."

"And blamed Rob," Kim put in.

Rob put his hands on the table. "So I took the sail back to the loft and destroyed it."

"Was Ruth definitely convinced the sail was legitimate?" Tim asked.

"She was. She said she was going to quash the rumor of the unauthorized sail in her *Westport Voice* report. She was still wandering around the yard in her inflatable life jacket when I left."

Rob's wife said, "I convinced Rob to give up the idea of getting a license to make sails for Olympic class boats. It's not worth it. He agreed for now at least to stick to making sails for one-design boats that don't insist that they come from a licensed sail loft."

"Yeah," Rob agreed. "Like Snipes or Lightnings. Plenty of business making sails for those boats without having to get their association's authorization." He took a big chug of beer. "I've already taken some measurements for Snipes. Thanks for helping, Tim. I wonder if it's all right if I come to the boat club tomorrow to measure for Lightnings?"

"Sure," Tim said. "No problem."

Anne and Tim walked back to her house in silence. Finally, Anne voiced what she was sure Tim was also thinking. "I wish we hadn't mentioned Rob to William's public defender. What Rob and Kim told us at the Sea Shanty sounded fairly credible."

"I know. I feel really bad now. We put Rob on the possible suspect list." Tim ruffled his hair. "Did you get the idea he and his wife knew we'd done that?"

"They didn't seem to. Let's hope they don't find out."

37

Suspicious congratulations

Anne couldn't get the idea out of her head that Ruth's laptop might contain some useful information. How complex a password had she set? Certainly the police had tried her address, her birthday, her husband's birthday. Well, maybe not her husband's birthday. Anne decided to go back to the school.

As expected, the principal, Lucia, was there, now watering the rubber plants, jade plants, zebra plants, African violets, and peace lilies that lined the windowsill and every bookshelf in her office. Anne helped her finish her rounds before saying she wanted to check again in Ruth's desk.

She knelt down and crawled under the wide center drawer. Bingo! Taped to the bottom was a paper labeled *Passwords*, which she gently peeled off.

"Now how did you ever know to look there?" Lucia tittered.

Anne pulled herself up, a little dizzy. "Just a hunch," she lied. The truth was she kept her own list of passwords taped under the center drawer of her home desk. "I'd like to get this to the police, who have Ruth's laptop and haven't been able to open it."

"Sure, Hon. I'd call them myself, but there's lots to do getting ready for the substitute teacher who's going to replace Ruth. Besides, when I called the police to come get those papers we found in Ruth's desk, they looked at me funny. Gave me the creeps. I wonder if you …."

Anne didn't relish the idea of going to the police station for another encounter with Sergeant Carrs, either, but it was better to take them the list right away. There wasn't much time before William's preliminary hearing when a judge would decide if there was enough evidence to take William to trial for murder. Anne took a picture of the list of passwords, filled her lungs, gritted her teeth, and drove to the police station.

"Ah, Ms. Anne Bateman. Have you come to confess?" Sergeant Carrs stroked his sharp nose with the tip of a finger. A sign that he was only kidding? But it was too late. Anne already felt her face was red hot. She held Ruth's list of passwords up between forefingers and thumbs without a word.

"Ooh, my, my. Look at what we have here," the police clerk Ms. Trimble sang out, leaning forward from her desk next to the sergeant's. "What do you think, Sergeant? Should we call the IT guys off the case? Or let them keep tweaking those zeroes and ones a while longer to justify their salary?"

Sergeant Carrs took the paper from Anne. "I'm assuming you believe this is Ruth Neucomb's list of passwords." He seemed to sniff it.

"I found it taped under her school desk. So, yes."

"I see. This may or may not be helpful. The laptop was found in her house." He gave a weak snort. "It's doubtful the victim identified and recorded the name of her assailant *before* the murder occurred."

"I thought it might be interesting to see what she *did* type in before the murder occurred."

Sergeant Carrs looked over the list. "Ronstheman, ronstheman1, ronstheman2, ronstheman3!!"

"I'm guessing Real Estate Ron," Anne suggested.

The sergeant went on. "Dontparkhere, don'tparkinfrontofmyhouse."

"No ones or twos?" Ms. Trimble chuckled.

Sergeant Carrs gave her an amused glance. "Oh, yeah. This series goes up to—let me see—five. No, six."

"Anyway," Anne said. "I just wanted to drop the list off."

The sergeant slid back his chair. "Once again, I have to remind you not to leave the area without notifying us."

Anne lifted her hand thinking to give a mock salute but then chickened out.

"Let me ask you before you go. Tim Griffin was told not to leave the area without notifying us. When I came upon you and John Neucomb in his cabin, it was actually Tim I'd gone to talk to. I hadn't been able to reach him by phone. Can you tell me where he was? He didn't leave town, did he?"

"You can't suspect him of the murders?"

"He found both bodies. Both a short distance from where he lives. Our investigation is still ongoing."

"Well, if you told him to notify you before leaving town, I'm sure he would have."

She wasn't sure at all and decided not to ask Tim. After all, he was already back.

Anne had brought with her in the van the red psychology book Ruth had taken home from school the day before the regatta. After leaving the police office, she drove to the Severn Heights College library to return it. Before getting out of her van, she decided to take a closer look at the book. Anne had been intrigued that Ruth was interested in psychology and wondered why she had whisked it off her desk so quickly and put it into her bag to take home. Was Ruth having some psychological problem? Before returning the book, Anne skimmed through it. She found a bookmark buried between two pages. A lengthy passage was underlined in pencil. Anne decided to hold onto the book a little longer before returning it and, instead, drove home.

As she stepped from her van, in the corner of her eye Anne saw Ms. Beatrice tapping her way along the sidewalk. Anne pretended not to see the Westport sentinel, but Ms. Beatrice stopped her. "I suppose you've heard. It's what everybody is talking about."

"I don't—"

"Mr. John Neucomb has found himself a new belle." With a decidedly gleeful turn of her lips, Ms. Beatrice added, "I'm so sorry to have to be the one to tell you."

"Don't let it upset you, Ms. Beatrice."

"They say she's a doctor who's been featured in the *Colonial City Magazine*. Very beautiful."

"An anesthesiologist?"

"I don't know what her religion is. They say she has money. But I don't like to gossip."

"A good policy."

"Well, take care, Dear. You'll find somebody someday."

Anne went straight to her kitchen, warmed some leftover crab casserole she'd brought back from the Sea Shanty, and sat down to let the creamy flavors clear her mind. It worked for a while, until the reality of actually being a murder suspect made her hands sweat once again. And Tim was a suspect, too? Or at least the police hadn't eliminated him. Just because he found the bodies?

Sergeant Carrs hadn't mentioned Rob Green. Had William's public defender passed on to the police what Anne and Tim told her about Rob's possible motive for wanting both Ruth and Petra out of the way? If she had, Rob and his wife didn't seem to know about it yet during that dinner at the Sea Shack.

Anne had a hard time believing any of the police's suspects would commit murder. Of all the possible motives, John Neucomb's desire to punish his wife and get possession of their house seemed the most credible. But John Neucomb was a wuss.

She put the dirty dishes in the sink and opened the red psychology book on the table. Each chapter analyzed a different approach—the biological, cognitive, humanistic, socio-cultural, and behavioral methods, the last of which was the chapter where Ruth had put a bookmark. Anne shook her head. Why was Ruth reading up on behavioral psychology? Then she had to laugh. Ruth's behavior certainly could have used some modification. She was overly harsh with her students and haughty towards the other teachers. Anne wondered if the passages Ruth had underlined might be a clue. She read them carefully, unable to see how they applied to Ruth specifically.

At the sound of a light tap on her door, Anne closed the book. William's mother stood there, lips trembling and fidgeting with her white-gloved hands.

"Mrs. Jamieson, come in. You look upset." Anne took her arm and led her to the couch. "Let me get you some tea."

Mrs. Jamieson waved off the offer. "Ms. Sullivan came and talked to me again. I can't believe what she told me this time. The police think maybe William was paid to kill that teacher. And maybe also that sailor. 'Murder for hire,' that's what they called it." Mrs. Jamieson drew a tissue from her sleeve to wipe away tears. "Ms. Sullivan asked about you, Ms. Anne. She said the police suspect something about you and John Neucomb that I just can't believe."

"I know what they think. It's not true, Mrs. Jamieson. There's nothing between me and John Neucomb."

"That's what I told Ms. Sullivan. I told her you were a good woman, very kind to me and William." Mrs. Jamieson sniffed. "She said she was going to talk to you herself."

"She did. She talked to me again after the police got the idea this might be a murder for hire. I told her William would never do such a thing."

William's mother inhaled and sent out a stuttering breath. "Thank you, Dear. I hope the police come to believe that."

"Let me walk you home, Mrs. Jamieson. Or would you like to stay here with me for a while?"

"You're kind. But I need to be home in case Ms. Sullivan tries to contact me again."

Anne took Mrs. Jamieson to her house and then went straight to the boat club. Tim was giving Molly a bath with a hose. He whisked a playful spray across Anne's bare legs.

"Hey!" Anne ran and grabbed Tim from behind. "Give me that hose." She tried to pull it from his hands. No way. He tried to twist around to spray her again, but she held on tight behind him. "Oh, no you don't. I'm not letting go."

"OK with me."

"Drop the hose."

He dropped it. And stood motionless.

Anne kept ahold of him. "Promise not to pick it up?"

Tim covered her hands with his. "Hmm. Let me think."

Anne squeezed tighter.

"I'm still thinking."

Before Anne, embarrassed at her excitement, let him go, the phone in his pocket rang. She stepped back to let him answer it.

"Hi, Kim," Tim said.

Anne gulped.

"No, Rob hasn't got here yet to take Lightning sail measurements. Oh, no. I'm sorry. Don't hang—"

"That was Rob Green's wife. The police have taken Rob to the station for questioning."

"Oh, no. She told you the police took Rob, then just hung up?"

"Yeah, she was a nervous wreck."

"Maybe we should go talk to her."

38

Sails and kimchi

Anne and Tim clattered up the narrow wooden stairway of Green Sails that led to the loft on the wide-open second floor. It was almost the size of a basketball court. Three scattered pits were cut into the smooth wood floor where women in white head scarves sat at chin level to the floor as massive Dacron sails were slid past their industrial sized sewing machines. The whirring of the machines was enough to keep anyone from noticing Anne and Tim's arrival. On a walkway alongside the loft floor, Anne noticed steep ladder-like steps leading up to a kind of raised pulpit where Rob's wife Kim sat behind two computer screens directing the work below. Tim had to raise his voice to get her attention.

Kim backed carefully down the steps, keeping one hand against her stomach. Anne held her arm as she took the last few steps. "Kim, do you think you should be climbing up there when you're pregnant?"

Kim didn't seem to hear Anne. She held her face in her hands. "It wasn't Rob's fault. He told that woman not to use that sail. Why did the police take him?"

"They're just trying to get as much information as they can from as many people as possible," Tim assured her. He added, "About that woman's death, not about anything to do with sails."

"They questioned me and Tim, too," Anne put in. "Please don't worry. Rob will be back soon."

Kim took Anne's hand. "Thank you. We're going to have our first child. I think that's what makes me so scared."

Tim looked out over the loft floor. "The ladies seem to be finishing up with those sails. How about coming with us to get some lunch?"

"We all bring our bento boxes with food that we like. But

thanks." In fact, the sewing machines at that moment fell silent, the women climbed out of their pits, and in moments the smell of kimchi steadily replaced the mildly resin smell of treated Dacron and the oily smell of the machines.

"Maybe when you have a day off sometime," Anne offered. "Meantime, don't worry about Rob. Take care of that baby you're carrying."

When they left the loft, Tim said, "You seem a little down, Anne."

"I'm thinking about my mom now. I was planning to visit her in Florida as soon as school was out. Do you think I could go? I mean before the police catch the murderer?"

"Well, I slipped up to New York and back without the police realizing it."

"I know. The police asked me where you were when they couldn't contact you. All I said was I'm sure Tim would have notified them if he left town. The sergeant either believed me or didn't care that much. I'm the one they think has a motive for murder."

"Let's go to Clyde's. Maybe some pizza will cheer you up."

Anne drew the still-wet bottom of her shorts away from her legs with a finger. "I'd like to go home and change first. And call my mom."

"I'll walk with you, then go feed Molly. I'll come back to get you in about an hour."

Anne pulled on a new pair of black jeans and hung her tan shorts up on the shower curtain rail to finish drying. The bathtub served as a shower. The sink was almost touching the toilet. She and her mother could get by with one small, old fashioned bathroom. And two cramped bedrooms. But lately she'd, briefly, allowed herself to imagine Tim living in the same house with her. Stop dreaming, she told herself.

She called her mother.

"Annie, Dear. So nice to hear from you. I was just picking out a birthday card for you in the supermarket the other day."

"That's right, my birthday's in a couple of weeks. I'm still planning to drive to Florida to see you and talk about you selling the house and moving up here to live with me, but things are crazy right now."

"You should come down to visit me. I can send you the plane fare."

"Thank you. That's nice, but I was thinking I'd come in the van so, in case you agree to come live with me, we could bring some of your furniture back here."

"Furniture? Oh, I have plenty of that. Don't worry about bringing me anything, Sweetie."

"I think I'll write you a letter or send you a card, Mom, before I come. Just to be sure we're on the same page about everything."

"I'm the one who's going to send you a card, Annie. It's your birthday coming up."

"Thanks, Mom. I miss you."

Anne had assumed she and her mother could live in this house. They could stay as long as Anne kept paying the rent. Now, unless Real Estate Ron's plan to evict her was foiled, she'd have to find somewhere else for them to live.

Anne recoiled at the thought of contacting John Neucomb to ask if any progress had been made towards getting Real Estate Ron's license taken away. Besides, John seemed to have forgotten about doing that once he met Vivian Witherspoon. Anne decided to call Real Estate Ron's office herself.

"Hello, this is Madeline Rich," Anne lied. "I'd like to make an appointment to meet with Real Estate Ron."

"I'm sure I can help you. Ron is too busy to take on new clients at this time, but we can put you in touch with one of our other agents."

"Oh? When do you think Ron himself will be available? I've been so impressed by his ads, I had my heart set on working with him personally."

The real estate receptionist paused before answering. "I'm

afraid Ron is very much tied up with other work right now. Our other agents—"

"I'll wait," Anne insisted. "Would you have him call me as soon as he's free?" She ended the call before the receptionist could reply.

Real Estate Ron was "tied up with other work." Did that mean tied up by the ethics investigation that John Neucomb had set in motion? Anne hoped so. But for now she would just have to wait.

Lucia's car was parked in the principal's spot when Anne and Tim passed by the school on the way to Clyde's. The car was still there when they came back from savoring Clyde's crab soup and lemon butter shrimp on rice. "I'd like to talk to Lucia," Anne told Tim. "Let's say good night here."

Anne knocked on the thick, locked door. Lucia's head checked through the high glass window, then let Anne in. "I was just going to call you," Lucia trilled. "I've been getting things ready for the new teacher. County human resources forms, our Westport Elementary procedures and regulations, the Welcome to New Teachers packet you helped me write up. The only thing missing is a laptop. I can't find Ruth's. The new teacher's supposed to inherit hers. I was going to ask you to—"

"The police have Ruth's laptop. They took it from her house when they searched it looking for evidence."

"Oh, no." Lucia put her hands to her cheeks. "I'm responsible for the laptops loaned to teachers. The county says they can't afford to buy any more."

"Maybe you could call the police. They might be finished examining it."

"Call the police?" Lucia was wringing her hands.

"I know the number of the sergeant leading the case. I can dial him for you."

"Oh, my. Well, if you think—"

Anne held out her hand for Lucia's phone, dialed Sergeant Carrs, and gave the phone back to a trembling Lucia, who after several false starts stuttered out enough information to make her request clear. "You mean," she asked in a high voice, "I am to pick it up myself? Yes, I understand. Tomorrow morning."

Lucia told Anne the police would only give the laptop to the Westport Elementary principal. "I'll have to sign some papers. Oh, my! I hate to drive in the Colonial City traffic."

"I'll drive you there. Did Sergeant Carrs say the police don't need the laptop?"

"They copied it. Something like that. They said it had nothing but school stuff."

Anne knew she wouldn't be able to fall asleep easily that night. She took the thick red psychology textbook to bed and turned on the black gooseneck reading light her mother had always called an atrocious monstrosity. Rather than read from the beginning, she skipped to the chapter Ruth had put a bookmark in. As Anne went through it, she found more sentences and paragraphs underlined. She tried to find a connection among these passages. They were all basically explanations and critiques of the work of behavioral psychologists. As far as Anne remembered, Ruth had never indicated any interest in this field. Ruth's EdD was in education.

Light off, book on the bed table, Anne set her alarm for eight o'clock and tried to stop wondering why Ruth had underlined these passages.

39

A snoop

Lucia sifted through her bulky purse when she got into Anne's van. "The policeman told me I need to prove I'm the principal. Show him the county rule about laptops needing to be turned in when a teacher leaves the school. I think I got it all."

"Good. Relax, Lucia."

When Anne pulled into the police department lot, she encouraged Lucia. "You'll do fine. I'll be waiting here for you."

"You're not coming in?"

Anne didn't want to tell Lucia that she herself was a suspect in the murder. And she definitely didn't want Sergeant Carrs to think she had anything to do with reclaiming the laptop. Even though it didn't make much sense, she told Lucia the police would want to return the laptop to her alone.

Lucia was in the station close to an hour. When she came out, the laptop was sealed with red evidence tape, and Lucia was flustered. "Sorry you had to wait so long. You wouldn't believe the hassle I had to go through, the papers I had to sign and they had to make copies of."

Back at the school, Lucia asked Anne to come in with her. They sat in the principal's office. "What kind of tape is this," Lucia groused. "It shreds when you try to take it off. Ouff. There. I'm going to ask you to help me set this up for the new teacher. Delete all of Ruth's personal items and make sure it has the latest standard stuff we put on them. It's all on this." She handed Anne a thumb drive. "Everything she needs is on here. I'll give you a new temporary password that the new teacher can change."

This was just what Anne had been hoping. "Sure. I'll take the laptop home and make sure it's ready to go."

Anne fired up the laptop feeling like a snoop but determined to find out what Ruth had been up to before she was murdered. What to look through first? Her emails? Was that stooping too low? But the police must have already checked them out. What harm could it do if Anne had a look herself? Quite a few were from Real Estate Ron. Anne gritted her teeth and read.

"You won't believe how much money a four-story condo in Westport can bring in, Ruth."

"Ruth, you are the love of my life. We are going to be a great team."

"I can't see you this evening, Ruth. There's an important meeting I need to go to. Love you." (This message tended to appear once or twice a week.)

"Any chance the construction on your house can start before the divorce is final? I have potential tenants lined up."

Anne clicked Ruth's Sent Box and read her emails to Real Estate Ron.

"My husband is pathetic. Always trying to be something he's not. I prefer a man who knows how to get what he wants. Like you, Ron."

"I'm still thinking of last night. Ron, you know how to please a woman."

Anne decided not to read any more of these and went back to Ruth's In Box, where she found some interesting messages from the human resources department of Severn Heights College.

"We have received your application for the position of president of the college. The selection committee will review all the applicants. Just a reminder: the position requires a Ph.D. or Ed.D. degree."

And later:

"The selection committee has ranked the applicants for the position of president of the college. Notices to the top ranked applicants will be mailed out this week."

Then there was an email from someone Anne didn't know but who seemed to be a teacher on the Severn Heights College selection committee. "Ruth, please keep this email secret. I shouldn't tell you. But you are second on the list of applicants the Board of Trustees is considering. Cross your fingers."

Anne took a breath and glanced at the items that cluttered Ruth's computer desktop. One that immediately attracted her interest was a link to a pdf document entitled "Doctoral Dissertation: A Practical Analysis of B.F. Skinner's Approach to Training, by Lawrence A. Bullock." Next to it was a document called a "Similarity Report." Anne clicked that open. It was a Turnitin.com report on Bullock's Ph.D. dissertation. His dissertation was coded yellow, meaning that twenty-five to forty-nine percent of the text matched text found in other documents. Anne scrolled through the report, which produced the whole of Bullock's dissertation with various phrases, sentences, and paragraphs highlighted in colors that identified where the text was found in other published books. The majority of these highlighted passages came from the red psychology book that Ruth had borrowed from the library and made pencil underlinings in.

So Bullock's dissertation was at least twenty-five percent plagiarized. And Ruth had known that.

Tim called to see if Anne wanted to go to lunch.

"Not now. Tim, can you come over here? I want to show you something."

Tim came in sweating in a tight-fitting T-shirt that ended above his waist. "What is it, Anne? I rushed over."

"Oh, uh, yes." Anne turned her head. "Can you look at this?"

Tim read the title of Bullock's dissertation. "Didn't Bullock mention that Skinner guy in his ridiculous speech before the regatta?"

"He did. And look at this report. Ruth was aware that his Ph.D. dissertation was partly plagiarized." Anne studied Tim's eyes, waiting for his reaction.

"You think there's some link between Bullock and Ruth?"

"Seems like it. Because look at these emails. Ruth had applied for the position of president of Severn Heights College."

"The job Bullock was expecting to get?"

"Yes. And after the regatta he did get it. At least he was chosen, according to my friend Lily. She says Bullock's holding out for the college to buy him a membership in the Colonial City Golf Club before he accepts."

"What do you make of all this?"

"Look at this email. Severn Heights College emphasizes that applicants must have a doctoral degree. If Bullock's degree is invalid, he's not qualified. Look at the Turnitin.com date. Ruth found out his dissertation was plagiarized two days before the regatta."

"I'm starting to—"

"And look at this email from a friend of Ruth's at the college. Ruth is second on the list of applicants the Board of Trustees was prepared to approve."

Tim's blue eyes widened. "All she'd need to do is reveal the plagiarism and disqualify Bullock."

"Or convince him to withdraw his application."

"You think she tried that?"

"Ruth's whereabouts are unaccounted for after the race committee meeting ended. She didn't go home. At least that's what her husband says. And Rob the sailmaker says Ruth told him she had something to do and was still wandering around the yard in her inflatable life jacket when he left."

"You think she went to talk to Bullock on his boat after everybody left?"

"It's possible. Bullock announced that his boat was for sale and invited anybody interested to come look at it after the regatta." Anne grinned. "None of the women in the regatta went, I'm sure. The guy is too creepy."

"So maybe Ruth went and threatened to reveal his dissertation was plagiarized unless he withdrew his application?"

"That's what I'm thinking. She probably kept her inflatable life jacket on because she was afraid of boats."

"Do you think the police are aware of all this?"

"They copied everything from Ruth's laptop, but they told the principal it just contained 'school stuff.' So it doesn't look like they suspect anything on the laptop suggests Bullock might have a motive for killing Ruth."

"They should take another look. I haven't fed Molly yet. Walk back to the club with me?"

With a beep of the horn, a yellow sports car swished into the boat club lot. Vivian Witherspoon slipped out and approached in a tight, silky dress. "Hello, Anne. There've been a few developments since we last met."

"Oh?" Anne replied innocently.

"I thought you might have guessed. John Neucomb and I have become friends. That's one thing."

"Yes?"

"And I'm at my wit's end. My husband called to tell me not to sell the boat. But I'm determined to sell it to John."

"Doctor Bullock is still in South Carolina?"

"He is. The exclusive country club there has accused him of cheating at golf, and he's searching for a lawyer willing to threaten a lawsuit unless the club retracts the accusation. As soon as my husband finds a guy, he's coming back to 'take possession of the boat,' he told me."

"He was so intent on selling it. I'm surprised he changed his mind."

"I think he got the idea from those country club people. He now wants to join the Colonial City Yacht Club here, but to join a *yacht* club, one of the requirements is that one must have a yacht."

"Yet you still want to sell it?"

"Yes, I do. I want to sell it before he gets back."

Anne introduced Tim and explained that Vivian was the owner of *Knot on Call* and that John Neucomb had agreed to buy it.

Vivian added, "I wasn't able to show John the boat because the hatch is locked. And the documentation showing me as sole owner of the boat is locked inside. My husband says he gave the key to you, Mr. Griffin."

"Yes, he said he was going to give me the key, but he never did."

"He told you to show the boat to potential buyers, correct? I need those papers to complete the sale."

Tim said, "If you get the key from your husband when he—"

"I'll be glad if he never comes back. This is unconscionable. I'll find a way. I'll buy a lock cutter, if I have to." Vivian stomped back to her car, leaving Anne and Tim gawking as she sped away.

Anne put her hands on her hips. "That boat shouldn't be removed before the police have had a chance to search it. I'm going to call William's public defender." She used speaker phone so Tim could hear. "Ms. Sullivan? Anne Bateman. Have the police mentioned anything to you yet about what was on Ruth's laptop? No? Well, here's what I found." She gave Ms. Sullivan a full account.

"All this might put a new light on the case," Ms. Sullivan agreed. "I'll ask the police to take a closer look at the laptop files they copied."

"And one more thing. Could you suggest they ask Bullock's wife what time he got home the night of the regatta?"

40

The smell of blackmail

Jorge pulled into the club yard in his huge red pickup truck, Jessie sitting in the passenger seat, a red and white Miller's Marina cap on her head. Jorge helped her climb down. "Jessie wanted to give you something," he grinned. Her face a deep pink, Jessie nervously handed Anne an envelope. "It's a résumé. I don't know—"

"She's hoping to volunteer at Westport Elementary," Jorge finished for her.

"Fantastic," Anne said. "We need tutors for after-school classes. I'll pass this on to the principal. But, Jessie, isn't it a bit far to drive from where you live?"

Jessie gave an embarrassed giggle. "I applied for a job at Medtech in Colonial City and they took me right away."

"You'll drive here through the traffic every day?"

Jessie's face turned a deeper red. "Well, I—"

"She's staying with me for the time being," Jorge explained. "In my room over the Miller's Marina office."

"It's exciting. You can see all the boats from the window," Jessie trilled, hands on her cheeks.

"I should probably look for a bigger place," Jorge admitted.

"No. I'm fine in your little room," Jessie insisted.

"Anyway," Jorge said, "we're on our way to meet Lily and her husband Vince at Clyde's to celebrate. We want you to come, too. They have a pan fried bluefish special today."

Lily and Vince were already there. As Anne and the others joined them, out of recent habit Anne glanced around hoping John Neucomb wouldn't be there. He was. He was eating at a table in the corner with two men. One, sporting a shiny bald patch on the top of his head, was spreading pictures in front of the other, who wore a dark gray suit. Anne recognized the bald private detective John had hired. The man in the suit, she hoped, could have been with the National Association of Realtors.

Tim caught Anne's attention and rolled his eyes towards the men, pursing his lips to hide a smile. The gray suit man pocketed the photos, and the three men stood, shook hands, and left. With any luck Real Estate Ron's license was about to be in trouble.

Vince ordered a bottle of chardonnay and toasted Jessie and Jorge's "new friendship." Lily took Jessie's hand. "Congratulations. You'll love being with Jorge. After all, he's the kind of person who rescues baby eagles."

The friends lingered over the dinner, and Jorge and Jessie gradually grew restless, refused dessert, and said they needed to get going. "There are still some boxes I haven't unpacked yet," Jessie explained.

"Uh-huh." Vince grinned. "Gotta get back to those boxes."

When Jessie and Jorge left, Anne asked Lily if Doctor Bullock had accepted the Severn Heights College job yet.

"The Board of Trustees is still waiting for him to officially accept the position. They haven't agreed to buy him a golf club membership yet. They vote on that next week. My dad will vote against it," Lily added, "but Bullock has a lot of influence with some of the other board members."

Anne told Lily that Bullock's wife wanted to sell *Knot on Call* to John Neucomb but Bullock now wanted to keep it so he could get into the Colonial City Yacht Club. "Apparently Bullock's wife Vivian and John Neucomb are a 'thing' now."

"You're kidding!"

"That's right. John wants the boat so he can feel like a true Westporter, and Bullock wants the boat so he can join the yacht club."

"They both ought to take lessons on a Laser," Lily quipped. "That's the best way to earn their salty credits."

"Or drown," Vince added. He took a sip of chardonnay. "Or simply die of fright."

Anne walked with Tim to his cabin after dinner. Tim started rummaging in a wooden tool chest in the corner. "If you're worried that Bullock will take the boat away before the police search it, here's an idea. We'll put a second lock on it before you go home." Tim pulled out a hefty brass combination lock.

"You still know the combination?"

Tim gave her the numbers.

"Is that a date or something?"

"Yeah."

"That was two years ago. I can't help being nosy. June sixteenth. Something special about that day?"

Tim gave his neck an embarrassed rub. "It's the day I helped you repair a fitting on your Laser."

Anne felt her mouth gape as she caught her breath.

"Anyway," Tim said, "let's go lock up the boat. If Bullock comes to get it before the police can search it, we won't open it."

Anne clutched Tim's arm to steady herself as they stood in the cockpit of the boat still gently rocking from when they jumped aboard. She tried hard to chase from her thoughts the picture of Ruth hanging from the boat lift hook, a white plastic bag tied around her head.

"You seem edgy," Tim observed.

"I'm having second thoughts. Maybe it's better if we don't put another lock on Bullock's boat. Let's not give the police the idea that we had anything to do with it."

Tim nodded and put the lock in his pocket. "I see what you mean. Come back to the cabin. I'll fix you a cup of hot chocolate before you go home."

Anne held the warm cup in both hands, breathing in the steam and the kindness that Tim always exuded. She had only taken a few sips when William's public defender called. Again Anne switched her phone to speaker so Tim could hear.

"Anne, I went to the police right away as you suggested and encouraged them to have another look at the information they got from Ruth's laptop. I told them what you found."

"Did they agree it was important?"

"Sergeant Carrs and Captain Blunt stared at me with bored faces like the one I probably wear when a certain friend of mine decides to lecture me on what foods I should and shouldn't eat. As you know, the police believe they know best how to pursue a case and aren't likely to appreciate any advice." Sergeant Carrs told me, 'No need for another look. We're quite aware of what was on the laptop.'"

"But—"

"Anyway, that police clerk, Ms. Trimble? She caught the cops' attention by droning, 'What's that smell? I'm smelling something. Anybody smell blackmail?' Then Captain Blunt turned to me and said not to worry. They routinely take all evidence into consideration."

"So if it looks like Ruth might have gone aboard Bullock's boat to convince him to drop his application for the job as college president, will they come and search Bullock's boat?"

"They didn't exactly say that, but we can only hope."

"Did you suggest they ask Bullock's wife what time he got home the night of the regatta?"

"As I said, they weren't very open to suggestions. But as I got up to leave, I dropped that on them. I saw Ms. Trimble give a slow nod."

"Have you told William about any of this? How is he doing?"

"I don't like to get his hopes up. So I haven't mentioned anything about Bullock yet. William is depressed. He thinks he lost his chance to be exonerated when he lied and didn't admit from the start that he hoisted Ruth's body onto that hook."

"Depressed? I hope you've been able to talk to him. Do you think I can?"

"No, Anne. As things stand, you're still a suspect yourself."

Tim kissed Anne good-night on her porch. "You still seem

tense. Want me and Molly to come in for a little while?"

"I don't have anything to offer you. I'm out of wine, beer, dog treats."

"When I was worried, my mother used to give me a massage."

Anne lay on the couch while Tim massaged her shoulders, neck, and back. She must have fallen into a deep sleep because when she awoke the next morning, she was still on the couch.

41

A torn suit

If Anne couldn't talk to William, at least she could talk to his mother. It was Sunday morning. Mrs. Jamieson would be going to church. Anne put on a long-sleeved white blouse and black slacks and walked over to Independence Street to wait in front of the Mount Zion Church as the parishioners began to trickle in. When the usher closed the door for the service to begin, Mrs. Jamieson hadn't appeared. Fearing something was wrong, Anne hurried down to the woman's house at the end of the street.

Mrs. Jamieson opened the door only a crack, peering out in a flowery nightgown. "Oh," she said. "I'm not—"

"I hope you're not feeling sick, Mrs. Jamieson. I thought I might find you going to church."

William's mother opened the door just a little more. "Truth to tell, I'm embarrassed to show my face at church these days."

"You mean …."

"My William in jail for murder. Nobody says anything, but I see the look on their faces."

"Oh, Mrs. Jamieson, I'm so sorry. This will all change when William is found innocent."

Mrs. Jamieson took a tissue from her sleeve, whisked off a tear, and opened the door to let Anne in.

"I came here," Anne explained, "to tell you the police have some new information that suggests somebody else might be guilty. It's too soon to know what they'll find, but there's still a chance they'll decide to drop the charges against William before his preliminary hearing. That's not for ten more days."

"Lord, hear my prayer. I know my William would never hurt anybody."

"So don't despair, Mrs. Jamieson. William's public defender is working hard for him."

Mrs. Jamieson sniffled a thank you.

"I wonder if Pastor Brown could remind the congregation that William is innocent until proven guilty. Do you think he would do that?"

"He already did. Without mentioning William's name. But you know how people think. I can't blame them, of course."

With a long hug, Anne urged her not to give up hope.

Heading to Clyde's for coffee and a croissant, Anne got a call from the Westport Sailing Club commodore. "I'm calling because Tim said to run this by you. He didn't say why."

"Yes?"

"We have to get the club operating again. It's been three weeks. The Soling fleet already had to cancel their regatta. Members are calling to ask if it's safe to come into the yard. I want to send a message to all members assuring them the club is open."

"I'll help with the phone calls and texts," Anne offered.

"Thanks. And I asked Tim to tow Bullock's boat back to its mooring. We need the space for our boats to tie up after launching."

Anne didn't want anything to prevent the police from coming to search Bullock's boat. She didn't know what evidence they might find on it but hoped there would be some direct proof that Ruth had been aboard and confronted Bullock with her knowledge of his plagiarism. "I'm afraid, though," she told the commodore, "the police might want to search Bullock's boat."

"Why the hell would they do that? I called Bullock days ago to ask him to get his boat off our dock. His wife said he was out of town. That's why I asked Tim to tow it."

"There's some new evidence suggesting that Ruth Neucomb might have gone onto Bullock's boat that night and tried to blackmail him."

"Oh great! You mean the police will come and tape off that

whole launching area again? We have our Fourth of July feast coming up on Friday."

"How about I check with the police and get back to you?"

"All right, Annie. Better you than me. Tell them we need that boat out of here by Thursday morning at the latest."

"I'll tell them, but they might not care."

"Then how about this instead? We get Tim to tow the boat back to its mooring on the other side of the drawbridge. Done. Let the police inspect it there if they want."

Anne, however, wanted to see for herself what was on the boat. She might have a chance to do that if the police searched it at the sailing club. "Well," she said vaguely, "I'll tell Tim your idea."

Tim had taken Molly to the vet for a booster shot when Anne called him. He stepped outside to take her call. "I agree we shouldn't move Bullock's boat, at least not before getting permission from the police. They've known since yesterday what you found on Ruth's laptop. We could ask them if they need to search the boat."

"We? You mean I could?"

"Heh-heh. I mean you're the one who figured out that Bullock might have had a motive to get Ruth out of the way. You could explain—"

"The public defender already explained it to them. The police didn't tell her whether they were going to follow up on the theory or not."

"I see. All right. I'll call and tell them I'd like to tow the boat back to its mooring. See what they say."

"Would you, Tim? The police still think I had a motive for wanting Ruth dead."

"The John Neucomb thing. Right. I'll call them."

"Thank you. I'll bring a coffee and croissant to the club for you."

"Maybe an iced coffee. It looks like I'll be stuck in the waiting room with Molly for quite a while. My cabin door's open."

Anne slid the boxed croissant and iced coffee onto Tim's table with unsteady fingers. The commodore's call had brought back the tenseness in her back that Tim's massage had managed to remedy the night before. She had to face it. The thought of being grilled again by the police made her palms sweat, despite the fact she'd done nothing wrong in examining Ruth's laptop and library book. She tried to comfort herself by realizing she was not alone. Lots of innocent "persons of interest" must have to suffer through police interrogations. She wondered how William managed to get through it. She'd heard of innocent people caving in to pressure and admitting to crimes they hadn't committed, and she realized it might have been an unspoken dread in the back of her mind all along that William would give them a false confession.

Tires squealed. Anne looked out the cabin doorway and saw a black sedan that was vaguely familiar turn into one of the club's parking spots. Doctor Lawrence A. Bullock ducked out, his stodgy body crammed into a shiny black suit, and made for the cabin like a bear on the prowl.

Anne stiffened. It was too late to close the door on him. He seized an arm. "Tim Griffin. Where is he?"

"Let go of me."

"I'll let you go when you tell me where Griffin is." Bullock's bulbous eyes scanned the cabin.

"He'll be back soon. Would you like to wait outside on the bench by the creek? Take your hand off me."

Bullock dragged her from the cabin. "I need to get some papers from my boat so my wife can't sell it." Keeping hold of Anne's wrist, he pulled her towards the dock where the boat was tied up. "The boat's no longer for sale, you understand."

"Your wife says she's the sole owner. Let's call her and see if she agrees."

"My wife's a liar. Get in." He pushed Anne from the pier into the cockpit, then dropped in behind her, causing the boat to rock, and steadied himself by gripping her around the waist. When the boat steadied, he fumbled in his pocket for the key, yanked off the padlock, and started throwing the companionway boards onto the deck. "You seem to work here. You must know about boats. I need to get those papers. Maybe you can give me an idea where they're usually kept." He slid back the hatch and went down into the cabin.

"They could be anywhere," she called to him. If there was any evidence against Bullock inside the boat, Anne didn't want the police to suspect she'd put it there, so she didn't want to go below deck. Instead she knelt in front of the steps down into the cabin and began videoing the interior as Bullock opened cabinets and drawers. "I'll shine my phone flash to brighten things up," she called. As soon as she did, she saw a blue sneaker dangling from the top step rail. "Look over there," she called, shining the video flash onto a counter next to the galley sink—and on the long kitchen knife lying there beside a box of small white trash bags. "Look above the starboard settee. Slide that panel back." While he did, she focused on a beige headscarf lying on the settee partly covering a small object with a leopard skin cover.

"Where did that bitch hide those papers?" Bullock roared, sliding panels open and slamming them shut.

Anne had videoed all she needed. She stepped up onto the main deck to peer above the row of trailered Solings to see if Tim had returned yet but couldn't see much of the yard from where the boat was docked. She jumped back down into the cockpit as Bullock came out of the boat empty handed. He seemed to look at her closely for the first time. "You're a pretty thing. What's your name?"

"I'm a friend of Ruth Neucomb and Petra Fields."

Bullock froze. "I never met those women, but I've heard what happened. It's sad."

"Didn't know them? But you saw Petra, right? That day you came here after the hurricane you told me you wondered what a drunken woman was doing poking around here late at night. You didn't get that information from the news. It was never reported, so you must have seen her yourself."

Bullock grabbed Anne's neck and squeezed. She managed to knee him below the belt, and he lost his grip just as Anne heard Tim's little pickup truck pull onto the lot. "Help!" she screamed. "Tim, help!" Bullock seized her neck again, but a black shape leapt on him, knocking him down in the cockpit. It was Molly. Tim followed, panting harder than Molly, who held Bullock's arm in her mouth.

A screech of tires sounded in the boatyard. "That's the police," Tim said. "This way," he yelled, cupping his mouth with his hands.

Sergeant Carrs ran to the pier and stood a moment, hand on gun, taking in the situation. "Call off the dog," he commanded.

Bullock scrambled to his feet. "This dog attacked me. I'm filing a complaint."

"Lawrence Bullock?" Sergeant Carrs eyed him closely. "We have some questions for you at the station."

"Why me? Look at what this dog did to my suit. He bit my arm."

Sergeant Carrs called for an ambulance. "Sit down right there, Sir. Medical help is on the way."

Tim held Anne's shoulders. "Your neck is red. What happened?"

"Bullock choked me."

Sergeant Carrs called for backup. "Stay on the boat, Mr. Bullock. And Ms. Anne, walk over here with me and tell me what happened."

42

A holding tank

Bullock had refused to be taken to the hospital when the ambulance arrived and had sent it away. He was still sitting in the cockpit nursing his arm when Captain Blunt and another policeman arrived. The three cops, along with Anne, Tim, and Molly, stood on the dock. "We have reason to believe there's important evidence on your boat pertaining to recent murders," Captain Blunt told Bullock. "Do we have your permission to search it?"

"What did that woman tell you? She's never been inside this boat."

"I'll tell you why they need to look for evidence," Anne cried out. She took a deep breath and began. "Ruth Neucomb learned that this man, Doctor Bullock as he insists on calling himself, had plagiarized his doctoral dissertation. After the Laser regatta three weeks ago, she accepted his invitation for anyone to join him on his boat and told him she had proof of the plagiarism, which would disqualify him from the position of president of Severn Heights College for which both he and Ruth had applied. Ruth either told him she was going to expose him or offered to keep the plagiarism quiet if he withdrew his application. Bullock took a white plastic trash bag and suffocated her, sealing the bag around her head with duct tape."

"Outrageous," Bullock cried. "How can you listen to these lies?"

"Be still, Sir," Captain Blunt ordered, "or we'll have to restrain you. Go on, Ms. Anne."

"It was a little after 9 p.m. by then. Mr. Bullock took Ruth's body and tossed her overboard, not realizing she was wearing an inflatable life jacket. But there was a witness. Petra Fields, who had an appointment to meet William Jamieson near here, had arrived sometime after she left Blake's Pub at nine o'clock. She either heard something on board Bullock's boat and jumped onto it in time to see him kill Ruth. Or she saw Ruth's body floating next to Bullock's boat and jumped onboard probably to get a boat hook to rescue her. Either way, she came aboard, tangling and losing one of her blue sneakers on the steps. Bullock, to eliminate a possible witness to the murder, took a knife and stabbed Petra in the upper abdomen. The autopsy report says she was dead before she hit the water."

"You already have the murderer," Bullock roared. "Why listen to this nonsense?"

"William Jamieson is innocent," Anne continued. "He got off work at eleven o'clock and came here to meet Petra. He saw Ruth's body floating by the dock and tried to rescue her by lowering the boat lift, hooking it onto her life jacket, and raising her out of the water. Before he could swing the lift around to the dock and lower her, this dog, Molly, barked and William ran away, possibly afraid he'd be accused of something."

Bullock started to get up, but Sergeant Carrs held him down. Bullock bellowed, "I'm the president of Severn Heights College. It's absurd to think I would do anything like this."

Anne stretched open the collar of her blouse to show her neck. "And yet he did this to me a few minutes ago."

The captain and the two policemen put Bullock into the captain's car. Captain Blunt called for the forensics team.

When the team arrived, Sergeant Carrs described the video Anne had shown him. "Get a photo of everything where it is first," he told the photographer, who was followed by two white-gowned women who soon came out of the boat with clear plastic bags containing Ruth's beige headscarf, her leopard skin cased phone, Petra's blue shoe, the knife, the box of white trash bags, and a roll of duct tape.

Tim had been watching the whole process by Anne's side. As Sergeant Carrs was about to leave, Tim stepped up and asked, "Sergeant, the commodore of our sailing club has asked me to remove

Doctor Bullock's boat, which we've only allowed to be docked here temporarily. We need this space for launching our boats. Now that the search is complete, can the boat be removed?"

"Not just yet," the sergeant answered. "I'm going to tape off this area until the Department of Natural Resources can send a Marine Police boat to tow it to their secure facility at Sandy Beach. They'll probably do it tomorrow."

With the area taped off and the forensics team and police driving away with Bullock in custody, a huge sigh of relief cascaded from Anne's chest. She and Tim sat on the clubhouse stairs shoulder to shoulder. After a moment, Tim took out his phone. "I'll call the commodore, tell him the club will soon be back in business." He switched to speaker phone in time for Anne to hear Commodore Dan let out a "Boo-yah!"

Tim told the commodore, "We can start texting the members to let them know. I'll add all the club members to the group message I had already set up for the Laser fleet."

Anne offered to email the members who don't list cell phone numbers. "And I'll put a notice in the *Westport Voice*."

The two of them went up into the clubhouse to get the membership list. Anne had just finished making the calls and posting her message when Sergeant Carrs phoned her. "Ms. Anne, after interviewing Doctor Bullock with his lawyer, we need a formal, signed statement from you, and there are some things we need you to clear up. We'd like you to come to the station as soon as you can."

Sergeant Carrs asked Anne for her phone. "What's your password? We need to copy that video I understand you made of the boat. And would you state for the record everything you told me today at the boatyard?"

"Sure."

"What's that you have there, Ms. Anne?"

"A library psychology book I picked up at the yard sale John

Neucomb held to get rid of Ruth's things. I found passages Ruth had underlined that Bullock had plagiarized." She handed the book to the sergeant. "Of course, it'll have to be returned to the library sometime."

Sergeant Carrs gave her a look. "Let's get your statement." The sergeant showed Anne a phone in a plastic bag. "Can you identify this phone as Ruth Neucomb's?"

"Yes."

"And this tan headscarf—"

"Beige," Ms. Trimble called out from her desk.

The sergeant ignored her "You can identify it as hers, correct?"

"Yes. I saw it in Bullock's boat. To me it looked like she had hidden it under her headscarf. I wonder if she was recording her whole encounter with Bullock. You have the list of her passwords. Have you charged her phone and listened?"

"I'd rather ask you the questions," Carrs said. Anne glanced over to Ms. Trimble's desk to see her give a discreet nod to affirm that the police had indeed listened to the recording.

When she'd finished answering all the sergeant's and the captain's questions, Anne signed the statement that Ms. Trimble had typed up. The captain went back to his office, and Anne asked the sergeant, "Doctor Bullock, is he—"

"Being held until tomorrow," the sergeant told her, "when he'll be indicted."

"For … ?"

"The murder of Ruth Neucomb."

"So the charges against William Jamieson will be dropped, obviously."

"I'm afraid not. The phone recording along with the trash bags and duct tape is evidence that Bullock killed Ruth Neucomb. But there is no evidence that Bullock killed Petra Fields."

"The knife beside the galley sink. Petra's body had a single wound by an object like that knife. And the blue shoe in the boat cabin was hers."

"We haven't been able to determine that the shoe matched the one found on her body. That one was more faded and greenish than blue."

"I'm sure that happened when it was in the water all that time. But what about the knife?"

"No blood on it."

"He probably washed it off."

"Then he did a good job. We haven't found a trace."

Anne thought a moment, then told the sergeant, "Cruising boats like Bullock's usually have small separate holding tanks to capture water from the sink rather than sending it overboard. If Bullock washed the knife, traces of Petra's blood would still be in the holding tank. You might be able to get a DNA sample even from blood that has been diluted with water."

Ms. Trimble at the desk next to the sergeant's began to nod. "Um-hum, um-hum, we did that in a case last year. Did your guys collect that holding tank water, Sergeant?"

His mouth in a pucker, he picked up his phone. "I'm about to send them back right now."

"So. Want me to set up an analysis with the biology unit of the county police forensic services?" Ms. Trimble's eyebrows lifted in an admonishing arch.

"Yeah. Go ahead." The sergeant scratched his nose with the end of a finger and commented to Anne, "Even if we find Petra Fields' blood in the sink, what's to say William Jamieson didn't stab her with that knife?"

"You could ask Bullock's wife."

"What do you mean?"

"I was hoping you'd already asked her what time Bullock got home that night. If you haven't—"

"We asked her. She says he got home in time for the sports on the ten o'clock news."

"So William didn't kill Petra."

"I don't see how—"

"Bullock locked up his boat when he went home that night. Nobody has been able to get into it without the key until today when he got back from South Carolina."

"I still don't—"

"William didn't leave the bar until eleven o'clock, when he got off work. Bullock had already locked up his boat and arrived home by then."

Sergeant Carrs tilted his head. "And you're saying the blue shoe and the knife—and maybe the blood—were locked up in the boat when William got there? All right, the prosecutor still has a few more days to decide whether to drop the charges against William. Meanwhile, we'll try to get a DNA match on that blood."

A man in civilian clothes brought back Anne's phone and set it on the sergeant's desk. Carrs rolled back his chair and handed the phone back to Anne. "Here you go. Thanks for coming in."

43

A gambling problem

Anne parked in front of her house and walked to the club. Tim's little truck wasn't there. In its place was Vivian Witherspoon's yellow sports car, the driver's door hanging open. The police must have notified Vivian that her husband was being charged with murder. Anne found her beyond the row of Solings, in medical scrubs, staring motionless at her taped-off *Knot on Call* and the boat launching crane near it. Choppy little waves from the bay lapped against the stern of the boat, and a seagull landed on one of its spreaders with a squawk. Vivian stood stiff, frozen in place. Anne stopped, giving the woman space to process what had happened.

Vivian turned, wiping away tears with an arm, and noticed Anne. For a moment, neither found words. Anne's heart beating heavily, she stepped up to Vivian and wrapped her in a hug. "This must be a terrible shock," she murmured in Vivian's ear.

Vivian clung to Anne's shirt. "The police called me at work. They said they have evidence to show Lawrence, my husband, killed a woman. That woman who was found hanging from the hook over there."

"I'm so sorry for you."

"I never thought he would go this far. I shouldn't have pushed him to find a job with a decent salary."

Anne remembered Lily saying Bullock had only held part-time teaching jobs before applying for the president's job at Severn Heights College.

"We could have lived on my pay alone," Vivian whimpered. "His gambling debts could have been paid by the sale of the boat."

"So that's why you wanted to sell it. It sounds like the debts were ... substantial."

"He always gambled. But it got worse in the past few years. He got mixed up with some shady people, although he managed to hide this side of his life and put on a good show. The Fellowship Club thought he was a wealthy benefactor." Vivian tisked. "It was my money that he was giving away."

"But your husband changed his mind about selling the boat."

"Yes. When he got the job at Severn Heights College, he thought he could use his salary to start paying off his debts. He said he needed the boat—and a golf club membership—to impress and entertain potential donors to the college."

Anne couldn't come up with any consolation except, "Well, *Knot on Call* is still yours. When this is all over, you'll be able to keep it or sell it, whichever you want."

"I know. The police told me. I'm not responsible for my husband's gambling debts."

"If he's found guilty, are you …."

"No, I won't stay with him. The police say the case is 'open and shut.' They found a recording and made me listen to it to confirm it was my husband's voice. You could hear that woman Ruth threatening to expose him for plagiarism if he didn't withdraw his application to be president of Severn Heights College. The phone picked up him threatening to hurt her and, when she held her ground, you could hear the sound of him choking her and her gasping. There were sounds of struggle followed by a more distant splash. After that the phone's battery seemed to run out and it went dead." Vivian burst into tears and sank to the ground.

Anne bent down and put her arm around her. "I don't know what to say. This must be devastating." When she heard Tim's pickup drive into the club, she helped Vivian up and walked her back to her car. Tim held a bag of food he'd bought at Harry's Grocery. "Oh, Mrs. Witherspoon. This must be a sad day for you. I'm sorry."

Vivian nodded. "I'll be going now. I need to find a good lawyer."

"I guess Doctor Bullock will be needing one," Tim agreed.

"Not for him. For myself."

When Vivian drove away, Anne followed Tim into his cabin. "I was hoping to call William's mother with good news as soon as I left the police station, but they're still holding him for Petra's murder."

"The knife and the shoe that were already locked inside the boat when William got to the club—that wasn't enough evidence to prove it was Bullock who killed Petra, not William?"

"They want something more conclusive," Anne said.

"Hm. While you were at the police station, their forensics guys came back to the club looking through Bullock's boat again. They carried away a container of something."

"Oh, good. I suggested they could get Petra's DNA from blood in the holding tank under the boat's sink."

"Thinking he stabbed Petra and washed the knife in the sink? Sounds like if they found her blood, that would be conclusive."

"Yeah. I don't know how closely the police keep William's public defender in the loop. I think I'll call her with an update."

Ms. Sullivan was out of breath when she answered. "Hi, Anne. I'm running up the parking garage steps to keep in shape. What do you have?"

Anne told her about the police search of Bullock's boat and the recording they found. "They've charged Bullock with Ruth's murder."

"Great news for William. I'm sure they'll release him soon."

"No. They're still holding him for the murder of Petra." Anne told her the whole story.

Ms. Sullivan said, "These DNA tests can take some time. They're probably going to wait till they get the results back before they tell me about it. But I'll call to confirm they're doing the tests and let William know. And … I don't know if I should get his mother's hopes up too soon."

Anne didn't think so. "This morning I told his mother the police had new evidence that might help William's case. Then, when

I found out the police were definitely charging Bullock with Ruth's murder, I wanted to call and tell her that but decided not to because I'd have to tell her they're still holding William for the murder of Petra."

"You've already given her a little hope. I think you're right. It might be best to leave it at that for now. Let's keep in touch."

Tim was putting a large porterhouse steak into his tiny fridge when Anne's phone rang. The connection cut off before she could answer.

"That has to be my mom," Anne told Tim. "She's still confused by the buttons on her new cordless phone." Anne called her back. "Hi, Mom. It's me. You don't have to hold down the Talk button while you talk. Anyway, I was going to call you. Things have started to settle down here. I think I'll be able to drive down and see you soon."

"Annie, so good to hear from you. I have great news. I've met a man."

"What's that, Mom?"

"Yes. Mr. Maynard Banks. Very handsome. We play pickleball almost every day. I'm hoping he'll move in with me."

Anne's mouth opened but no words came out.

"I'm sorry, Annie. I didn't hear what you said. Anyway, I'd like to fly up to Westport for a quick visit on your birthday."

"Why quick? You can stay as long as you want."

"But I can't stay long. Maynard wants to come with me, and he has something important coming up." A high octave giggle escaped her mother. "Just don't try to take him away from me."

"Gosh, Mom. I'm happy for you. How long have you known this man? The last time we talked you didn't mention him *at all*."

"Tall? Yes, he's tall and, uh, well-built. I think that's the best way to describe him."

"Mm. The Maritime Republic of Westport is having its own little Fourth of July parade on Friday. Why don't you come up for that. Come up on Thursday, the day before."

"Sweetie, can you tell me exactly when would be good time to come up?"

"THURSDAY, Mom. Four days from now."

"Tuesday? I don't know. How about Thursday, Annie. We can be there for the Fourth of July and your birthday the next day."

"Thursday will be great, Mom. I'll pick you up at the airport. Send me your flight information."

"Oh, here's Maynard tapping on the door now. I have to go. See you on Thursday."

Anne had a hard time imagining what a conversation might be like between her mother and her tall, well-built pickleball player. Maybe new love spoke louder than unheard words.

The glitter in Tim's eyes showed he'd followed Anne's half of the conversation and tried to imagine the rest. He asked if her mother would be here for her birthday.

"You know my birthday's coming up soon? I never told you."

"I happened to notice it on the registration form for the Laser regatta."

"Ah."

"It's this coming Saturday, isn't it? We'll have to celebrate."

"Thanks, Tim. I'll feel more like celebrating if the police release William. Let's see how that goes."

"Then let me make you a non-birthday dinner right now. We can at least celebrate Bullock being charged for Ruth's murder instead of William. I bought some Idaho potatoes and a porterhouse steak at Harry's Grocery. If you don't mind a dinner of meat, potatoes, and wine ...."

While Tim cooked, Anne thought about her mother's current life change. At least that's what it seemed this might be. Anne had been planning for her mother to come live with her in Westport— even though she only held the lease on her house until the first of September and would have to find them another place to live after that. But if her mother was happy in Florida now with her "well-built" friend, Anne could put off for a while worrying about finding a new place to rent. Besides, there was still hope that Real Estate Ron would lose his license and have to cancel his deal with the owner. In that case, Anne could just stay where she was.

44

Sleeping arrangements

On her walk to Clyde's for a morning coffee and croissant, Anne ran across Ms. Beatrice, who held up a hand to stop her. "Shocking, isn't it?" the neighborhood sentinel gasped. "The lady doctor featured in *Colonial City Magazine*? The word is she filed for divorce just after her husband was appointed president of Severn Heights College. Can you imagine that?"

Ms. Beatrice obviously hadn't heard yet that Bullock had been charged with murder. Anne just offered her a "tisk" to acknowledge the information, wondering how she'd obtained it.

"I've been keeping my eye on John Neucomb ever since his wife was murdered. As you might have noticed," Ms. Beatrice sniggered with raised eyebrows. "Anyway, this morning I saw John Neucomb talking to a contractor in front of his house. And of course I stopped to ask what he was planning. He told me a woman he'd hoped to marry had filed for a divorce. He didn't want to tell me who she was. I knew it wasn't you because you're a widow. And besides, your latest interest seems to be the dockmaster at that sailing club. Tim something, right? What is his family name?"

Anne offered only a blank stare.

"Anyway, I'd seen John Neucomb with that lady doctor holding hands before, and I figured it out." Ms. Beatrice's lips stretched into a scornful grimace. "Giving up a college president for John Neucomb. The woman must be crazy."

Anne gave a unconcerned shrug. "To each her own, I guess. Maybe we don't know all the facts."

"I agree," Ms. Beatrice said. "And I'm going to keep looking into this."

Vivian Witherspoon's divorce plans were confirmed to Anne by John Neucomb himself when he sat down at her table in Clyde's.

He couldn't keep the grin off his face. "The police haven't announced it yet, but they're charging Doctor Bullock with Ruth's murder. That's what Vivian told me. Who would've thought a guy in his position would commit murder? Vivian told me she refused to be married to a murderer. She's already contacted a lawyer to file for divorce." John leaned closer to Anne and lowered his voice. "I'm hoping Vivian and I will get married. I wanted to ask you not to mention to anybody the future plans you and I made previously. Vivian doesn't know anything about that."

Now Anne had to grin. "You can be sure the secret rests with me."

John reached to shake her hand. Anne recalled the lawyer's adage that a verbal agreement wasn't worth the paper it was written on, but John seemed to be satisfied with a handshake. Obviously as much as Anne, he preferred that none of his previous attention to her be put in writing.

With a sigh of relief John got up to go, but Anne stopped him. "I wanted to ask you about any progress in getting Real Estate Ron's license revoked."

"Oh. I gave a representative of the National Association of Realtors some pictures of Ron using that house he listed for rent as a tryst house. I haven't heard back from him yet, and I've been busy with other things."

"When you hear something, would you let me know? Real Estate Ron has brought the owner a client's offer to buy the house I'm renting, and the owner, some man in D.C., wants me out by September first so he can sell it."

John Neucomb's lip curled. "I'm sure Real Estate Ron's client wants to buy it and turn it into a multi-story condo like he wanted to do with my house. OK. You keep our past little affair secret and I'll get right on it and get back to you."

On the way back to her house, Anne's brief buoyant feeling at the thought that she might be able to keep the lease on her house was eventually deflated by the sad thought of William Jamieson still in jail and his mother worrying herself to death. William's public defender had told her that DNA tests took some time, and his freedom seemed to depend on that test, which would be a specialized one on a diluted blood sample. How much time would that take? There was somebody she knew who might be able to answer this question, Petra's former partner Jessie, who had just got a job in a Colonial City medical lab.

"Jessie, sorry to call you at work. I have a question about DNA samples you might be able to answer." She told Jessie what she knew.

"We did DNA tests on blood diluted in water at the place where I used to work. We used a special process to find the blood, then another process to extract it before we could analyze it. It took a couple of days. Is this related to Ruth's murder?"

"Um, no. Actually to Petra's death." Anne took a breath. "I know you assumed it was an accidental drowning. I'm sorry to tell you, but the police have learned she was killed before she fell into the water."

"Oh, no. The poor dear. I can't believe anybody would want to kill Petra."

"Petra might have witnessed Ruth's murder," Anne explained. As far as Anne knew, Jessie had never been told that Petra was once a suspect in Ruth's murder. With luck, it could stay that way. "The police have reason to suspect the man who murdered Ruth also killed Petra."

"And a DNA test might prove he killed her? After he killed Ruth?"

"I think so. Yes."

When Jessie was silent for a moment, Anne said, "I have some other news. My mother and a friend are coming up from Florida for the Westport Fourth of July parade. Maybe we can get together."

"That would be nice. Soon after I moved in with Jorge, I called my parents, too. When they asked about the 'guy' I was living with,

I didn't have to lie any more. Jorge suggested they fly here for the parade. He said it's small but fun. But my parents would never come to a town where somebody had recently been murdered. They're kind of particular or judgmental about lots of things, but that would push them over the edge. I didn't mention coming here to them."

"Maybe in the fall when this has all passed over," Anne suggested. "They could watch the Maritime Republic of Westport versus Colonial City tug of war. I'll tell everybody not to mention anything about the murders. Or about Petra, if that's what you'd prefer."

"Thanks, Anne."

A Boston Whaler-sized boat drifted up to the Westport Sailing Club dock just as Anne got there. Tim had called to say the Natural Resources Police were coming to tow Vivian's boat to their secure facility at Sandy Beach. Anne stood watching on the dock beside Tim. There was shouting as uniformed men and one woman motored their boat up to the stern of *Knot on Call*. The woman climbed up the still-folded transom ladder and un-cleated the lines holding the boat to the dock. She put a long coiled line on the Beneteau's bow cleat, pushed the boat away from the dock with a boat hook, and skillfully tossed the line directly to a man in the police boat. She dropped down into *Knot on Call*'s cockpit to steer while they towed it away.

Tim cupped his hands by his mouth and called out, "OK to take down these security tapes now?" and someone on the police boat called back, "The police will get right on it." Doctor Bullock's boat, or more accurately his wife's boat, was gone. The Westport Sailing Club operations could resume.

As Anne and Tim walked back to the clubhouse, they noticed a couple of Snipe sailors getting their boats ready to trail to the regatta at the South Bay Racing Club. "Too bad," Tim muttered to Anne. "It's too late to bring the regatta back here to the Westport club."

"Hey!" someone called to Anne. "I came here to talk to you." It was Lily, helping a sailor raise the mast on his Snipe. Lily held the mast while he attached the shrouds to hold it up. "I told Daryl he could look on the bulletin for a crew," Lily explained, introducing the young man.

Lily walked back to the clubhouse with Anne and Tim. "My dad gave me some shocking news. He said it will be on TV tonight. It's Doctor Bullock who killed Ruth."

Anne nodded. "We know. Ruth found out Bullock had plagiarized his dissertation. She confronted him hoping he'd withdraw his application. She wanted the job at the college herself."

"And Bullock killed her for that." Lily put her hands to her neck. "Choked her. And that bag over her head. Horrible."

Anne asked if Bullock had already accepted the position. "I know he was waiting for the college to pay for his membership in the golf club here."

"He hadn't formally accepted yet. The college still hadn't responded about the membership."

Anne said, "I guess the Board of Trustees withdrew their offer now that Bullock is charged with murder."

"They did. Finally. Two members of the board kept insisting that, you know, Bullock is innocent until he's proven guilty. They wanted to wait and see if he's convicted."

"There's not much doubt he will be," Anne said indignantly. "There's a recording on Ruth's phone of him killing her. I can't imagine why a person like Bullock was being considered in the first place."

Lily said she knew why. "One man on the board has a cafeteria franchise. My dad is sure Bullock had committed to switch the college contract to his company. The other guy has a construction company, and the college was about to offer a contract for a new math building, so ...."

Tim stepped in. "We're pretty sure Bullock also killed Petra. Waiting for a blood test to prove it."

Lily gasped. "My dad hadn't heard about that."

"It's true," Anne told her. "Petra seems to have either witnessed Ruth's murder or seen her floating in the water and boarded Bullock's boat to get a boathook to save her."

Lily stood silent for a moment, slowly shaking her head. "I never thought William could kill anybody. I hope they can prove Bullock killed them both. I want to put this whole thing out of my mind."

As Lily was about to leave, she stopped, taking Anne's arm. "Anne, you should apply for the job as president of the college yourself. You have the qualifications."

The suggestion took Anne by surprise. "Oh, no, Lily. I love my job at Westport Elementary. I can't think of working anywhere else."

Lily smiled. "I know. It was just a thought. Want to come over to my house for tea?"

"I would, but I'm going to help Tim get ready for the feast on July Fourth. Plus, my mother's coming to visit. I need to get ready for that, too."

"It would be great to see her again. How's she doing?"

"She's coming with a man."

Lily's mouth dropped.

"Some guy she met down in Florida. They're staying with me." Anne shook her head. "I don't know what to do about the sleeping arrangements."

Lily held a hand over her mouth but couldn't suppress a giggle.

"I mean I just have two bedrooms, so …."

"I think you just have to ask your mother."

"Yeah. I wanted to but couldn't do it. She dropped this on me so fast. If I call her back, how should I word the question?"

Tim excused himself, saying, "I have some things to do in the clubhouse."

"Besides," Anne said, "Mom's hard of hearing. She mis-hears me half the time."

Lily gripped Anne's arm. "Then forget it. Let the chips fall where they may, as Vince says."

Anne bit her lip. "That's what I'm going to have to do."

When Lily went home, Anne walked into the clubhouse to help Tim get volunteers for the Fourth of July feast and order ears of corn, kegs of beer, ground beef, hotdogs, rolls, and huge cans of baked beans. "And the crabs?" she asked.

"The prices are sky high. Commodore Dan says since Bullock won't be supplying them, we might have to do without them."

Anne shrugged. "I never wanted to eat Bullock's crabs anyway." She told Tim she needed to go get some food supplies and spend the rest of the day cleaning up her house for her mother's visit.

45

Good sportsmanship

Washing the windows, kitchen counters, and bathroom took Anne the rest of the day, and the next morning she washed and dried towels, bed sheets, and a lot of her clothes, then vacuumed the whole house. She had just flopped down on the couch when Tim called. "Have you checked the TV news? It's official. The police have charged Lawrence A. Bullock with the murder of Ruth Neucomb."

"Still no word about William?"

"No. But at least we know Petra didn't kill Ruth. So I'm going to call the commodore and ask if he's been in touch with her parents. Now that we know Petra's not a murderer, we can let them set up an endowment in her name."

The commodore met Anne and Tim at the club. "Petra's not a murderer," he reasoned. "But several women have griped to me about her, uh ...."

"Cheating?" Anne suggested.

"Exactly." He scratched the back of his neck. "I suppose that would be forgotten over time. Petra's parents are coming to town tomorrow to make arrangements for Petra's transport back to Rhode Island for burial. They said they're ready to set up a Petra Fields Memorial Endowment. I told them I'd get back to them."

"If we let them establish it," Anne reasoned, "I'm sure there would have to be some kind of endowment agreement drawn up. Maybe the endowment could state that the purpose of the Petra Fields Endowment is to foster good sportsmanship and integrity?"

Both the commodore and Tim turned towards Anne.

"What?" she retorted. "You're not thinking of me to draw it up? Just because—"

"You're a teacher?" Tim grinned. "That's right."

Anne looked away towards the Laser racks where she and Tonya had borrowed Petra's boat. "What I would like," she said, "is to make the endowment for eight- to twelve-year-olds who can't afford to buy a boat and pay for sailing lessons."

"Sounds good," the commodore said.

Tim rolled his eyes. "I suppose Petra's name would have to be on the endowment."

"That sticks in my craw, too," Anne admitted. "But I've come to see Petra as a victim of sorts, a victim of her parents' raising her to think that winning is everything. Of her parents' seeming to love her for her accomplishments rather than for herself. You've talked to her mother, haven't you, Tim?"

"I have. And I got the same impression." He thought a moment. "I wonder if the endowment is a way for her parents to assuage some feelings of guilt."

"Uh-huh. And don't you wonder if that might be true about any endowment, from those established by the robber barons in the nineteenth-century continuing up to today?" Anne shrugged. "Not saying there's anything wrong with that. It's better than doing nothing, isn't it?"

Commodore Dan broke in. "Let's not worry about their motive. We'll put Petra's name on the endowment. We have to. As far as the Westport Sailing Club goes, we don't know anything about Petra Fields."

Anne agreed. "It could be the Westport Sailing Club Youth Program supported by the Petra Fields endowment."

"Perfect," the commodore said. "Anne, it's your idea. Would you help Petra's parents draw that up?"

Anne spent the rest of the day at home talking on the phone with Petra's parents' financial advisor. He told her Petra's parents had learned from the police that Petra was murdered and were more determined than ever that an endowment should be set up in her name. As for the wording of the endowment, Anne expected some pushback when she insisted on omitting references to Petra's own character or sportsmanship, but luckily the advisor had a less than positive impression of Petra from past discussions with her about a stipend her parents set up for her and was easily convinced.

The financial advisor suggested that the commodore be designated the local administrator of the fund, but when they called him, he declined. "Between my job and the club, my hands are tied up," he explained, suggesting Anne as the administrator. But the thought of running a fund with Petra's name on it brought a sour taste to Anne's mouth. Then she had an idea. She'd suggest Jessie.

"A member of the Westport Sailing Club?" the advisor asked.

"No," Anne said. "But wouldn't it be better to have a neutral party administering the fund? Jessie's a scientist, not a banker or whatever. But she knew Petra, lived with her, admired her."

"I'll put her down tentatively," the advisor said. "Mr. and Mrs. Fields and I are flying down tomorrow to arrange for Petra's burial. Let's meet before that in the morning at your Westport Sailing Club. Bring Jessie. We'll see what Petra's parents think of putting her in charge."

As soon as Anne got off the phone, she called Jessie. "Sorry to bother you at work again. Something's come up." Anne told her about the Petra Fields Endowment, emphasizing its benefit to children who couldn't afford the club membership or buy a boat. "The fund administrator needs to make sure the money is spent correctly and wisely. We think you're the best person for the job."

Jessie was silent for a minute, but then in a trembling voice agreed. "If you really think I can handle it."

"Of course, you can. Can you meet me at my house at nine tomorrow morning? We'll go to the boat club together. Petra's parents want to make arrangements for her burial after the meeting."

Anne put on a long sleeved white blouse and her best slacks, brushed her waves into place, and had finished a hurried breakfast by the time Jessie appeared on her porch. She was wearing a black dress. When Anne widened her eyes, Jessie explained, "If Petra's parents are going to, um, view the body, I'd like to go with them."

Cliff and Winifred Fields were leaning over a table in the clubhouse across from Commodore Dan and Tim. The platinum blonde hair on Petra's mother was teased into wiry curls that looked so stiff it might hurt your hand to touch them. Heavy makeup gave her face the same fixed-in-place look, and a hefty string of pearls swayed from her sallow neck as she turned from the commodore to Tim and back.

Petra's father and their financial advisor wore identical navy blue suits. Her father had white hair and a thin salt-and-pepper moustache. The advisor was bald and had reading glasses perched on his nose. He stood when Anne and Jessie were introduced, causing Petra's father to initiate a token half-rise. They'd been poring over a draft of the Petra Fields Endowment agreement that the advisor had drawn up after talking to Anne on the phone.

Jessie said, "I'm so sorry for you loss, Mr. and Mrs. Fields. Petra was …." With shaky hands she took a tissue from a small black satin purse and wiped her tears. Anne took her arm and showed her to a chair at the table. Petra's mother looked at Jessie with a dog-like tilted head, as if assessing whether she was for real.

The financial advisor cleared his throat. "We have an appointment with a mortician at noon to view the deceased's body at the forensic medical center in Baltimore and make arrangements for transport and burial. Maybe we could get on with the business at hand."

Jessie burst into a flood of tears. Anne put an arm on her shoulder, and Petra's mother gave Jessie a red-lipped grin of approval. With no show of emotion, Petra's father picked up the document, scrolling through it with a gold ballpoint pen. He tapped twice on one passage. "It says 'funds to be distributed at the discretion of the local administrator,' whom it names as Ms. Jessica Belinski." He turned to Jessie. "This is a heavy responsibility, Ms. Belinski. Do you think you're capable of carrying it out?"

Before Jessie could reply, Petra's mother slapped her palm on the table with a rattle of bracelets. "She's perfect. Can you think of anybody else who knew Petra so well and would be willing to do it? This young lady is going to be our administrator."

An hour or more passed while the group went over the financial details of the endowment. The principal would be invested in a national bank with the interest and dividends going to the Westport Sailing Club. Anne was thrilled to learn how much this was estimated to be. The local administrator would authorize expenditures and send financial reports to the donors, Mr. and Mrs. Fields, and take care of tax reporting. Commodore Dan spoke for the first time. "You seem troubled, Jessie. Are you willing to take on this responsibility?"

Jessie sniffed. "I am. I'll do a good job." Then she added, "But I have one request. I want to go along when Petra's parents go to view Petra in the medical center."

Tim took the Whaler to fill up at Fred's marine gas station. Anne rushed to the schoolyard with news of the endowment. The soccer game had been getting bigger as the summer went on. Now there were full teams on both sides, and the shouting was continuous. Anne stood at the fence watching until Tonya noticed her and came over, out of breath and dripping with sweat. "Ms. Anne, we heard on the TV that a doctor murdered somebody at your sailing club."

"It's not another murder, Tonya. It's the same one. They just found the person who actually did it. He's not a medical doctor. But anyway I have some good news." She told Tonya about the endowment sailing program for eight- to twelve-year-old kids.

"Time out, guys!" Tonya shouted. "Come over here."

Jorge's nephew Roberto and Luis, the son of the waiter Pedro at Clyde's, were the first to run up. They were followed by others. Anne told them she'd be coming by some day soon with a written announcement, in English and Spanish, for anybody who wanted to learn how to sail to take home to their parents. "You won't need to pay, and you won't need your own boat. You'll just have to prove you can swim pretty well."

A chorus of "I can. I can swim. I'm a great swimmer" rang out, and Anne described the program. "The smaller kids will learn to sail in Optimist dinghies. Anybody who's too big for that will learn on Lasers. As you get better at sailing, you'll be able to crew in two-person boats like the Snipe. Snipe sailors are always looking for crew. In a few years I'm hoping to turn out some excellent sailors who started when they were in Westport Elementary School."

As excited as the children, Anne went home to eat a ham sandwich and unwind. She hadn't had much sleep the night before and fell asleep on the couch as soon as she lay down. She didn't wake up until early evening when Jessie phoned her. "Oh, Anne. I could only peep at her face between my fingers. It was so horrible. I couldn't breathe. Mr. Fields had to help me out of the room."

"I'm sorry. But you should be proud of yourself for going through with this. I hope seeing Petra gave you some closure."

"It did. I called Jorge before you. I think I'm totally ready to move on with my life."

"Good for you, Jessie."

"And I have good news. We went back to the club to get the commodore's signature on one of the papers. He invited Petra's parents to announce the endowment at the Fourth of July feast. Petra's father asked if they were going to have Maryland style steamed crabs. He wanted to try them. When the commodore said the club couldn't afford them this year, Petra's mother said they would pay for them."

"Nice to have mon—you know, the means to do something like that."

"And the commodore told them you'd volunteered to be the kids' instructor."

"I did. I told him I'll teach them how to sail and race but I'm going to stress fair play and honesty even more than racing skills."

"Of course. You wouldn't think that was something that had to be taught. By the way, are you coming to the church children's workshop tomorrow?"

"If I can. My mother hasn't told me what time she's getting here yet. I have to call her."

When the call ended, Anne called her mother. "Hi, Mom. I'm really looking forward to your visit tomorrow. When are you arriving and what's the flight number?"

"Right number? Of course it's the right number, Annie. I didn't change my phone number."

"When does your plane arrive tomorrow, Mom?"

"Yes, we're coming tomorrow, Sweetie. Hold on. I'll read you the flight information." She and Maynard Banks were arriving at the airport at six in the evening. "It's a little late, I know," Anne's mother apologized. "But we got a great deal on the flight."

"Can't wait to see you, Mom."

46

Could have been yours

Tim called, and they talked for a long time about arrangements for the coming Fourth of July feast and the Petra endowment until Anne went to bed for the night. The next morning was the children's workshop at the church, and she'd told Jessie she would attend if she could.

Pastor Brown took Anne's hand to welcome her and drew her aside. "I'm concerned about Mrs. Jamieson," he admitted. "Since word got out that her son is accused of a terrible crime, she hasn't come to services even though she's always been one of our most faithful parishioners. She told me some people in church seem to 'give her looks.' That's how she put it. I told her they're looks of sympathy, not blame. I told the congregation I visited William soon after he was arrested, and he swore to me that he is not guilty and I believe him. I reminded them that we're innocent until proven guilty. I said I've known William for a long time, he volunteers in the church's children's workshop, and I've never known him to do anything other than good."

Anne lowered her voice. "Maybe you've heard that a different person has been accused of Ruth Neucomb's murder now. I'm hopeful that any day that same person will be charged with Petra Fields' murder, too, and William will be released."

Pastor Brown bowed his head with closed eyes as if offering a silent prayer, then led Anne into the workshop. Jessie and Jorge were there, side by side setting up a colorful model of a double helix in what seemed to be a project they'd planned together. Anne found a seat next to Jorge, who smiled. "I'm learning about this along with the kids."

Anne's phone rang. She took it out of her pocket intending to silence it but saw the call was from Terry Sullivan in the Office of the Public Defender. "Really sorry," Anne told the group. "I have to go outside and take this call."

"I only have a few minutes before I have to be in court on another case," Ms. Sullivan said. "The DNA test identified Petra's blood in the holding tank of Bullock's boat. The police got the report late yesterday. Since the blood was already locked into the boat by the time William got there, charges against him have been dropped. They aren't charging him with failure to report a dead body or anything else. He's being released any minute. I called his mother. She doesn't drive. Could you—"

"I'm on it. I'll pick her up and drive her to the detention center. Conifer Road, right?"

Anne led Mrs. Jamieson into the public lobby of the detention center. They went up to a curly blonde with purple lipstick staring into a computer monitor behind a high wall. The woman didn't look up. "Excuse me," Anne said. "We've come to pick up William Jamieson."

Her eyes still on the screen, the woman snapped, "Photo ID."

"Um, our IDs? It's William Jamieson we've come to pick up."

The woman tapped a long fingernail on top of the wall she sat behind, which came up to her nose level. "Photo ID," she repeated without looking up.

"Oh, dear me," Mrs. Jamieson murmured, starting to rake through her purse. "I don't have a driver's license. I have a Medicaid card. And a library card."

A sound something like *Whamp-whamp-whaaah* burst from the woman's computer, and she looked down at Anne and Mrs. Jamieson. "Family only. All visitors must present a picture ID."

"We were told William Jamieson is to be released today," Anne tried to explain.

"Hold on." The purple-lipped woman clicked something on her computer. "Unconditional release at eleven o'clock. No ID? You can wait outside."

They waited in the sun in front of the flat roofed brick building, leaning against the yellow pole fence at the sidewalk until William walked out of the door a free man. He wore the same blue work shirt and tattered jeans shorts he'd had on when Anne last saw him testing his dinghy. His mother took hold of him in a long hug. "You're so thin. You're wasting away," she moaned. "Didn't they feed you in there?"

"They fed me, Mom. I wasn't very hungry." Still in his mother's arms, he turned to Anne. "Ms. Sullivan told me you were a big help getting me out. Thank you, Ms. Anne. You believed me all along."

"And I was right." Anne clapped a hand on his back. "Let's get out of here. My van's over there in the parking lot."

As they drove over the drawbridge to Westport, Anne had a thought. "The children's workshop at the church will still be going on when we get back. I bet they would like to see you back in the group, William."

His mother uttered a kind of moan. William said, "I don't know. I don't know."

"Pastor Brown told the congregation he always believed you weren't guilty, William. Showing up a free man today would prove him right."

"I guess I could ignore the looks I get," William said. "Once you're accused of something, it's hard to get that out of people's minds." His mother nodded. "But God help us, William. We have to face everybody sometime. I think Ms. Anne is right. Let's walk in there right now and get it over with."

The chatter of the children stopped the minute they entered the room. The brief silence was drowned by spontaneous applause and cheering, everyone standing and some of the children running up to take hold of William's hands. Pastor Brown came out of his adjoining office and raised William's hand like a prize fighter. "Innocent!" he shouted. "Not guilty!"

The pastor then raised Mrs. Jamieson's and Anne's hands. "William's mother prayed for justice, and Ms. Anne worked for it.

Justice prevails!"

Anne was anxious to tell Tim the news, but first she needed a moment to sit alone on her couch and think. Would Westport ever be convinced of William's innocence? Would they ever be able to move on and put the murders behind them? She logged onto the *Westport Voice*, scrolled to the postings about Ruth's murder, and added a post announcing that all charges against William had been dropped. "A different person has been charged with the murder of Ruth Neucomb," she wrote, logging off without mentioning who it was or mentioning Petra at all. There were sure to be questions and comments, some of them instantaneous, but she wasn't going to deal with them.

Now to tell Tim at the club that William was released. When she crossed over to Tiller Street, John Neucomb, in a dark suit and wearing black leather shoes *with* socks, was ahead of her, walking in the direction of the sailing club. She slowed, hoping he would walk past the club entrance, but he turned in. Anne reluctantly followed.

John Neucomb opened the glass door covering the bulletin board and ripped off the *For Sale* notice for Vivian Witherspoon's *Knot on Call*, replacing it with a different notice. He looked around for Tim, saw Anne watching him, and did a little jump. "I'm not buying that boat," he said. "Not after Bullock murdered two people, including my wife, on it. Vivian agrees. She's listed it with a dealer on Bay Creek." He pointed to the new *For Sale* notice for *Knot on Call*. "We'll find a different boat."

"Ah. You and Vivian together? Joint ownership?"

John's face reddened. "Vivian's going to file for a divorce. I'm going to ask her to marry me. Both of us will own it equally."

That had been the problem with the house John and Ruth owned together, Anne thought. Apparently the possibility of another divorce didn't occur to him.

Tim walked up, and John filled him in. "Viv and I aren't going to sail in a boat two people have been murdered in."

"Murdered by Bullock," Anne added for Tim's benefit. "He's charged with both murders now. William is free. All charges dropped. I picked him up today and brought him home."

John nodded. "Viv told me. Something about that other woman's blood being found in the boat. The police told Viv that Bullock's going to claim he killed the woman in self-defense."

Anne and Tim looked at each other. She knew what they were both thinking. Petra might have seen Bullock throw overboard a body with her head in a plastic bag. When Bullock went back below deck, she might have stepped aboard to confront him. If that's why he killed her, it wasn't really self-defense.

John spoke up. "It doesn't matter. There's no way Bullock won't be convicted for my wife's murder. And I can't believe his lawyer could ever convince the jury the second murder was self-defense, but even if he does, Bullock's still a murderer."

When John turned to leave, Anne followed him. "You look quite spiffy in that suit. I can't help wondering—"

"Too late," John grinned. "You had your chance. I'm off to propose to Viv just now." He took a small black case from his jacket pocket and opened it to reveal a diamond ring. "Could have been yours," he teased.

"Ah, well," Anne sighed dramatically. "Actually I was wondering if the suit ... and socks," she added glancing down, "meant you might be filing a court complaint against Real Estate Ron."

"No. The real estate commission is handling him. Don't be surprised if all of Ron's *For Sale* and *For Rent* signs get replaced soon with signs from a different realtor."

Tim had offered to take Anne to pick up her mother and her new friend at the airport, then take them to dinner, but Anne wanted to meet her mother alone before dealing with the question of who Tim was. Her mother loved what people now called "comfort food" more than anything, so she prepared a meatloaf and macaroni and cheese to serve with a salad of nothing but iceberg lettuce and what her mother used to call Russian dressing, which was simply mayonnaise mixed with ketchup. Anne set the dining room table with dishes handed down to her by her mother, rushed around the house dusting the furniture again, and then moved a quilt and pillow into the downstairs closet in case she ended up sleeping on the couch. She'd already stocked in plenty of wine and beer.

Before driving to the airport, she swung by the house that Real Estate Ron had used for his trysts. *For Rent by Harbor Real Estate*, the sign said. Anne raised a fist, shouting, "Yes!" as happy as if she'd taken first place in a regatta. Her trip to the airport was slowed by traffic, and her mother with newly bleached blonde hair and bangs and Maynard Banks with short gray hair and long sideburns stood waiting at the curb with their bags when she drove up. Anne jumped out and gave her mother a hug. Maynard gave Anne a firm handshake. "So glad to meet you," he said in a deep voice. "Your mother talks about you all the time." Attesting to his "well-built" designation, Maynard lifted both suitcases into her van together, one in each hand.

Dinner went well. Anne and her mother drank wine, and Maynard drank beer. He talked loud, and her mother seemed to understand everything he said. At least she pretended to. The more wine Anne drank, the louder she talked, too. The main topic of conversation? Pickleball. Anne had to promise she'd give it a try sometime.

Maynard gushed over the meatloaf. "Even better than what we get at the Cracker Barrel," he swore.

"It's my recipe," Anne's mother bragged.

The topic of the Westport murders didn't come up. Anne wondered if her mother had told Maynard about them. In any case, Anne wasn't going to bring it up. They took a walk around the neighborhood after dinner. Bumblebees hummed around the hollyhocks and lavender that many villagers had planted in front of their porches. "And look at those black-eyed Susans," Anne's mother gushed.

Before they reached the corner of the street, they ran into Ms. Beatrice, who stopped in front of them. "My mother's visiting," Anne told her. Ms. Beatrice said, "Welcome to the Maritime Republic of Westport. I thought your father died, Anne."

Anne's mother appeared not to have heard. Maynard corrected Ms. Beatrice. "I'm not Anne's father, actually."

"Oh," said Ms. Beatrice. "I see." She tapped away.

Despite the health benefits of playing pickleball acclaimed by Anne's mother and friend, both were ready to go to bed early. "There's only one bathroom," Anne said. "We can go up and get ready one at a time."

Maynard went upstairs first while Anne and her mother looked at some pictures her mother had brought with her. "I'm going straight to bed," Maynard called down. "Which room?"

"The back bedroom with the blue walls," Anne called back. "I have ice cream," she told her mother.

"Maynard doesn't care for it, but you know I do." Her mother finished a large bowl of cherry vanilla, then gave Anne a pat on the hand. "I think I'll go up now, too, Annie. See you in the morning."

Anne listened to the shower, waited. A door opened and closed. Anne waited a little longer before she tiptoed upstairs. The back bedroom door was closed. The door to her own bedroom was open. Nobody was in it.

47

Oooh, Ahh

The Westport Fourth of July parade always assembled in the outlying stretches of the neighborhood in the broad parking lot of the Heights apartments, where most of Anne's students lived, then marched into the peninsula proper along Windward Street and eventually right by Anne's house. Anne peeped out her bedroom window just at daylight to see her street already lined with beach chairs claiming spots to watch from. Anne smiled to herself. As long as she could keep living in this house, she could always watch from her own front porch.

Her phone rang with a call from Terry Sullivan, William's public defender. "Sorry to call so early, Anne, but I have a request. William told me he's going to be in the Westport parade. I came here to watch it with his mother. She said the best view might be from your house. I wonder if she and I could possibly watch the parade from your porch?"

Anne dressed quickly and went down to check the local NOAA weather report. It was going to be a sunny day, winds light and variable. Not good for a regatta, but great for a parade. When would her mother and Maynard wake up? She was about to wake them when she heard stirring upstairs.

She served pancakes, her mother's favorite breakfast, and fried some bacon and eggs to go with them in case Maynard didn't like pancakes. He liked it all. "Better breakfast than we get at Waffle House," he boomed. Anne's mother nodded with a mouth full, "Mm." Anne got the idea they ate together in restaurants and didn't cook much.

Terry Sullivan helped William's mother up onto the porch. To keep things simple, Anne introduced Mrs. Jamieson and William's lawyer simply as friends. "Mrs. Jamieson's son William is going to be in the parade," she explained. No need to mention anything more about William's recent history.

"Your father is so handsome, Anne," Ms. Jamieson crooned loud enough for Anne's mother to hear. Anne realized Ms. Jamieson had never met her father.

"Oh, we're not married," Anne's mother declared, "but we're going to move in together."

Anne studied Mrs. Jamieson's face for a reaction. "My father died almost two years ago," Anne explained. Would the conservative church-going lady be scandalized by the idea of her mother and Maynard living together? Quickly changing the subject, Anne said, "I'll go bring out some ice tea for us to drink while we watch the parade."

A horse-drawn cart with a *Clyde's Café* banner led the parade, Clyde himself driving in the cleanest white apron Anne had ever seen him wear, while Pedro and his son Luis stood in the cart waving American flags. Children gathering on Windward Street cheered as the white horse clomped by.

"Clyde's Café uses a horse to deliver?" Terry Sullivan's mouth dropped open.

"His grandfather did," Anne explained. She pointed to an advertisement draped across the horse's back for the *Colonial Woods Riding School*. "I'm guessing that's who lent Clyde the horse."

Following slowly behind came a shiny silver convertible with its top down, Vince driving with a tall Uncle Sam hat on his head and Lily in the passenger seat waving. A sign on the car read *Colonial City Mercedes*. "Lily!" Anne called out. "Happy Fourth!" Lily turned and blew her a kiss.

The Blake's Pub float came next, drawn by a three-wheeled motorcycle. "William!" Mrs. Jamieson shouted, recognizing her son driving the cycle. "Hurray, William!" echoed Terry Sullivan. William waved and tipped a red, white, and blue hat to the group on the porch.

Walking along after the Blake's float came Harry, pushing a festooned wheelbarrow containing a giant plastic roasted pig—of course with *Harry's Grocery* written on its side. Behind him Howie came whirring along on a Harbor Hardware riding lawnmower sporting a huge American flag. He was followed by Bill from the Small Boat Tackle Shop in a classic MG open sports car, flags flying from its antenna and Sousa's *Stars and Stripes Forever* blasting from its radio. An Eastern Sails van followed with a spinnaker inflated above its roof by a huge fan. Anne recognized the driver as Tom, her brief Blake's Pub acquaintance. Close behind him Bob Green followed in his smaller van with a red, white, and blue Snipe sail waving on a mast strapped to the rear bumper.

The Westport Elementary principal Lucia, wrapped in a red, white, and blue chemise, marched ahead of the school band, six nervous kids playing *Yankee Doodle* with the help of Anne's colleague Gloria on the tuba. The band was followed by a cluster of Westport kids on bicycles with ribbons woven through their spokes led by Jorge's nephew Roberto. Tonya swerved close to the sidewalk and called out "Happy Fourth!" to Anne.

Another Westport teacher marched behind the bikes twirling a red streamer next to her husband, who waved a banner reading *Morales Travel Agency – Let Us Show You the World*. "Hi, Marge!" Anne called out. Behind them came the *Westport Voice* entry, a huge replica of a cell phone pulled on a wagon by two girl scouts and flashing consecutively on its screen the messages *Our Community News*, *Happy Fourth of July*, and its website address.

Anne stood up to see the next entry better. It was Tim driving a motorcycle with Molly in the sidecar. He was pulling a trailered Laser with a huge American flag raised on its mast. A sign on the hull said *Ask about the Westport Sailing Club's New Youth Program*. Anne put her hands to her mouth and called out to Tim, who turned and waved while Molly gave her a quick yelp.

Even before they came into view, Anne heard the Mount Zion Church choir, directed by Pastor Brown, standing in brown robes on the flatbed of a truck and singing "Oh Happy Days" to recorded organ music. On Anne's porch William's mother clapped to the rhythm along with the villagers watching on the street while this grand finale drove by. As Anne watched the end of the parade, something made her chuckle. For the first time in her memory, no Real Estate Ron float had made an appearance.

Anne, her mother, Maynard, and Terry Sullivan walked Mrs. Jamieson back to her house after the parade. William arrived, smiling, soon after they did. "Happy Fourth, everybody. It was a blast driving that motorcycle. And I have good news. Blake's Pub is keeping the cook they hired when I was, um, away. I'm going to be the chief cook. They need me to teach him how to make fish tacos." He beamed at Terry and Anne. "Thanks to you guys."

The door to the shed in the backyard was open, and Anne noticed William's dinghy inside. "I have another idea," she told him. "The Westport Sailing Club is going to start a program for kids who can't afford to buy their own boats. We'll need to supply them with Optimist dinghies."

"I know those little boats," William said. "I always wanted one when I was a kid."

"Did you also know the best ones are still made of wood? What if the club contracted you to build them for us? They have to be made according to certain specifications."

William's eyes widened. "Yes! Yes! I can do that. I promise they'll be first-class."

Folding tables and chairs had already been set out when Anne brought her mother and Maynard to the club for the feast. Tim was lighting the grill, and men were rolling in kegs of beer and tapping them. Men in white aprons poured water, vinegar, and National Bohemian beer into a tall stockpot set over flaming propane burners while others pulled live crabs from a basket with gloved hands, dropped them into a strainer, and sprinkled them with Old Bay seasoning. When the water was boiling, the crabs were lowered into the pot, held above the water by the strainer, and the pot top was put on.

Maynard stood watching and videoing the process. "We can get live crabs in Florida, too. I'm going to try cooking them like this."

Anne's mother needed to show Maynard how to open and eat them. They sat at a newspaper covered table, splitting the shells open and pounding the claws with wooden hammers to get to the meat. "Spicy," Maynard said. "Now I see why all the beer."

Lily and Vince sat next to them. Anne's mother gave Lily a pat on the leg. "Lily, how are you? You and Anne used to be such good friends. I saw you in the parade riding in that beautiful car."

"Want to buy one?" Vince joked. "I can get you a *deal*."

"It looked more silver than *teal*," Anne's mother replied. "Good to see you again, too, Vince. This is my friend Maynard."

Reggae rhythms beamed from Tim's cabin, and some of the young club members got up from their tables and started to dance in the space around the boats. Tim, followed by Molly, came up to Anne's table with a platter of hamburgers and corn on the cob. Anne introduced him as "my good friend" and noted her mother's rolling eyes. Maynard held up hands reddened by crab juice and seasoning. "Maybe I won't shake your hand right now."

Up on the platform at the top of the wide club stairway, Jessie and Jorge sat with Commodore Dan and Petra's parents, Jorge showing Cliff how to eat crabs. Bob Green and his wife were with them. Dan stood and signaled to Tim to cut the music. "I have an announcement to make." He waved his hand for the dancers to come near. "Let me introduce Mr. and Mrs. Fields, who have generously offered the club an endowment in honor of their daughter Petra that will support a new program for children whose parents lack the means to join the club or buy a boat." Petra's parents stood to applause by all the club members at the feast. Dan asked Bob Green to stand up, too. "And Green Sails has offered to donate sails for the program," Dan shouted. "We expect this new youth program to develop some impressive young talent for the Westport Sailing Club."

Tim turned the music back on, and the party continued for hours. As club members, families, and guests finally began to leave, Tim asked them to fold their tables and bring them to the clubhouse storeroom. "Leave the chairs for the fireworks," he told them.

"Tim excused me from helping to clean up for the fireworks," Anne told her mother as they walked back to her house. "Because you and Maynard are only here for a quick visit."

"Um-hum," her mother mumbled. "And who is this good-looking Tim? I saw you two smiling at each other."

"A friend. We're good friends."

Her mother nodded with pursed lips and raised eyebrows. "I see. I noticed there weren't any men's clothes in either bedroom armoire, so …."

"How did you like the crabs, Maynard?" Anne asked, changing the subject. "Good? I wish you guys didn't have to go back tomorrow."

"Pickleball tournament. Your mom's my partner."

"Well, good luck. How about we all take a little nap before the fireworks," Anne suggested.

Coast Guard cutters had cleared the water of boats where Town Creek meets the open bay, the location where the fireworks would be set off from a barge. Residents of Colonial City and the Maritime Republic of Westport knew that the best place to view them was at the Westport Sailing Club. Anne had brought her mom and Maynard early to claim a seat at the top of the clubhouse stairs. Tim wasn't to be seen. Anne knew he was in his cabin preparing to reassure Molly, who didn't appreciate fireworks.

The chairs below were quickly filled, and all available space in the clubhouse yard was crowded with people standing to watch. Some members sat in their trailered boats. Cheers rang out when the first rockets shot up, filling the sky with blue and white spray. A "flying fish" display followed leaving a trail of green sparks. "Ooo, and ahh," the crowd roared as the sky kept lighting up with booms and dazzling cascades of colors.

"Quite impressive," Maynard admitted. Anne's mom was sticking to "Ooo and ahh."

The display lasted longer than it had the previous year. Each year it was more remarkable than the year before, Anne had noticed. Towards the end, a sparkling simulation of the American flag rose from the barge, closely followed by the grand finale of loud bursts of colors exploding in the sky.

48

No problem

When Anne went to help pack the next morning, her mother pulled from her suitcase a package wrapped in striped paper and tied with a red ribbon. "Happy birthday, Annie. I hope you soon have an occasion to wear this." It was a silky white blouse embroidered with delicate designs along the collar, the button front, and the cuffs.

A lump rose in Anne's throat. "It's so beautiful," she croaked. "Thank you, Mom."

"I told Mrs. Jamieson today was your birthday, and she said she would bring you something."

"You shouldn't have—"

There was a knock on the door. Anne rushed downstairs to find Maynard marveling as he let Mrs. Jamieson in carrying a tall cake with vanilla icing and a ring of cherries on the top. "It's a Smith Island cake," she told him. "My specialty. For Ms. Anne's birthday."

Anne's mother put the tall cake on the dining room table. "Annie, you must call that Tim to come help us celebrate."

"Oh, I—"

"I insist."

Tim brought a little bouquet of pink zinnias. "Picked these behind my cabin," he said, blushing. "Thanks for inviting me."

Anne's mom made a fuss about finding a vase to put the flowers in. As they sat at the table, Anne said, "Now please don't sing—" But she was interrupted by a round of *Happy Birthday*, led by Maynard, who then volunteered to cut the cake. "How do you like it?" Mrs. Jamieson asked him. He swallowed. "Best cake I've ever eaten."

"I wish we could stay longer, Annie. You'll have to come visit us soon." Her mother gave her a long hug.

"I'll teach you how to play pickleball," Maynard chimed in.

Her mother looked at her watch. "I hate to leave so soon, but, you know flights are cheaper at certain times. Maybe we should get on the way."

"I'll drive you to the airport," Tim offered.

On the way out, Anne checked her mailbox. There was a letter from her landlord in D.C. *I am rescinding my previous notice canceling your lease on September 1. You are welcome to extend your lease for another year beyond that date. Please ....*

Since Anne had never mentioned the lease cancelation to her mother, not wanting to worry her about it, she folded the letter into her pocket without comment. She'd tell Tim the good news later.

Anne felt tears in her eyes when they dropped her mother and Maynard off at the airport. Her mother held her hand. "We need to get you to move to Florida, Annie. There are all kinds of activities in our community."

Anne smiled. "I'm not retired yet, Mom. I'll come and visit, though."

On the way back from the airport Anne asked Tim if the boatyard was cleaned up and in good shape after the crab feast and fireworks.

He grinned. "Sort of. There's still a lot of trash on the ground, and the chairs and tables are just piled up and not put away right. I'll need to spend some time—"

"I'll help you."

"Not on your birthday."

"I want to. Oh, and I have good news. I got a letter from my landlord. I can stay in the house at least another year."

"Great! That's what I was hoping when I saw you tuck the letter into your pocket."

The work at the boatyard was heavier than Anne had anticipated. All the tables and all the chairs had to be un-piled and taken into the storage area under the clubhouse. It took two people to carry each table. Huge, leaking garbage bags had to be dragged out to the street. The whole yard needed to be hosed down. By the time they finished, the sun was starting to set. Both Anne and Tim were soaking wet. They collapsed onto the bench by Town Creek. "I'm hungry," Tim said. "How about you?"

"I am, but I just need to rest here for a minute."

"Me too. But then I want to take you to dinner at the Palais de Paris for your birthday."

"Really? Oh, thank you, Tim. But look at me. I'll need to go home and clean up first." She tapped him on the back of his wet shirt. "Maybe you should, too."

They motored over across the creek in the club's Whaler. Anne had showered, washed and dried her hair, and put on the elegant blouse her mother had given her. Tim wore a white shirt, no tie, and a dark blue blazer. They tied up at the Palais de Paris, and a restaurant doorman in a brass-buttoned coat helped them onto the dock. Anne held her breath to keep from giggling.

The menu was in French. And very expensive. "Why don't you order for us," Anne suggested as the waiter approached.

"Sure. I don't know French very well, but I downloaded the menu and I've been practicing." He ordered Prosecco as an *apéritif*. With it the waiter brought pieces of salmon tartar for an *amuse bouche*, and Tim ordered a scallop *entrée* and boeuf bourguignon for the *plat principal* with a bottle of Bordeaux. This was going to be a long dinner. Anne was hungry. She ate everything put on her plate and drank all the wine poured into her glass. Then came *Camembert* and *crème brûlée*, and, yes, Anne ate that, too.

"Thank you so much, Tim," she said as they left the restaurant. "What a wonderful birthday this has been."

With the gentle rocking of the Whaler on the way back, Anne caught herself falling asleep. Tim helped her up onto the club dock. "Want to come into my palace for a while?" he asked.

"I would, but I'm so sleepy. And a little groggy. Right now I think I need to go home and go to bed. I'm sorry, Tim."

"No problem, Annie. I'll walk you home."

About the Author

For years Rea Keech sailed in Laser and Snipe regattas and sailed a J29 in longer-distance races. He taught American and international students for over thirty years before retiring. He has previously written seven novels, several of which are the result of his extensive overseas experience, but On the Hook is his first attempt at a cozy mystery.